A LITTLE TURN

A Novel

By

Alexandra Y. Caluen

A LITTLE TURN
Copyright 2020 by Alexandra Y. Caluen
All Rights Reserved

Cover design by RK Young

Cover photo by Brian Kyed @brnkd *unsplash.com*

A LITTLE TURN*

The Playlist:

Separate Ways – Journey

Lose Yourself – Eminem

Born This Way – Lady Gaga

Wash Me Clean – k.d. lang

I Want to Know What Love Is - Foreigner

A Matter of Minutes – Josh Little (Gay's the Word)

In the Still of the Night – The Five Satins

Walk This Way – Aerosmith

I'm Too Sexy – Right Said Fred

Our Day Will Come – Ruby & The Romantics

*on the catwalk

A LITTLE TURN

Chapter 1	1
Chapter 2	10
Chapter 3	22
Chapter 4	35
Chapter 5	48
Chapter 6	60
Chapter 7	73
Chapter 8	86
Chapter 9	98
Chapter 10	111
Chapter 11	126
Chapter 12	141
Chapter 13	150
Chapter 14	163
Chapter 15	179
Chapter 16	188
Chapter 17	201
Chapter 18	216
Chapter 19	236

Chapter 1

April 2010

Bob Anderson stood in the gym, staring at the woman he'd proposed to the night before, the woman who'd just put the ring box in his hand. He felt almost detached, as if he were watching this play out with two different people. As if it were a scene in a movie, the part of the romantic comedy where there's a big misunderstanding, but you know they'll get together in the end. Those scenes were never this final.

She was saying, "I shouldn't have let this go so far. The truth is I'm in love with somebody else."

It didn't matter, but he asked anyway. "Who?"

"Someone I can't be with. I thought I should try, and I tried, but it isn't fair to you. I'm sorry." There was a pause, as if she thought she should say something else, or maybe as if she expected *him* to say something. What on earth could he say? "So. I'd better go."

"Yeah. Well." He looked at the ring box. "It was worth a try." Did he really say that? What did it even mean? Did he mean for Sharon, or himself?

"You'll find someone who deserves that ring." She popped up on tiptoe to kiss his cheek, then turned around and left. He stood there, feeling cold, until he became aware that he was being stared at. He hated that. *Put this in the gym bag and pretend it never happened.* Maybe someone would steal it, and he really could pretend that.

A bit less than two hours later, he was in the bar at Callender's, for no other reason than that it was the only bar close to his apartment that he'd ever been in before.

1

He was wearing his business suit for no other reason than that he couldn't exactly go to a bar in his sweaty gym clothes. Those were sweatier than usual because after Sharon gave him the ring back, he had to work out harder than usual. He was, in fact, feeling a little shaky. Exhausted, hungry, and upset. All the reasons why he was upset were jangling around in his head. Having a drink or two and some greasy bar food was exactly the wrong thing to do in this situation. Going back to his apartment alone didn't seem any better.

There was nobody to talk to about it. He hadn't told his family that he was proposing. Had only mentioned in passing that he was seeing someone. Maybe he knew all along that Sharon didn't want to marry him. They'd only been dating for a few weeks, it was too soon, but that didn't matter because she was in love with someone else anyway. At least, that's what she said. And why shouldn't it be true? She was blonde, beautiful, smart, funny. Everything an up-and-coming sports agent in Los Angeles could want. Everything any man should want. He was convinced that he wanted her, as much as he'd ever wanted a woman. *Did I actually want her.*

That was the question he'd asked himself every time a relationship didn't work out. He did the right things, or so he thought. Good manners, decent clothes, a clean car. A careful progression of dates that he always paid for. He took them to bed once an indication of willingness was given. What happened in bed was a mystery. Who did a guy talk to about how to make love to a girl? Was he doing it right? They always acted like it was all right. Was every one of them faking it? How was he supposed to know? If he asked whether they had a good time and they said yes, was he supposed to assume they were lying?

2

He liked the kissing part. Liked being touched, being close to someone, skin to skin. Actual intercourse was not all that inspiring. All the reasons why that might be weren't jangling. They were buzzing at the bottom of the jangle, like an overloaded power line, or a computer hard drive that was about to self-destruct.

The bar was too exposed. He couldn't sit with his back to the room. After a few minutes, the host found a booth for him at the inside end of the bar, a few feet away from the piano that nobody was playing at this hour. He had no idea if anybody ever played that piano. Maybe it was for Sunday brunch. He'd never been here for that.

The server who showed up a few minutes later coached him through a drink selection and suggested some food to go with it. Bob didn't care. Anything was better than nothing, he didn't have any food allergies, he didn't care. He drank whatever was in the glass, ate whatever was on the plate, let the server suggest another drink for him. He was sitting there staring at it when someone sat down across from him. "You look like you've had a shitty day."

Bob looked up. It was almost like looking in a mirror, and yet nothing like that at all. Slim blond white man with good bones. Wearing not a suit, but an aggressively trendy casual shirt. Hair not in a businesslike cut but swept back, brushing his collar, and highlighted. Half a dozen colors, from platinum to spicy reddish-brown. One ear pierced. Shaped and tinted eyebrows. And was that eyeliner? Maybe he frowned. The other man pressed his lips together as if suppressing a smile. He reached across the table. Bob reflexively extended his own hand, realized that the offered hand was palm-down, thought *what the fuck am I supposed to do with this*, and made a confused sound.

3

Jade would have been shocked if the guy in the suit actually did what his offered hand invited, and kissed the back of it. He did the usual thing, which was to take it in a hesitant way, let go of it as soon as possible, and retrieve his own hand. Jade learned long ago that this was the very best way to avoid having his hands damaged by an overly-aggressive grip. Some men wouldn't touch his hand at all when he presented it that way. "My name is Jade Derecha."

"Bob Anderson. You don't look Latino." The second he said it Bob cringed. Of all the clumsy things to say.

"I'm not. Before I changed it, the name was Jake Wright. Wright, right, derecha. I'm from Ohio."

"I'm from Utah."

"What are you doing in Los Angeles?"

"I live here." Bob couldn't have been more confused if they were speaking Martian.

Jade heroically suppressed a laugh. At least now the guy wasn't staring at his drink as if he wished it were hemlock. Instead he was staring at Jade trying to figure out why they were talking. It wasn't the first time he got that reaction. "I live here too. I'm a stylist. What do you do for a living?"

"I'm a sports agent."

The agent part wasn't surprising. The sports part kind of was, but Jade rolled with it. "And instead of being out with some athlete talking about how to make the both of you some money, or out with a team from your office talking about who's making the most money, or out with the hot Los Angelena who is surely somewhere waiting for a good-looking guy in a suit, you're at Callender's by yourself looking like you want to go find a fast-moving bus to stand in front of."

4

Bob closed his eyes, hoping that when he opened them again this completely inappropriate person would be gone. Maybe it was his imagination. Maybe this was his brain projecting a version of his subconscious, telling him what was going on. Except he still didn't know what was going on. Maybe he should simply play along. Keeping his eyes closed, he dug in his pocket and pulled out the ring box. He only even had it because he didn't want to send it through the wash with his gym clothes by accident. Set it on the table. Sat back and opened his eyes to see what happened.

Jade picked up the box, opened it, took a moment to appreciate the tastefully-huge diamond ring inside. Not the average boring solitaire on a slim gold band; this was a platinum filigree band, nearly three millimeters wide. A trio of stones were set across the top, a square-cut one point five carat (if he were any judge, which he was; he'd seen a lot of fine jewelry) in the middle, flanked with half-carat triangles. He thought wistfully about how good that would look on his own graceful hand. Then he thought *screw it* and took it out of the box. Was it the right size? He slid it onto his ring finger. It fit as if it belonged there.

Across the table, Bob's mouth actually dropped open for a second. What the hell was this guy doing? How could that – okay, it did fit, his hands were fine-boned, but – what the *hell*. Had it fit Sharon? He couldn't remember, but surely not. That couldn't have helped with the yes-or-no decision. Except it didn't matter.

Jade was aware of the speechless incredulity on the other side of the table. He took the ring off regretfully, inserted it in that pillowy slot, closed the box again. Set it down and nudged it toward the other man. "I take it you offered this to some woman who said no thank you. Did she at least say thank you?"

Ordinarily Bob would have put the box back in his pocket. He left it sitting there because it didn't matter. And instead of saying 'what the hell was that about' he said, "I don't remember. She said she was in love with someone else."

"And are you crushed? Ruined for life? Suicidal?"

"I'm confused." Bob couldn't figure out why he was talking to this person at all, much less telling the truth. "I felt like, oh God not again, another one bites the dust, what do I keep doing wrong. And then I was … relieved."

"Do you make a habit out of proposing?"

"No, this was the first time. I thought it was time. I'm thirty-six."

"I'm thirty-five. I've never proposed to anybody."

Of course you haven't, Bob thought, *if you're not gay I'm Elizabeth Taylor.* Then he shook his head as if to dislodge that thought. Why the fuck was it always a woman's name when he had a thought like that? Why did he not think, if you're not whatever I'm Muhammad Ali? And why did he buy a ring like that instead of a nice safe delicate solitaire? Why a ring that looked right on a man's hand? "Oh fuck me," he said, awash with horror.

Jade watched the realization bloom. It wasn't what he'd expected, but it immediately made sense. His gaydar was usually very accurate. And now he could almost hear the litany of denial, denunciation, desperation. Could almost have spoken it out loud, confident that he wouldn't miss a thing. Decades of cultural abhorrence, brainwashing, and fear. This poor guy. "Could I call you Robert?"

6

"What?" It was faint, a reflex more than conscious speech.

"Mr. Anderson. I don't think you look like a Bob. I'd love to make you look like a Bertie, actually. I think you're perfect for the Edwardian style. Hey." The guy made eye contact. It looked as though it was painful. Jade leaned in a little, with his elbows on the table, and spoke very low. "I can guess what's going through your mind right now. You don't know me, but I've been where you are. Please believe you will be okay. You are a decent, worthwhile person, and whatever happened today doesn't change that." He was making some assumptions there, but this was not the time to say 'you're *probably* a decent, worthwhile person.'

Bob was nearly in tears. This was the worst thing in the world. The worst conversation. The worst thoughts to be having. He clutched at a life preserver. "It can't be true." Didn't mean to say that out loud.

"Why not?" Jade was still leaning in. The last thing this guy needed was for anyone to move away. How many people had left him before tonight's girl? How many times had he watched someone walk away and thought, what's wrong with me? He tried again. "There is nothing wrong with you." A movement caught his attention. The server was hovering. "Could we get the check please?" It came quickly. Jade took it before the other guy could. Pushed the ring box toward him, watched to make sure it landed in the suit pocket.

A few minutes later they were outside. Jade had a strong impression that Bob *ugh no I hate that name* barely remembered where he lived at the moment, much less how to get there. "Where's your car, Mr. Anderson."

Some struggling instinct to deal with things made him say, "Call me Robert." A desperate need to connect

7

with someone who seemed to recognize him, and wasn't walking away.

He was processing; that was good. Plus the full name was much too Matrix. All too close to home, really; the guy had clearly been living in an artificial world. Now he was trying to find his footing. Jade didn't want to leave him alone. He had a friend who got him through that first awful week. Who did this poor fucker have? "Your car," he prompted.

"It's over there." Bob pointed randomly. He couldn't think of himself as Robert right now. He'd always been Bob. But Bob wasn't real.

"Robert, I have a suggestion. I live nearby. I walked over here. There is a place we can park your car. I think you should come with me. I don't think you should be alone."

"You didn't even eat."

Thinking about someone else: that was another good sign. Jade had met his share of agents. The ones he liked all had the helper personality, underneath the mercenary hustle and the sharks-with-lasers focus. "I was really only there to get a whiff of pie. Once a month or so I let myself have a slice. Come on, take me to your car. I'll drive."

Robert started moving. Not so much because he wanted to, more because the other man was offering to help, and he seemed to actually understand what was going on, which was more than Robert could. Or maybe he could understand, simply didn't want to. Didn't want to look at his whole thirty-six years of life and wonder how much of it was actually his. *Who was Bob Anderson? Who is Robert Anderson? Oh sweet Jesus am I gay? How could you do this to me?* He handed over his keys as if someone else were controlling his body.

8

Got in the passenger seat. Noticed that Jade had to move the driver's seat up a notch; he was a couple inches shorter. He didn't say a word during the short drive. Jade was talking, in a soothing tone, about his day. Robert let it wash over him. He didn't pay much attention to models, actors, Hollywood events. His clients, even the ones who had advertising deals, didn't move in that world. He knew this was only to make the point that he wasn't alone. If he hadn't been wallowing in misery, he would have said 'thank you.'

Jade didn't expect a 'thank you.' He was hoping this silent distress was as bad as it got. It was going to be a while before Robert felt like thanking anybody for anything. He was at rock bottom right now. On the way up there might be rage. If so, whoever was nearby was likely to be in the line of fire, which meant taking him home was probably really stupid. He parked the car, got the guy out of it, and walked him into the building. Still talking. He knew Robert wasn't listening. The only reason to talk was to consciously engage. Yes you are with a person, yes this person sees you, yes this person is interacting with you, yes you deserve it. Upstairs to the apartment, unlocking the door, moving the guy through the kitchen and into the small living room. "Robert, I suggest you get as comfortable as possible. Take off your shoes. Take off whatever you want, actually. I'm not going to make a pass at you. Nobody's going to mess with you. This is a safe place." Then, more prosaically, "The bathroom's over there."

Robert didn't move for a few seconds. Then he started on his tie.

Chapter 2

Jade darted into the bathroom himself, washed up with much less attention to detail than usual, and made it back to the living room in time to see Robert placing his shoes with exaggerated precision under the coffee table. His suit jacket was draped over the back of one of the chairs in the breakfast nook, the tie folded neatly into the chest pocket. Jade gave him an expectant look. Robert nodded, walking past him to the bathroom. There was a brand-new toothbrush, still in its package, on the vanity.

He refreshed himself, somewhat mechanically. Noted the way the bathroom was actually designed, much as the bathroom in any given woman's apartment had been. Nothing was overtly feminine, but nothing was random. There weren't multiples, the way there were in his own bathroom, because he sometimes forgot exactly what he usually used and ended up buying something else that he didn't like as much, but never threw out the unsatisfactory product. And everything went together. No off-the-shelf bottle of hand soap here, or naked box of tissues. Those containers coordinated pleasantly with the towels, the rug, even the light-switch plate. Wanting to learn more about this situation he was in, he opened the medicine cabinet. Told himself it was simply to find the toothpaste. Examined the other contents, somewhat clinically. There were a lot more products than he used. Some were products he'd noticed at the drugstore and thought 'I wonder if I should be using something like that.' None were cosmetics. Maybe his host kept those somewhere else. He was a stylist. Maybe he kept things at his ... not an office. A salon?

Robert dismissed the temptation to think about his host instead of his own situation. He had to figure this out, and he might as well start with what was in front of him. Maybe his own bathroom was so unplanned because he never wanted to think too hard about these things. Never wanted to examine the implications. It wasn't a great theory; he knew a lot of straight men who were obsessed with grooming. But it was a theory, one that made more sense the more he thought about things. He remembered the way the server coached him through the menu tonight. He'd been letting people do that forever, maybe because on some level he didn't care to ask himself what he wanted. Even about something as innocuous as what to eat.

He closed the cabinet and brushed his teeth, staring at himself. Maybe he should be absolutely freaking out right now, but he wasn't. The initial avalanche of horrified WTF had settled. Now his brain was working, sorting through the jangle from earlier in the evening. Applying 'because this' to answer a lot of questions. He'd never had anything close to an answer before. And he wasn't convinced about this answer, but if he really was gay, then there was an actual reason why none of those relationships with girls worked out. They weren't supposed to. Maybe the girls realized it somehow. Maybe they knew he would never be a perfect husband, because he didn't actually want them.

But how could he be gay and not know it? He'd never kissed a man. Barely even hugged a man. The bro hug, sure. He couldn't remember hugging his father, or his brother. He'd never wanted a man. Or at least not to the point that he recognized the feeling. Watching with appreciation, okay, but desire? He'd been inside an awful lot of locker rooms. Had played sports himself starting at age four, even though he was always a bit on

11

the delicate side. Five eleven and one-sixty now, which made a suit look great but had surprised more than one woman. It was a turn-off for some. There had been more than one sharp-edged joke about looking fat next to him. Of course they didn't, and he didn't care anyway. His focus was always on their faces and personalities. Because ... fuck.

Jade must weigh one-fifty, tops. Robert thought about it, very deliberately. Was he attracted to this person. *Accept the possibility and conduct the analysis from there.* If he was gay, then he was gay. Everything he'd been told growing up led him to absolute revulsion, but how much of that was true? If he was actually gay, then he was what a gay person was. And he was not a pedophile, or an exhibitionist, or a rapist. He was not any of those awful things. There was nothing wrong with his brain, he believed he was capable of love – he *did* love, he loved his family and his friends and some of his clients – and he was obviously not promiscuous. Since he'd made it to thirty-six without even asking himself if he might be gay, he was either a master of control or a master of denial. Maybe both. He would need to come back to this and look for context clues he must have missed.

Do I think he's attractive. Well, of course. Anybody would. But did that mean Robert was attracted to him? The two things weren't necessarily the same. All he was sure of was that Jade was none of those awful things either. He was a person who saw someone having a shitty day and came to see if he could help.

"Everything okay in there?" Jade didn't like to hover, and it wasn't as though there was an obvious way for a person to do himself an injury in the bathroom (the kitchen was another matter), but it was awfully quiet.

Robert opened the door. "Thanks for the toothbrush. And everything."

Already at thank you. That was both surprising and reassuring. "You're welcome. How are you doing?"

"I don't know. Am I gay?" Might as well ask. This guy seemed to have recognized something.

Jade shook his head. "Only you can answer that question, my friend. Do you want to sit down and talk about it? Don't worry about how late it is. I don't think you should go to work tomorrow and I don't have anything till noon."

"Why are you helping me?"

"Because somebody helped me. Come and sit down." Jade led the way, as if Robert could possibly have forgotten where the living room was. Looking back to make sure he was following. If the guy's process had already arrived at this point, maybe this wouldn't be a disaster. Robert looked a lot calmer than he had at Callender's, that was for sure. Jade told himself not to think about the way he looked. The way he moved. The shapely forearms and wrists, accented by golden hair and a stylish watch, exposed now that the man had rolled up his sleeves. They sat down. "What made you say oh fuck me at the bar."

Robert huffed out something close to a laugh. "You said that thing about how you never proposed to anybody, and I thought of course you haven't, if you're not gay I'm Elizabeth Taylor." Jade laughed. "And then I thought wait one fucking minute. Why do I always put some glamorous woman's name there? Why not, like, Mike Tyson?"

"And you realized?"

"I'm not sure if I could call this realization. I'm still questioning. How could I not have known who I am for

13

all these years?" He was quiet for a minute, absorbing the fact that he'd said 'who' and not 'what.' On some level, it seemed, he never had believed all those bad things. "How did you know?"

"I was fifteen," Jade said. "I grew up in a religious household. I noticed other boys. I watched Luke and Han, instead of Leia. They were just more interesting. It wasn't until later that I realized why. I thought if I ever touched another boy I was going to hell. But somebody touched me."

"In a bad way?"

"Mmm." Jade shook his head. "It was a friend. I did makeup and costume for everything at the school. My parents told their friends I was artistic. I was on the baseball team, too. Had a paper route, rode all over on my bike. I was enough of a guy that I guess they didn't see the signs. Lucky for me," he added. "Anyway, I was cleaning up the dressing room when this friend, a musician for a play we were doing, came in and closed the door. I was all, did you need something? And he said yes, I need to kiss you. I thought fucking *what*?"

Robert smiled. It was the first smile he'd managed since he saw Sharon at the gym, before she gave back the ring. "You didn't run for your life?"

"I stood there like my feet were nailed to the floor. I didn't know what to do."

"Stood there until he kissed you."

"Mm-hmm. It might have been his first kiss too. He sure wasn't very good at it, at least not at first. Then it started getting good, and I realized I was getting turned on, and I pushed him away. He said Jake, it's okay. I won't tell anybody. I just love you, that's all. And I started crying because nobody ever said that to me."

"Nobody?" Robert was horrified all over again, for a completely different reason. At least his parents did say that. His siblings. He heard 'God loves you' a lot more often than he heard 'I love you,' but he did at least hear it. *Maybe not from here on out*. The thought hurt.

Jade saw the flinch and thought he knew what that was about. He also saw the sympathy, and appreciated it. This guy was definitely handling things better. Well, he was older. Maybe wiser. And maybe even though his first thought was 'oh fuck me' his second was 'well now everything makes sense.' He couldn't help wondering how fast the process was going to be. Robert was already at roughly day four of Jade's process. "It took about a week to come to terms with it. The only person I could possibly talk to was my friend, and it had to be in private, and privacy barely existed in that community. It was a small town." Robert nodded comprehension. Jade took a calming breath. He hadn't told anyone this story for years. "We ended up going for these long walks. I ditched baseball, he ditched band. I was angry, upset, couldn't keep my temper. I felt like God had betrayed me. Because I didn't go looking for that, you know? I was trying to be who I thought I was supposed to be. I got in trouble at school, got in trouble at home. Finally told my parents I thought I was gay, and my father hit me."

"Oh no." Robert wanted to reach out, as if that injury were fresh instead of twenty years old. *Well, that answers the question of whether I'm attracted. What the hell do I do now? And why am I not screaming at myself that this is wrong?*

"They didn't throw me out of the house, but it was a close call. My friend was out to his parents, not to anyone else. I told him what happened. He talked to his parents, they talked to mine, and we came up with a way

15

to get through high school. My part of the deal was that I wouldn't come out to anyone else. I would have been afraid to anyway. And I had to swear I wouldn't touch anyone while I was living under my parents' roof." He shrugged. "I lied about that."

Robert was laughing silently, full of admiration and envy and still-jangling dissonant conflict because he simply couldn't believe this was happening, and yet it was. "It was very kind of you to sit with me tonight."

"I didn't know what your trouble was, but it was clear there was something. I am not a guy who minds his own business. That said, if it looked like you were going to throw a punch I'd have skated."

"I've never hit anyone in my life."

"Well, good. I've been in a few fights in my day but it's not my idea of fun." He'd dismissed his concerns as soon as Robert said 'thanks.' Maybe someday they could talk about how (and why) Jade learned to use elbows, knees, and feet. *Don't be ridiculous, he doesn't care. You'll probably never see him again.* He glanced down at his manicured hands, startled to realize that he wished that weren't true. When he looked up again they made eye contact.

Robert gazed at Jade across the width of the couch and asked himself, again, why he wasn't crouched in a corner with his fingers in his ears yelling No No No. Asked himself if the warmth in those big hazel-green eyes was for him, or if it was simply Jade being Jade. Jade who was beautiful in such a male way. Alluring, but wary and tough. Robert could almost smell the testosterone. This wasn't a person who would require protection. This was a person who would stand beside you. "Is that when you really knew? When your friend kissed you?"

Oh really, Jade thought, with a frisson of half-alarm, half-delight. The other man's expression was speculative, not frightened. Curious, not appalled. "I'd say yes to that." He could have been answering Robert's spoken question. He could also have been answering the unspoken one.

"You live alone here."

"Yes. I'm single, if that's what you're asking. Have been for a year or so. My last lover moved to Sonoma to be a winemaker. With someone else."

Robert thought about that for a minute. Jade did not seem heartbroken. But if his last lover was the one who moved, and that was a year or so ago, then he wasn't only single: he was celibate. That was not something Robert had been taught to associate with gay men. He'd been taught they were all promiscuous. That they'd go with anybody, do anything, anytime or all the time. That sex was all they wanted. And obviously that wasn't true. If he'd ever really thought about it before, he would have already erased that for the slanderous bullshit it was, because he knew plenty of gay men. Most of them were in committed relationships, the kind that would have been marriages if that were legal. He had not ever thought 'they should be allowed to get married.' Had bowed out of those discussions, because it was none of his business, and it was like having an opinion about the conflict between Shiite and Sunni. He wasn't part of that community, so he shouldn't judge. "I'm trying to figure out why I'm not up on the roof looking for something spiky to jump onto."

"Well," Jade said slowly, drawing it out, "maybe you've discovered that you don't actually believe some of what you were told?"

Robert sat forward, as if to close some of the distance between them. "It's like, if I am gay, which I'm still not sure

17

but there's evidence for that conclusion, then I am a representative gay man. And I am not what I was told gay men are, so what I was told has to be wrong. You're not that either."

"It's a small sample size." Jade couldn't help smiling.

"Yeah, but I know other gay men. And those men aren't what I was told either. It's like I've just been hit upside the head with the fact that all these unquestioned statements are based on nothing. There were verses from the Bible, I'm sure you heard all of those too."

"Oh, yes."

"But there's a lot in the Bible that we *don't* believe, or we ignore. My family, the church, the whole freaking state. If you went through it line by line and said is this what we practice, at least half the time the answer would be no. So then I have to ask myself, why is it so important to them. Why are *these* people demonized. What exactly is the threat here. I mean, in a church where the fundamentalists believe in polygyny, you would think they would *want* all those unpartnered men to get together."

"You're making the jump from confused to politicized awfully fast."

Robert laughed out loud. He suddenly felt a little bit high. "I'm probably going to be on a rollercoaster for the next week, at least. But." He stopped.

Jade studied him for a few seconds. "Hang on." They'd been talking for a while. He went to the kitchen, brought back two glasses of water. "Here." Sat down again, not so far away.

Robert drank some water, set down the glass, looked at Jade again. "Out of all the miserable men in bars in Los Angeles, how the hell did you roll up on me?"

18

"Pie?" Jade offered. "I was really only there for a whiff of pie." *And then I saw you at the end of the bar and couldn't stay away.*

"Would you kiss me?" He blurted it out, then sucked in a breath and held it. Couldn't believe he said that.

Jade took a mouthful of water, held it for a second, swallowed. Set down his glass, not looking at Robert. *Is this even the slightest approximation of a good idea.* He had no intention of kissing the man when he brought him here. It was only to give him better odds of surviving the night. Wasn't it? He glanced over; Robert was still not breathing. "Exhale." Studied him again. "You want to find out if kissing a man feels right, or if it disgusts you." It wasn't a question. Robert nodded anyway. "And you are inclined to not be disgusted by me because I was kind to you, and because you know I'm single and therefore not cheating on anybody." Another nod, with a faint blush. "I know *you're* single. For the record, I'm not disgusted by you. At all. And I won't be even if kissing me makes you run for the toilet." That thought had obviously occurred to Robert. "It might be better if you tried kissing me. I'll stay right here. I won't touch you." There was more he could have said.

Robert thought things through for a few seconds. There was something Jade hadn't said. "You want me to be clear that this is something I'm doing. My choice. Not something being done to me." A silent nod. Robert wondered what his life would have been like if, some night at summer camp, he turned around and kissed a boy. Had he wanted to? Had he simply not recognized the impulse and the desire? Or had it triggered such immediate rejection that he buried it? Well, here was his chance to find out. With a consenting adult. He was trembling with nerves. He edged closer on the couch.

Jade could feel the tremor, though Robert's face gave little away. He must be an excellent negotiator. His approach was slow. It was as if each six inches of proximity gain necessitated a moment to regroup. "Robert." A sharp intake of breath. "Yes, that's what I was going to say. Keep breathing. And remember, you don't have to do this. Not with me, not with anybody. Not tonight, not ever."

"I want to." His voice was shaking now. "How else will I know? I'd rather *know*."

Yes, of course, you want to know if there's a reason. If this is the reason. Thirty-six, you poor lonely bastard - . Jade's thoughts cut off abruptly because Robert finally made contact. His lips were trembling, but they were pressed against Jade's. His eyes were closed, as if he didn't want to see what was happening. His breath was audibly short. Jade wanted very strongly to touch him, hold him, soothe him. He kept his hands to himself. Didn't do anything. Simply sat and waited. Robert gasped a little, as if he needed more breath. Of course that meant his lips parted. He closed them, but slowly, because Jade's lip was between his. It took a real effort of will not to move now. To sit and experience this virginal kiss. The re-shaping of an entire self-image, decades of experience re-framed, all through this nearly-innocent contact. Jade had received more enthusiastic kisses from women. He was momentarily distracted by a flash of memory, his own second kiss. His friend inviting, but letting Jade initiate. He tried to do that now, so focused on Robert's mouth and on listening for breath – he didn't want the man to pass out on him – that he missed the moment when Robert put one hand on the back of the couch so he could lean in.

He didn't miss the moment when Robert's lips parted again. This time it was intentional. A stifled sound, his head angling, and the lightest touch of tongue. Jade thought hazily *I never said I wouldn't respond*, and opened his mouth.

Chapter 3

Robert's thought process was so disrupted that he barely knew what he was doing until the moment Jade's mouth opened. Then he was lost in a flood of sensation, battling with a flood of internal monologue. This mouth, so different from a woman's mouth. The slight rasp of stubble. *Are his eyes closed? Does he like it? I always did like kissing. Oh wow.* He should have asked more questions. Should have asked what else he could do. Was it okay to put his hand in Jade's hair, or on his neck.

"Mmm." Jade broke the kiss because he could sense a hovering hand, and they needed to get a couple of things clear. "You can touch me. Can I touch you?"

"Yes. Oh God –" Jade's arm went around his back, his other hand was in Robert's hair, which suddenly seemed much too short because Robert had a handful of Jade's and it felt so good. This was better than the best kiss he'd ever had with a woman. This was *right*. He gave up thinking. All he wanted to do was taste and feel and get closer. The next time he had a conscious thought, it was *I am about to come*. Jade was underneath him with one leg hooked over Robert's. His body was strong and firm and the right size. They were both moving, both vocalizing. Jade's erection was hard against Robert's belly, and if he moved once more it was going to be too much. He grunted with the effort of going still, turning his head a few degrees away from the kiss, panting until he could speak. "I didn't mean to do this."

Jade unwound his leg. Removed his hand from inside Robert's pants. Smoothed that hand down his back, because he didn't want this memory to end with

22

'he stopped touching me' if that wasn't what Robert actually wanted. "I know."

"I mean, I didn't mean to pounce on you. Pin you down. Hump you like a horny dog." Robert wasn't looking at Jade's face until he felt the laugh. He glanced up; the other man was smiling. "I almost came in my pants."

"Well, Robert. I think you're gay."

"I think I am."

"Are you going to be okay with it?"

He honestly didn't know. "I feel like I took advantage of you." He realized he was still lying on top of Jade, and hurriedly pushed back. "Shit, I'm sorry."

"It felt good." All of it felt good. The kisses, the touches, the right-sized body on his. Jade didn't move. He lay there feeling frustrated and abandoned, holding eye contact with Robert, who was now curled up in a ball against the far end of the couch. He didn't look like he was going to run for the toilet. He looked as though he wanted to stretch out again. Jade very deliberately took the hand that had been on Robert's back a moment ago, and ran it down his own body to his groin. Gripped himself through his pants. "I want to finish this. Do you mind?" He was one hundred percent sure Robert had never watched another man jerk off.

Robert swallowed hard and shook his head. He was still painfully aroused. He didn't know if he could watch this. Didn't know how he could possibly *not* watch this. Jade had his pants open. He pushed them down. Oh God, he was taking them *off*.

Jade wasn't sure what he was doing now. It wasn't seduction. More like confrontation: this is what happens when you're a man and you're aroused. When you're with another man and he's aroused. Finish it. He unbuttoned his shirt, pulled it off, and threw it somewhere. Robert made some kind of gulping sound, and a convulsive movement. Jade didn't know if that was desire or fright or revulsion. At the moment he didn't care. *That's a lie, you want him to want you.* He lay back, making himself comfortable, even though it meant his feet were on either side of Robert. *Yes, you're between my legs, and you're going to watch me, aren't you?* Stroking himself, eyes closed. This was more comfortable than rubbing one out through his clothes, but Robert's weight on him had been just right. Jade let himself imagine what the man looked like naked. He was slim. Long-legged. Probably not much body hair, and what he had would be light-colored, like Jade's. Was the tan on his arms a sign of sunbathing, or simply of walking around L.A. with short sleeves? Was he circumcised? Most American men were. Jade wondered what he tasted like. Pushing up into his hand, lips parted, imagining.

There was a minute when Robert's internal monologue was screaming *what the fuck are you doing watching this you sick bastard.* Then there was Jade's smooth pale skin, the way his body flexed, the pressure of his ankles against Robert's hips. The scent of his arousal. The planes of his face, and that mouth. The mouth that said 'there is nothing wrong with you.' Robert couldn't stand it. "Can I kiss you while you do that?"

"Mmm." It was the closest thing to a word he could manage, so Jade lifted his other hand and beckoned. He heard what sounded an awful lot like clothes coming off. *He processes fast,* he thought, in the moment before Robert stretched out again, half on top of him, weight on one side and mouth on Jade's. His erection was hot and leaking. Jade couldn't have said whether it was that

24

or the kiss or the warm skin pressed to his, but he bucked up into his hand a minute later, moaning into Robert's mouth for the length of his climax. There was an answering sound, something that might have been 'oh God' if his tongue wasn't in Jade's mouth. Jade tried to say "Can I," and whether Robert fully understood it or not he pushed his hips against Jade, who decided to accept the invitation. He ran his palm across the wetness on his belly, wrapped that wet hand around Robert's cock, heard something like a shout, and held still while Robert fucked his hand. Panting, gasping, braced on a hand planted beside Jade's head and with his teeth set in Jade's shoulder. There was no way he fucked women like this. No woman who got fucked like this would have said no to that ring. His cock swelled even more and he shoved hard into Jade's belly, crying out. Jade held on, counting the pulses. Letting his grip slacken, but not letting go entirely until Robert's dick softened. He wiped his palm unobtrusively on his hip, wondering what happened next. That was one serious, much-needed orgasm. Now if only he didn't have an existential crisis over the fact that he had an orgasm with a man. On a man. In a man's hand. He relaxed, his body weight resting mostly on Jade, who didn't mind at all.

It was a few long quiet minutes before Robert stirred again. He shifted his weight, settling against the back of the couch. Head propped on one hand, the other hand resting on Jade's chest. He was afraid to make eye contact. Forced himself to do it anyway. "You are either the most tolerant human being on planet Earth, or there's something about me that you like."

Jade laughed silently for a few seconds. "Possibly both?" They gazed at each other for another few seconds. "Of course I like you. I don't do favors. I let you see that I wouldn't mind if you kissed me. That allowed you to consider the possibility without having to worry about whether you were going to get rejected."

"But from kissing to, well, that got a little out of hand."

"That got *in* hand."

Robert snort-laughed. He didn't know why he wasn't freaked out. Maybe because for once he knew the person he was with had a good time. You couldn't fake that. "I feel like I should go."

"Why?"

"Uh." Robert blinked. Tried to remember the last time he spent the night with someone. "I just realized it's eight years since I spent the night with someone."

"Jesus, Robert. You're pretty hard on yourself, aren't you?"

"Would you mind if I stayed?"

"I'd *rather* you stayed." Another minute of eye contact. Jade had a lot of reasons for wishing Robert would still be there in the morning. He remembered the way his first had stayed with him, long past the point they should have gone home, so late that they both got in trouble. That period of not kissing, not touching, only talking. Plus the time spent silently together, the feeling of support and concern. The feeling that even though neither of them really knew what they were doing, they could figure it out and try to be good for each other. Carry their friendship forward, no matter what. Thinking of that helped him settle on a rationale that wasn't completely selfish. "You may feel off-balance in the morning. This is a lot. You started off the day thinking you might be engaged to a woman, and you ended it having sex with a man. I could have stopped this. Maybe I should have. I was greedy."

"Greedy." Robert's voice was soft.

Jade glanced away for a second, then back. "I wanted you to see me."

"You're beautiful." He could tell Jade liked hearing that. It wasn't the first time he'd thought that about a man. A lot of athletes were beautiful, in their way. It was the first time he'd consciously associated male beauty and sexual appeal. But obviously that appreciation was always there. It was inconceivable that he could have done what he did tonight if, somewhere deep inside, it wasn't what he always wanted. "If you're sure you don't mind, I'd like to stay."

"I'm sure." He rolled off the couch and stood up. Gave Robert a hand. Took a good look at the body as he did so. A runner's tan, a runner's body. "That's what I thought you'd look like." Robert was blushing again. "Make yourself at home. I'll be out in a minute." Jade went to the bathroom, determinedly casual, hoping the depth of his own confusion didn't show. He really didn't do this, not anymore. Didn't pick people up, didn't talk, didn't cuddle, didn't spend the night. And here he was, doing all that with the thirty-six-year-old virgin. If there was ever a recipe for disaster, it was walking around his apartment right now. The odds definitely favored a panicky flight in the morning after the implications sank in. He'd probably never see Robert again. Well, it was nowhere near the worst decision he'd ever made, and there were plenty of people he'd never see again.

He looked at himself in the mirror, dissatisfied. The color was good, but the hair was too long. It made him look frivolous. He'd get Shaya to cut it the next time they were both free.

Robert was in the kitchen when Jade passed through to the bedroom. He told himself it was so he

27

knew what the man liked to eat. The least he could do was offer some kind of meal. He said he didn't have anything till noon, so maybe they could have breakfast. He thought about that totally prosaic preoccupation as he washed up again. *Why am I not freaked out. I just fucked a guy's hand after kissing him while he got himself off. I should be a screaming ball of panic right now.* He simply couldn't panic.

The suggestion to take a day off was a good one. Robert didn't take a lot of days off. Didn't call in sick unless he felt deathly ill. But he needed to think. His business was entirely dependent on keeping in touch with people, and he was too distracted. All the questions were simmering away. What would happen now? His personal life wasn't generally a topic of discussion with his clients. They were mostly egomaniacs, like all entertainers, and mostly would have been offended at the suggestion that they *were* entertainers. Not all of them. The new guy, Jonathan Morris, definitely had a sense of humor about it. He was with the WWE. Maybe Robert could test the waters there. Drop a hint or two, see what kind of reaction he got. Not that he planned on re-doing his office with rainbows, but if this was who he was, then his life was going to change. Some of his friends might freak out. His family was definitely going to freak out. The first time he went out with that in his head, I am a gay man, and looked for someone to ask to dinner, he was going to be saying to the world, I am a gay man.

If it meant there was a chance for more nights like tonight, saying honest things honestly, and knowing the person he was with truly had a good time, he could deal with everything else. Thank God he lived in Los Angeles.

And thank God he might be through with going home after a date, even a date that included sex, feeling

28

vaguely dissatisfied. Frustrated, worried, and positive the other person would rather have been with just about anyone else. *I ought to give that ring to Jade. At least it fits.* The thought made him smile.

The smile as Robert came into the bedroom was a surprise. Everything about him was a surprise, actually. From nearly crying to 'I'd like to stay' in less than three hours. Jade said, "You're either the most adaptable human being on planet Earth or you're deep in denial about everything that happened tonight." Robert laughed out loud. He got into bed. Both of them were naked, because that was how Jade always slept and Robert didn't have much of a choice. "You're taller than the last man who slept with me," Jade said, watching for a reaction. He had his lamp on, mostly because it seemed passive-aggressive to turn it off and make the guy come into a dark room.

Robert knew it was absolutely none of his business what kind of men Jade might have slept with. If Robert had somehow managed to go to bed with a dozen women, Jade had surely racked up twice that many sex partners. The only thing he thought he should ask could be asked another time. If there was another time. "I have a queen bed too," was all he said, as if that comment had to do with comfort. He followed it up with, "Thank you, Jade."

"Let's see if you still feel like thanking me in the morning." Jade switched off the lamp. It took him longer than usual to fall asleep. He was very conscious of the other man. Listening to him breathe. Wondering if he was truly asleep or if he was lying there tensely quiet like Jade was. *Why am I tense. We've already had sex. If he hated the sight of me he wouldn't have asked to stay. Why is he so not freaked out.* Eventually, a long tiring day (even before bringing the virgin home) caught up with him.

A pornographic dream morphed into recognition that there was a real, warm body up against his. A real hand on his dick. A real person doing some heavy breathing into his hair and pushing a real erection against his hip. Jade turned his head; Robert was apparently having the same dream he woke Jade up from. The room was light. He turned his head the other direction to look at the clock, confirming it was past seven. He could easily lie here for hours and let Robert do things to him. But what the guy wanted in his dreams and what he wanted in full possession of his faculties might be two different things. Jade regretfully moved the hand off his dick and edged away. Robert rolled onto his front and started humping the bed. It was all Jade could do not to laugh out loud. He saw no reason not to take care of his own business while that was happening. He thought he could be forgiven for imagining that sleek body was on top of his again. Maybe with that very nice cock between his thighs. Maybe with that very nice mouth on his, kissing. They climaxed almost simultaneously, which was interesting. Robert was loud. Jade lost the fight not to laugh.

"Uh." Robert was very out of breath to be just waking up. *What the ... oh. Oh SHIT where am I what happened is this FUCK.* He stayed face down for a minute, moving his head only enough to get an unobstructed breath. There was no doubt. He definitely just rubbed one out on this bed. Was Jade in here? Was that the rudest possible thing he could have done? He turned his head. *You have to say something.* Jade was gazing back at him, looking very amused. Also somewhat post-coital, which because Robert was over here and Jade was over there had to mean he did it

30

himself again. *Damn it.* "Sorry about your sheets," he said after a few seconds to think about why 'damn it,' of all things, was his reaction. Jade laughed. Robert realized that same sound woke him up. "I am so embarrassed."

"About which part?"

"About this adolescent wet dream thing."

"How do you feel aside from that?"

Robert rolled onto his back – away from the wet spot – and gave it some thought. He woke up in bed with someone he met the night before. A man. A man he kissed, and had sex with. Yesterday he thought he was straight; today he knew he was gay. His whole life had changed. "What seems most important right now is I wish we did that together." He looked at Jade again; the expression was astonished. "I do not know why I'm not freaked out."

"I don't either. What do you want to do?"

Another moment's thought. "Kiss you. Take a shower. Take you out to breakfast."

"In that order?" Jade was smiling for real now. This guy was incredible.

"Yes. If you don't mind having breakfast with someone in yesterday's suit."

It wouldn't be the first time, but there was no need to say that. "I don't. Hang on." Jade slid out of bed and went to get a glass of water. He drank a little, then handed the glass to Robert while he went to take a piss. When he got back to the bedroom it was Robert's turn. Jade waited, wondering, a little bit nervous because this was new and he always assumed something new couldn't be trusted. He was sitting on the edge of the bed, trying to find parallels, when Robert returned.

He didn't get on the bed. Instead he went to his knees in front of Jade, not touching. Hands on his own thighs, looking up. "You are the absolute best person I could possibly have been with last night."

Jade thought with sudden clarity *he will fall in love with me if I give him half a chance*. He couldn't decide if that was what he wanted. Did he want to be someone's how-to-be-gay coach? Teach him the ins and outs, as it were? This man was very different from Jade's usual. On the other hand, none of those usual men had worked out for the long term (though not all for the same reasons), and Jade was tired of dating. Which would explain why he hadn't done any of that for a year. Because dating always seemed to mean sex, but only twice had it meant more. A new notch on his belt had stopped being satisfying a long time ago; now it simply meant 'that didn't work either.' He was truly tired of things ending. Tired of people wanting his support for their careers but not giving the same to him. Tired of jealousy, tired of infidelity – sometimes from the same partner, which seemed really offensively unfair – and tired of feeling like he had to perform. Had to be the swish Hollywood stylist at home, same as he was in the dressing room or salon.

A very different man might produce a very different outcome. But the man at his feet needed a minute to adjust. He focused on Robert, whose expression was uncertain. "I'm glad you feel that way," Jade said gently. "I think the two of us should maybe not have more sex until you've had time to really think things through. But I would like a kiss." He leaned down; Robert stretched up; they kissed. It was soft, affectionate, comfortable. Jade gazed into those very nice blue-green eyes. "Who gets the shower first."

Robert thought he hid the disappointment. "You go first. It matters how you look."

Jade appreciated the understanding at the same time he was slightly nettled by it. "Oh, so I'll have extra time for primping. Fine." He stood up, which put his junk pretty much right in Robert's face because the guy did not move back. "Jesus, when you decide you're doing something you really don't flinch, do you?" He stepped sideways and left the room, listening to slightly-hysterical laughter from his guest.

The walk to IHOP could have been awkward, if Robert hadn't remembered something from the night before and asked Jade what he thought about the start of the baseball season. They were still talking baseball when he picked up the check. It was only on the way back to Jade's apartment that he changed the subject. "I want to say thank you again," he said. "And, well. Can I call you?"

If not for that refreshing hour of being treated like a regular guy, Jade might have said no. Might have thought the potential for disaster was simply too high. Liking each other was not enough. Getting off together was not enough. Painfully-honest conversation was not enough. He'd had all those things with other men, and none of them stayed. None of them had ever talked to him about baseball, either, as if they'd paid attention not only to his words but to his tone when he mentioned it. Maybe it was stupid to be hung up on that, but it was the one thing he'd been really good at aside from styling. Well, and aside from sex; he was really good at that. But Robert wasn't equipped to judge that. He *was* equipped to judge whether someone knew what he was talking about when it came to sports. One sport, anyway. Jade would be the first to admit he knew nothing about most other sports. But that was situational. He hadn't dated anyone who wanted to talk sports since the golfer. And that guy mostly wanted to talk about how great he was. Wanted Jade to sit and listen admiringly to the endless recaps of this or that shot, or putt, or escape from the rough. *No wonder I don't like the name Bob*, Jade thought, stifling a laugh at himself. "Yes. You can call me." So they exchanged business cards before Robert went to his car. They might have exchanged a kiss if there hadn't been people around; Jade could see the wish in Robert's expression, and God knew he wished for that too. He held out a hand instead, in a normal handshake way. "It was nice meeting you, Mr. Anderson."

Robert took his hand gently. Simply held it, rather than squeezing. "It was nice meeting you, too, Mr. Derecha." He let go with probably-visible reluctance, sketched a wave, and headed for his vehicle. Resisting the temptation to look back and see if Jade was watching him go.

Chapter 4

The first thing Robert did at his apartment was call his assistant to say he wouldn't be in. "I'll be checking email and stuff from here. Touch of food poisoning, I think." It was a white lie, and a plausibly transient illness. No-one would question him not wanting to be in the office today, or showing up tomorrow as usual. Thank God he didn't have anything hot going on right now. Contract negotiations were recently completed for a few of his clients. Most of them were in multi-year deals. He'd go through the book at the end of the week, as usual, and see who still didn't have anything to do in their off-season. Start looking around for something he could shake out for them. Till then, he could give himself a day to do nothing but react and respond. And think.

He thought while he was attending to his suit. A misting of Febreze, hanging up the jacket in the living room where it could air. Then taking the steamer to the pants, hanging them up to let them settle. He'd take a look later to see if they needed to be pressed. He didn't love this suit. Took a minute to examine that. Did he care what he wore? Yes, of course. But he didn't like being looked at, so he didn't dress to be noticed. This suit was a greenish gray with a windowpane check, and now that he thought about it, he'd never liked the pattern. Even the navy pinstripe was better. The guy at the Men's Wearhouse tried to steer him to brighter blues or to rich blue-grays. Robert resisted for some reason. Was it because the guy said, these colors bring out the color of your eyes? Did Robert not want people to look at his eyes? Why did he not want to be noticed?

He thought about it all through the mindless task of stripping the bed, taking a load down to the building's laundry room, and waiting for the wash cycle to finish. He always stayed down there, because there was a person in the building who would hijack a paid-for wash cycle if you gave them a chance, until things went into the dryer. Usually with a copy of Sports Illustrated in hand. This time he stared into space and let his brain work on his problem. The sub-question of being seen wouldn't leave him alone.

Jade saw him. Really saw him. Was that why? Had Robert always dodged being noticed because he didn't want anyone to really see him? Did he not really want to see *himself*? It was all too plausible. The last time he'd really felt noticed it was the kind of situation that might have been traumatic. Stripped down in a locker room in high school, having recently shot up to his full height. Skinny, gawky, and half-hard after toweling off. Someone said something. He'd laughed it off like everyone else. Boxed it up and put it away for twenty years. Good thing you've got that, Anderson, 'cause from the back you look like a girl. *Fuck you*, he thought now, exactly the same as he'd thought then, before laughing. Ha ha yeah remember this in ten years when you're fat and I'm not.

Was there subtext? Was the guy saying, I'd like to fuck you like a girl? What would have happened if Robert said something confrontational? Well, he'd have gotten beat up, probably, and he still wouldn't have been ready to remember that he was watching that one guy while he was toweling off. The towel wasn't the only reason he was getting hard. All those half-glances, those stolen peeks at naked teammates. Those long looks at photos of shirtless men in the athletics magazines. Telling himself he was making comparisons, inspiring

36

himself to work out more. He'd never looked at straight porn in his life. When he took a girl out, he never looked at other women. That was one of the things girls liked about him, or so they said. He wondered if any of them ever suspected.

There had never been any question in his mind that he would marry a woman eventually. He'd really only been decent marriage material in the past few years. Before then, dating wasn't so intentional. It was simply the thing a guy did. Now his small college loans were paid off, and he was making good money at the agency. He had a reputation for fair dealing and smart deal-making. Sharon was the first woman he'd proposed to, but not the first he'd considered. He hadn't told the truth to any of those women. He'd never lied, but as soon as it was clear they didn't share his real interests he'd simply diverted. Let them take charge of the conversations, kept things trivially-focused on Los Angeles happenings, the latest movies, what they'd heard about this or that restaurant. There was plenty of trivia to talk about. It was exactly the kind of thing you shouldn't waste time talking about if you were trying to decide on someone as a mate for life. What an idiot he'd been.

The wash cycle was done. He transferred things to the dryers and went upstairs. Did a little more housework. He usually did it on Sunday mornings, when he knew his family would be at church. Telling himself cleanliness was next to godliness and not examining that either. Why he didn't go to church. Why he didn't miss the church. That was the one thing he'd lied to his family about. They thought he went to services. Talked about how great it was that he could go to the big temple. He'd been there once, so he could tell them what it was like inside. Considering he'd lived in

L.A. for more than ten years, the fact that he stayed away ought to have told him something.

Coming to L.A. was the result of a job offer. In retrospect, he could see he'd used relocation as a way to re-frame his life. To begin doing that, at least. None of his family had ever visited him here. He'd met them all down in Anaheim for a Disneyland family vacation once, when he was thirty. He knew they expected him to move back to Utah at some point, maybe after he got married. That was yet another thing he'd lied about by deflecting the question. He didn't want to move back. Especially not now.

The bathroom was always the last thing on his housekeeping list. This time he filled up the trash with all those products he didn't like. He hated to waste things, but there was nowhere to donate stuff like that, and it was going to waste anyway. Maybe he needed to walk down to the drugstore and get some of that moisturizer with sunscreen he'd seen in Jade's cabinet. The man's skin was perfect. "You shouldn't be thinking about that," he said out loud. Not about that, and not about the subtle scent of Jade's hair, or the way his skin might taste. Except why shouldn't he? Wasn't that *exactly* what he should be thinking about now? The first man he'd kissed, been skin to skin with, had sex with. Good grief, what a night. What a strange, wonderful, life-changing night.

Jade wasn't sure he was going to tell anybody about that strange and kind-of-wonderful night until the moment he started talking about it. At the salon, of course, with Shaya at her station next to his, glancing up at him in the mirror while her hands were busy. He didn't tell her everything. Other people were listening, after all. She didn't have much to say until her client

38

left. Then she said, "When's the last time someone treated you like an actual person?"

Jade blinked. "Well, you do." She made an impatient sound. "Fine, okay. Not since Robbie."

Shaya narrowed her eyes. She had her own opinion of the Robbie situation, but she mostly kept it to herself. "Tell me again about Eric."

"Jesus, why?" Jade stalled by concentrating on the last stage of the cut he was doing. Shaya didn't have another client for a while. She threw herself into her chair, legs crossed, swinging a foot, watching him cut as if she were judging a contest. Jade didn't let it distract him. The client pretended not to notice. When the guy was finally gone Jade cleaned his tools and tidied his station. Then he went to the back to assemble a couple of iced coffees. Not as good as what they could get down the block, but a lot closer to free. He handed one to Shaya, then sat down. "Eric and I dated for a year. He finished his sommelier course. He met a guy who owned land in Sonoma. They moved up there to open a winery. End of story."

"During that year, when you were talking him off the ledge multiple times as he was panicking over not being able to tell the difference between this vintage or that, did he ever once ask you about *your* hopes and dreams?"

"No."

"Did he ever talk about anything but himself?"

"No."

"Is that why you haven't dated anyone since?"

She knew it was. Jade sighed. "Yes."

"Are you going to see this guy again if he calls you?"

Jade averted his eyes. "Yes." He was strongly tempted to turn it around on her, ask why she wasn't dating, get all up in her business. Some other time for that. "This guy is not my usual. I couldn't help thinking, maybe if the guy is different, the outcome might be different."

"It's not outside the realm." Shaya was strongly tempted to push it, ask more about the guy, force Jade to think about his usual. Some other time for that. Instead she volunteered something, because they'd been friends for a long time. "My usual always sucks, too. I'm waiting for someone different." Time to change the subject. "Have you had any thoughts about the pageant?"

"Haven't decided what book to do. You?"

"I want to do Amelia Peabody. You know those books." Jade was snickering. "Well, come on. That's some serious styling, and a lot of people know those books."

"No, it's a great idea." They both supported the Los Angeles LGBT Center. When they heard about the September fundraiser, the proposed drag pageant, and its theme – fabulous ladies of literature – they both signed on immediately. "In fact, you just gave me an idea. I have to check and see if anybody else has already bagged it." He dug his phone out, logged into his email, and sent a query. By the end of the day he had an answer, and a brand-new idea. It was probably impossible. He was positive it wasn't worth mentioning to Robert. The guy would probably never call. Except he did, that very night.

The business card was on his nightstand. He hadn't yet put the number in his contacts, so when the call came in it was – for all he knew – spam. But an unknown number was a potential new client or other gig as often as it was spam, so Jade picked it up. "Hello?"

The voice on the other end was tentative. "Hi Jade, this is Bob. I mean Robert. You don't like the name Bob."

"No, I don't." Jade was smiling, he couldn't help it. "There's a story."

"Maybe you'll tell me sometime. I just wanted to thank you again. Well, that's not entirely true. I mean yes I wanted to thank you but that's not all."

Oh really. Jade stretched out on the bed, observed that he was overdue for a pedicure, and wondered where this was going. "What else?"

It sounded as though Robert was making himself comfortable too. "I've been spending the past couple of days deconstructing my entire life history and I'm sick of thinking about myself. Could I ask you something?"

"Sure."

"You said you did costume and makeup for school things. Is that what you always wanted to do?"

Jade blinked. After that conversation with Shaya, he'd been planning to spend a little time thinking about past men. Trying to tease out whether any of them ever had been truly interested in Jade the person, and whether he might simply have buried the memory of any such interest after things ended. "Oh, sorry," he said, realizing that he'd been silent for a beat too long. "I was thinking how to answer that, not deciding whether or not I would."

A stifled laugh from the other end. "You don't have to."

"Obviously. I could just hang up on you if I didn't want to talk to you."

"That's true." A pleased note in Robert's voice, as if he hadn't thought of that.

Jade was aware he'd as good as said 'I want to talk to you.' Well, he wasn't in the business of lying to people, unless they wanted him to. This person didn't want him to. "I wanted to be a baseball player. Right up until the end of my junior year."

"What happened then?"

"I got cut from the team. For a bunch of reasons, mostly boiling down to not big enough. A lot of guys on the teams in our state used steroids. Being my height and not juicing, I was about fifty pounds lighter than everyone else on the team. I was fast, I'm a pretty good hitter, and I've got a decent arm. But it was all about power. How about you?"

"I couldn't decide what sport I liked best. I was kind of good at all of them but I wasn't willing to pick one. And, like you. I was way lighter than most of the other guys. Pretty easy to knock me down. I knew the college teams would be even more aggressive. Didn't want to get injured. So what did you do after that?"

"Spent the summer sulking about it." A laugh at the other end. Jade was smiling again, or still. "At the same time, I was taking a good hard look at what my options were. They kind of sucked. I mean, in our part of the state, there were four big employers. Wal-Mart, Home Depot, an Army base, and a prison."

"Oh, shit."

"Yeah. If I wasn't going to get a ticket out with sports, what was I going to do? I wasn't a great student. No real interest in college. I knew my friend was headed to college. What was I going to be left with? It was kind of scary." An understanding sound now. This guy was easy to talk to. Jade said the next thing. "My mother sat me down and talked to me right before senior year started. She said, a couple of years ago we talked about you joining the service. I said, I remember. And that was all I said."

42

After a moment's pause, Robert said, "Was she saying they wouldn't expect that now?"

"I think she was. And I was saying no way no how. That was nineteen ninety-two. I wouldn't join the military *now*, much less then. Short skinny pretty blond kid? I'd have been lucky to survive basic training." He meant it literally.

Robert made a sound of disagreement. "You're not short. I'll bet you'd have been good at it. There are so many technical fields. You're smart."

Jade held the phone away from his face for a second, staring at it as if it would tell him something. Trying to remember the last time anyone said that to him. Had anyone ever said that to him? "How do you know?"

"The way you talk. The way you see things."

The way I see things. He was going to think about that later. "Mmm. Anyway, Mom didn't push it but that little two-minute conversation told me I needed to figure my shit out fast. So I spent most of fall quarter in the library. Talked to the guidance counselor, not that he was good for much. His job was to sort people into groups for those four employers. The people who weren't going on to college. He didn't know what to do with me after I said nope, nope, nope, and nope." Another stifled laugh from Robert. "It was actually my English teacher who said, have you considered working in the theater. And I was like, is that a job?" Robert laughed out loud. Jade wished he could see that. "She hooked me up with some people she knew from college, people who were working in cities. One of them was working out here. That person said, if you like doing costume and makeup there's a union. People can make a good living doing that in L.A. You could crash with me for a while until you get situated."

43

"Wow, that was nice. Or was it?"

Jade laughed. "No, it was. Another schoolteacher, married with children. They had a spare room. I got a job at a restaurant. Rented that room under the table for a year while I got my licenses. By then I knew some people. The next situation was a two-bedroom apartment with four of us sharing. That lasted a few years while I was getting established. But you made me realize something."

"What's that." Soft, warm, interested.

I want more. "I haven't thought about what I want to do for a long time. I've been, you know, working." He suddenly became aware of the time. "And I've really enjoyed talking to you but I have an early start tomorrow."

"Okay. Thanks for talking to me."

"Thanks for calling." Jade was tempted to say a lot of other things, starting with 'call me anytime,' but he disconnected. If Robert wanted to talk to him again, he would call, or maybe text. Maybe send an email. Jade added the contact, put the phone on its charger, and went to wash up for bed.

Not terribly far away, Robert sat on the loveseat in his den, halfway-listening to the sports commentary on TV, wondering if Jade was now thinking about what he wanted to do. Wondering if any part of that was 'talk to Robert again.'

Jade might have brushed off those half-serious thoughts about wanting more, about hopes and dreams, if not for a marathon day styling a photo shoot. After fourteen hours, mostly on his feet, he was so tired he wanted to cry. Lying on the couch that night, talking on the phone with Shaya, he admitted, "I'm not going to want to do this forever."

"You know how at the beginning a new stylist always comes in wearing something jazzy, and then by the end of a month or so they're in nurses' shoes and yoga pants?"

Jade laughed. "The new girl and those high heels. Oh God did I want to say something."

"She figured it out. You knew that gig was going to go long."

"I dressed for it. The money was great. But I'm like, damn. There is no amount of stretching and massage that will fix this twenty years from now. Is there?"

"You're asking me? I'm younger than you are."

Jade made an irritated sound. "Do you get massages?"

"Every day, no. Once a month, yes. I dated a massage therapist for a while, remember? Thought we could do the service swap thing. Well, I cut his hair, and did he ever touch my feet? No, no he didn't. Fuck him." Jade was laughing. Shaya ranted on. "Plus he was all incense and singing bowls all the time and I was like, I never knew people actually did that. I thought those were props, like those stupid little sandbox Zen gardens. Does it really chill you out, because I have to say it's making me homicidal." She listened to Jade giggling. "What do you want, baby."

"I want to get on the short list," he said without thinking. She knew what that meant. That meant being one of the top stylists in the industry, one of the dozen or so who were the first to get called when a movie or TV series was contracting, or one of the lucky few who were on speed-dial for an actual movie or TV star. He

45

sighed. "The only person I've really clicked with was Robbie."

And Robbie was dead. Shaya winced. The competition for on-set styling gigs was fierce. Jade had a lot of good connections and he worked steadily outside the salon. But for a stylist, finding that one celebrity who would say 'he's the one I want' was as much of a crapshoot as any given acting audition was. She certainly wasn't in a position to give advice. All she could do was offer support. "There's hot iron out there somewhere. You won't miss the chance to strike it."

Jade made a 'pssh' sound. "I couldn't strike a fucking balloon right now. I don't even want to go brush my teeth."

"So don't. Unless you have a hot guy in your bed." She put an interested spin on that.

He really wished he could say yes to that. That night with Robert had kind of wrecked his celibacy equilibrium; he was horny all the time. "Not tonight. Ugh. Guess I have to crawl to the bathroom. See you tomorrow." He heard her say good night, disconnected, set the phone on the coffee table. Thought seriously about not washing up. He seriously did not want to be on his feet for even five minutes. If he didn't, he'd lie there feeling gross and not being able to get to sleep, so he sat up, swung his legs off the couch, and stood up. Cursed, and hobbled to the bathroom. Next time he had a gig like this he was going to bring along his own goddamned director's chair. The one that was bar-height, the one that was folded up in his closet, the one that he told himself was too much trouble to load up.

"Never again," he told his reflection. "You're almost middle-aged. Adapt." It was not a thought he'd ever had before, and not one he was happy about having.

He shouldn't be waiting for hot iron to roll into the salon. He should be out there with a torch, heating some up.

Chapter 5

May 2010

A month after that momentous night, Robert was fairly comfortable thinking of himself as a gay man. Most of the time it simply didn't matter. His male co-workers were not the sort who organized outings to strip clubs. His female co-workers had always treated him as nothing more or less than a colleague. Most of his clients couldn't have cared less about his personal life. The only time he cared about theirs was when they had to get a publicist involved for some kind of damage control. He was looking forward to finding a way to detach his most-controversial client. There was a lot of work in agenting. Most of it didn't produce income. He would much rather spend time on the 'let's make money' side of things than the 'let's keep you out of jail' side.

He didn't change the way he dressed, spoke, or moved, though he paid a lot more attention to those things. Nothing about his professional life was different. A month wasn't enough time to manage a get-together with each of his particular friends, but he'd seen a few. When they asked about his love life, he told the truth. "I was seeing a woman this spring. I asked her to marry me and she said no." They inevitably asked how he felt, whether they were still dating, whatever. He said, "I was relieved. She said she was in love with someone else. Since then I've seen a different person. A man. It turns out I'm gay."

The resulting conversation was always long. There was always curiosity. In only one case had there been a negative reaction. It wasn't a 'never call me again' reaction, more of a subtle withdrawal, as if the person needed some time to get used to the idea. If they never did, Robert would be all right with that. He felt that type of reaction was about the other person, not about him. It wasn't a reaction to him specifically, but to preconceptions that person had. And it wasn't his job to address that. He was going to focus on the people who saw him for who he was. The people who said things like "Wow, that must be wild, how are you coping?" would be his real friends, going forward.

One of those was a colleague who repped a slate of actors. Since he wasn't in the sports group, they weren't in competition with each other. They didn't even work on the same floor of the agency. Robert had to go out of his way to open a conversation. He was doubly glad that conversation didn't happen at the office when he heard what was going on with Parker. "Divorce?"

Parker had another swallow of his drink and nodded glumly. "My best man said, I don't want to say I told you so, but I told you so."

"He did not!"

That almost got a laugh. "He never liked my wife. And you know, according to her I haven't done anything right since we got home from the honeymoon. Which is news to me, so maybe he had a point."

"God, I hate that. When someone hauls up a net full of ancient history and you're like why wasn't this ever a problem before. Or if it was a problem, why didn't you say something."

"Mmm. I'm trying to be above it, let the lawyers handle it. Thank God we don't have kids." Another hefty swallow from his glass. "So what's up with you?"

Robert told him the whole story, up to and including waking up in bed with Jade. "And I lay there looking at him thinking why am I not completely freaked out." He sipped his drink, shook his head, half-shrugged.

Parker stifled a laugh. "Still not freaked out?"

"Not at all. I'm processing a lot," he admitted. "There's cartons full of historical documents being rewritten."

"Never give up." Parker offered his fist.

Robert bumped it. Everyone in the agency quoted 'Galaxy Quest' constantly. "Never surrender." They sat in silence for a few minutes, long enough to finish their drinks and order more. Robert got some bar food, too; it seemed like this might go a little long. "I haven't told my family yet."

"Do you think it's going to be a disaster?"

"Pretty sure it will be. This guy Jade, he came out to his parents when he was fifteen. He said his father hit him."

"Oh, shit."

"Mmm. One advantage to doing it over the phone."

"If any screaming starts, you can just hang up. Well, I have to say, I never would have suspected. I mean, you're a metrosexual, sure –"

"Really?!"

Parker laughed. "Yes, really. What's been the biggest surprise so far, aside from not being freaked out?"

That was easy. "How *relieved* I feel. You know that woman I was seeing for a while. We weren't great together. I knew the sex wasn't fantastic. I knew she wasn't exactly waiting by the phone for me to call. But I was really trying to be the good boyfriend. To be good potential husband material. And she didn't brush me off until it got to that point. She didn't even say no right away."

"Probably wanted to play with the ring for a minute."

Robert nodded ruefully. "Maybe so. Anyway, once this landed it was like, of course. Of course she didn't want to marry me, because I didn't want to marry her, and she had to have known on some level."

"Lack of enthusiasm."

"Right! If you're in love with someone, really in love, shouldn't it be like God, I can't stand being away from this person?" He instantly wished he hadn't said that. "Shit, I'm sorry."

Parker was shaking his head, laughing. "It's been a long time, dude. Were you not pursuing?"

"No, I was, but," Robert tried to verbalize this, "from a distance. I called a lot. Took her out to nice places. Did things she said she wanted to do. But I didn't try to involve her in things that *I* like to do. On some level I think I was trying to not show her who I really am. I mean, it took about two minutes to determine that she could not have been less interested in sports." It sounded like a digression.

"And that's your bag. Did you not ever talk about work?"

"We talked about her job sometimes. We had some truly inane conversations." Parker snort-laughed. Robert smiled ruefully. "I'd like to think she would have said no even if I *wasn't* gay, because we were not right for each other. She was awfully pretty, though."

"Don't be so shallow."

"Oh, blow me."

"You know, that sounds really different now." Parker gave Robert a minute to laugh. "What does Jade look like?"

"Blond. Five nine, one-fifty. He's gorgeous." His tone might have been slightly wistful.

Parker might have noticed. He didn't call it out, though. "Sounds like he was nice, too."

"Best possible guy I could have had that meltdown with." His glass was almost empty again; the food was gone; it was probably time to go. And he had the worst possible guy to deal with again the next day. "I'd better get the check. It's another round with the biggest mess in my book tomorrow."

"You need to get rid of him."

"I'm working on it." It was only the germ of an idea so far. "I'm sorry about the, you know."

"Thanks. It'll be all right eventually."

"Do this again soon?"

Parker looked pleased. "Yeah, let's do that." They shook hands; Parker left; Robert took care of the check. When he got home he sent a text to Jade. It wasn't the first. This time he had a question: *Hi Jade, told a friend at work about you today. Wondered if we could meet up for a drink and talk about things?*

Jade told his friend Shaya all about seeing Robert again the next time he went to the salon. She had her hands full with a complicated cut, but she never let what she was hearing distract her. It was a skill every great stylist had to cultivate. There was a lot of 'uh huh' and 'really' and 'no kidding' until she sent that client on his way. Then she cleaned up her station, got herself a soda, and plopped down in her chair to watch while Jade finished a color job. Once his client and her fabulous new hair were out the door he said, "Are you done for the day?"

"Yes I am."

"Want to go down the street for dinner?"

"Yes I do." She already had her gear clean and packed. Waited for him to do his. Then they said good night to the two stylists remaining and went for a stroll down the block. There was a short wait at the Mexican restaurant. They used the time for low-voiced commentary on the hair, makeup, and clothing of every person around them. "We're so obnoxious," Shaya said once they were seated.

"We only speak the truth." Jade wanted a margarita and he wanted it now. "The thing is, I really liked him."

"Uh, yeah." Shaya's tone said that was obvious. "You don't go to bed on the first date."

Not anymore. Not for a long time. "It wasn't even a date!"

"Uh, yeah." Exactly the same tone. The server dropped off some chips and salsa, took their drink order, and disappeared again. "Was it fascination with his virginal freshness?"

Jade almost choked on a chip. "No. Ugh." He coughed. "Maybe."

"What does he look like?" He didn't answer, simply pulled up the agency website on his phone, found Robert's bio page, and showed it to Shaya. Her eyebrows went up. "Really cute, aside from the boring hair. And he's how old? Thirty-six? He does not look thirty-six."

It was true. If you saw him on the beach playing volleyball you'd think twenty-one, max. It was only at close range that Jade had seen the fine lines around Robert's eyes, and the roughness of the skin on his neck from many years of shaving. *Quit thinking about his skin*. "That has to be why he dealt with it so well. I mean, after the initial meltdown. I kept thinking he was going to dissociate or something, because that's what happened with me. I haven't ever been on the front line with someone having that experience."

Shaya snagged a chip out from under his hand. "They're going to need to bring more of these in about ten seconds. You did not have a good experience. Avoiding other people having that experience was smart."

"Except I ended up going from one smooth operator to another for too long. Falling for a confident presentation." He got the last whole chip, heard Shaya's 'tsk' sound, and laughed under his breath. "I might have been better off if I found another beginner for the first, like, ten years."

"Nooooo. Beginners are the worst. I remember this one time in college. True-blue virgin. All-American boy, God and country. He thought he was in love with me. And I, being a predatory vixen, got him into bed, which wasn't difficult. When he started talking about love and forever, which happened immediately, I was like sorry that's a no." She scrounged up the chip crumbs with a hateful look toward the server stand. "And he literally walked away through the dawn, heartbroken, jacket slung over his shoulder, never to call me again."

Jade bit his lip to keep from laughing. "I'll bet he looks back at that morning and thinks, what a drama queen I was. Probably wishes he hit it again before he left." Shaya laughed for a minute. Finally the server was back with drinks, to take their food order, and to promise more chips. After a committed slurp of his margarita, Jade said, "That's what I'm afraid of, actually. I mean, he's not a virgin, obviously. And I'd

54

like to think that ushering in the new age with me was better for him than doing it with almost any other gay guy I know."

"Well, of course."

"But if I'd kept him in bed that morning he might have been giving me the love and forever thing immediately. And what are the odds that would last? I mean, I'm sure your God and country boy didn't still love you a week later."

"Hey." Shaya let him laugh for a few seconds. "I hope not, I truly do. That was one of the three worst sins I ever committed. I was not a nice girl in college."

"Feeling like a criminal." Sometimes it seemed they could transition any conversation with a line from a song, or a movie quote. If they didn't know each other so well, that kind of shorthand would feel like avoidance.

"Mmm."

"I don't want to break his heart."

"Because you are a decent person," she said patiently, "under the bitchiness and the three hundred dollar color job." Finally, more chips. "Are you really afraid of breaking his heart?" She put a slight emphasis on 'his.' Jade shook his head. "That's what I thought."

Robert was trying to be conscious of other men. Trying to notice. What was attractive, what wasn't. Could he tell if someone was gay or not. Now that he thought about it, he'd always had a pretty good instinct for that. And he must have given off a don't-mind vibe, because so many people volunteered confirmatory information. At the same time he must have been giving off a don't-ask vibe, because nobody ever had. Things were different now. The first time he recognized flirtation from another man he had a conflicted reaction. It was equal parts alarm, excitement, and confusion. Since he was at a coffee shop, he had a good way to cover until he got himself in order. Cautiously, he tried flirting back. It was slightly strange, but not at all unpleasant. The other guy seemed to enjoy it too.

That led to exchanging cards, which resulted in a call. They arranged to meet for a drink at the Century City mall. That turned into dinner. And at the end of the evening, after they descended to the parking garage but before they went their separate ways, there was a kiss. Robert was nervous as hell, all too conscious of the fact that he was kissing a man. The first time he'd ever kissed anyone taller than he was. Physically, this man was very different from Jade, which was one reason Robert didn't deflect. The other was that he liked the guy. He was curious, there was a lot to learn, and why not. Let him take the lead, try to be observant at the same time he was enjoying it, accept that he enjoyed it. *What do I like about it, what's different, do I want more*. He wasn't sure he wanted more, so when they came up for air he said "I had a good time tonight. I'll call you." It was the same thing he'd always said to a woman after a kiss that seemed fine but that he didn't want to immediately progress. He always did call, and he meant to this time, if only to say thanks for a pleasant evening. He didn't know if the protocol was the same with men. Was a call expected? If so, was it the person who suggested the date that called? Or was it maybe the person who suggested turning one kind of date into another kind? Because the other guy said let's get a drink, but Robert said let's have dinner. He decided it was his job to call first. Then he was relieved to get voice mail, so he could leave it at 'thanks' and not have to make up his mind right away if he wanted another date. If the two of them decided the first date was worth repeating, one or both of them would eventually say so. There was no hurry.

That was the big difference, he decided. With a woman, he always had in mind that this might be the person he decided to marry. And with a woman, he'd always been conscious of her ticking clock. That was simply not a consideration now. He'd always assumed that with marriage came children; that he must want to get married; and that he must therefore want children. But he wasn't going to marry a woman, and he realized he didn't actually want children. It was strangely liberating.

And then there was Jade. Robert didn't blame the guy for saying let's step away for a minute. He also didn't believe the guy wanted to step away permanently. So he called or texted, not constantly but regularly. They went out for drinks a couple weeks after That Night. He gave Jade the rundown on what he was doing, who he was seeing, how he was feeling. Asked the same questions, listened to the answers, and wondered how long he should wait to ask for an actual date. If maybe he could do that now. But then he lost his nerve and turned the conversation to sports again.

Maybe it was the ultimate rebound situation. To feel close after a night like that was inevitable. He might have been infatuated with Jade even without the sex; everything else about that night was unique and heartwarming and, simply, encouraging. Robert wasn't set on making Jade his one and only. 'Open to the idea' would, however, have been an understatement. There were a lot of things he hadn't done yet as a gay man. He couldn't imagine anyone better than Jade to do those things with. The hardest thing he had to do was call his parents, and for that he definitely wanted backup.

Jade appreciated getting the regular updates. It would have been a little surprising, if he hadn't had that morning-after thought about how easy it would be to tip this over into something more serious than it should be. Or at least, than it should be now. He wasn't testing Robert, he told himself. Every sign pointed to consistent application of intelligence. The guy was approaching this life change as if it were a career change, or a move across country. And after a look at his bio, Jade was a lot less surprised about that. A person with a JD and an MBA was not a person who didn't think things through. He was glad he didn't know about those degrees before he sat down at Robert's table. He might not have had the nerve to assume he had anything to teach this guy, or that he could help.

But he could, and he had, and he was glad. That was one of the five most memorable nights of his life. So if anything, Jade was testing himself. The more they talked, the more he thought dangerously serious thoughts. While Robert might be primed to fall in love with him, he was equally primed to fall for Robert. That could be a very damaging thing to do, because Robert might truly find himself now. He might find that the things he wanted in life did not include a swish Hollywood stylist, or fidelity. He might decide he wanted to play the field. That didn't really seem in character for the guy, but you never knew. This wasn't the same sort of thing as discovering from one day to the next that yes, you actually do like avocado.

That was one of the two dozen reasons why he said yes when Robert asked if he would come over and keep him company for that call. They'd only seen each other the one time since the first night. It could have been a date, but it didn't really feel like one. It felt friendly, and that was all right. That was enough, except for that moment when Robert's gaze dropped to Jade's mouth. When their eyes met again, Jade thought *he wants to ask*, but the moment passed. Robert took it back to that regular-guy space. If it had felt dismissive, Jade would have been pissed. But it felt … respectful. As if Robert knew he wasn't quite ready, and he didn't want to get them more involved until he was ready, because that wouldn't be fair to either of them. It was a long time since someone tried to be fair to Jade.

He didn't wear a suit that night. Must have gone home and changed after work. Those long legs looked very good in jeans, and the shirt was well-chosen. Not the average straight-guy schmatta of souvenir sports jersey, or band tee-shirt, or aloha shirt. It was a short-sleeved henley that fit perfectly, in flattering indigo blue. Jade wondered if Robert knew it was sexy to leave all three buttons undone. Wondered if he was *trying* to be sexy. Wondered if Robert realized that Jade had dressed to impress, if not to seduce. Also in jeans, but in a long-sleeved collared shirt, close-fitting, made of a slinky fabric with a Japanese-inspired all-over print of wisteria. Top three buttons undone, and an amethyst stud in his pierced ear. Robert definitely noticed that.

And, truth to tell, Jade wanted him to.

Chapter 6

Going to the man's apartment was a whole new ball game. Jade was more nervous about this evening than he expected. He tried to be ready for anything. If Robert wanted to do something, Jade was not likely to say no. There was 'giving somebody his space' and then there was 'lying to each other about what you want.' He didn't think they'd lied to each other yet, and he wasn't going to be the one to start.

With that in mind, he left his own car in its secure parking space and took a taxi to Robert's building. If it so happened that he spent the night, he wouldn't have to worry about getting a parking ticket. Also with that in mind, he carried a few essentials in the messenger bag that usually did not go with him on a date. If this even was a date. If he wasn't simply lending support for what might be a tough conversation. *If that's all this is, be honored that he wants you here*. He pressed the intercom button at the lobby door. Robert answered. "Is that you, Jade?"

"It's me."

"Come on up." The door buzzed. Jade caught it and went in. It wasn't a big building. Robert was on the third floor. Jade took the stairs to burn off some nervous energy. The apartment door was already open when he reached it. He took a cautious step inside and looked around. Robert was across the room, adjusting the position of a small table between two club chairs. He looked up instantly, smiling. "Jade."

It sounded so warm. Jade smiled back. "Robert. You look great." He was in jeans again, this time with a plain white tee shirt. Barefoot. Jade almost missed the next thing he said.

"So do you. You cut your hair, though." It was not the only thing Robert noticed. There were the distressed jeans – distressed enough that he could see through the knee to the skin underneath – the purple Crocs, the ancient-looking Bionic Woman tee shirt that clung to Jade's body.

"My girl Shaya over in WeHo cut it. I thought it was too long." He stepped inside and closed the door. Kicked off the Crocs and looked around. "This place is huge."

Oh God he painted his toenails. Pearly multicolored stripes, like ribbon candy. Robert had never before wanted to put someone's toes in his mouth. He tried to focus. "It was built back in the fifties when people lived their whole lives in apartments. Before everybody fell for the must have a house propaganda."

"The last thing I want is a house. All I can remember is mowing this, re-shingling that, painting, ugh."

"Yeah. I'll probably never move out unless the rent gets crazy." Robert hesitated a second. "You want a tour?"

Since that would give them both a few minutes to settle down, Jade said he would. He dropped his messenger bag by one of the chairs. Robert didn't ask about it. They walked through the place, which was a one-bedroom plus den with one point five baths and a wet bar. It really was huge compared to Jade's place. It didn't have much style; the furniture all screamed Pottery Barn, which could have been worse – at least it wasn't IKEA – but didn't say a thing about who Robert was. On top of that, there was brownish carpet, beige paint, a brown laminate on the bar and tile countertop in the kitchen. Vertical blinds on all the windows. Jade couldn't hold back the sound of distaste.

"I know, they're awful. Impossible to clean, don't do a thing to keep heat or cold out, or muffle the noise from outside."

"Would they let you take them down?"

"Maybe." Robert studied the window for a moment, then studied Jade. "I'll bet if I had a professional stylist to help, I could turn this place into something worth looking at."

Jade grinned. "I'll bet you could. Got anything to drink?"

"You know I do." Back to the wet bar. Robert considered the rack of glass shelves over the sink. "What do you think, for this phone call? Something mildly sedative, or something stronger?"

"Mildly sedative is probably best." Jade leaned on the bar and watched Robert open a bottle of red wine. The guy was observant, that was for sure. He must have seen what Jade kept at his own place.

Without turning around, Robert said, "There's a few things for dinner if you could stay."

He didn't sound nervous, but the lack of eye contact was a dead giveaway. Jade said, "I'd like that."

"I went on a date this week." Still not turning around. Making quite a production out of filling those two modest glasses.

"How did you feel about it?"

Robert finally turned, setting one glass in front of Jade and holding the other. "It was exactly like a date with a girl, except for it being a guy." Jade laughed for a minute, leaning on the counter. Robert moved his glass out of harm's way. "It was drinks, then dinner. We met up at the Century City mall. He kissed me, and then we went home. Separately."

Jade really wanted to ask about the kiss. He didn't. Chose to believe that 'went home separately' meant 'didn't like it as much as I liked kissing you.' Told himself he should not be trying to find meanings like that. "You seem to be coping fantastically well."

Robert sipped some wine. "There was a minute. It was a shock. Turned my whole view of myself upside down. Well, you know." Jade nodded, drank some of his wine, and waited. Robert took a breath. "The thing is, I wonder if you had been a woman or a straight man, equally kind and supportive but minus the sex, if I would be handling it as well. The fact that it was you meant I was confronted right at the jump with the reality that being gay was not a bad thing. Despite everything I was told. I had myself to assess, knowing I was not a bad person. But it really helped to have that reinforced immediately. And to be shown, right in that minute when I could have gotten stuck on this being the worst thing in the world, that being with another man was not something gross."

Another mouthful of wine. "Well, for the record, it *can* be gross."

Robert laughed. "Having sex with a woman can be gross, too."

"What kinds of sex have you had?" He heard the question leave his mouth and almost choked. "Oh fuck I can't believe I asked that." Robert was cracking up. "None of my business, disregard, eject mayday eject." He was laughing now too.

"Maybe we could talk about that after dinner."

They both sobered up fast. There was a long moment of eye contact. Everything about Robert's expression said he was thinking of kissing Jade right that second. Jade swallowed, took a breath, and turned away. "We could do that. We should get this call handled."

"Ugh, yeah." Robert would have preferred to continue flirting with Jade (or doing pretty much anything with Jade) rather than make this call. But it had to be done. They sat down in the club chairs. Robert set his wineglass on the table, rolled his neck, and picked up his phone. Selected the number. As it started ringing on the other end, he put it on speaker with a glance at Jade, who raised his eyebrows.

Robert did a semi-comical 'I know but' thing, and then his mother answered. "Bobby! I wasn't expecting to hear from you. Is something wrong?"

He couldn't help wincing, because from her point of view the answer might be yes. "Hi Mom. I wouldn't say wrong but you might. I need to tell you something. It's kind of serious."

"Are you all right?" She sounded worried now.

"I'm fine. Is Dad there?"

"No, he's talking to the little league coach about your nephew. When are you going to give us another grandchild?"

Robert closed his eyes. This was not going to go well. "Probably never, Mom. I was seeing someone this spring, a woman I met at the gym. You would have loved her. I thought I loved her. I asked her to marry me."

"You did?!" Then she seemed to realize everything was in the past tense. "What happened?"

"Well, she said no, and I was relieved."

"*Relieved?!*"

"Mom, you should sit down."

64

"Bobby, what on earth. Okay, I'm sitting."

The only way to get through all this was to say it fast. "I had to think pretty hard about that, because why would I be relieved. And the fact is, I was relieved because I didn't want to marry her. I don't want to marry any woman. I don't want a wife and kids. I'm gay." He hadn't intended to attach that statement to the others, but it seemed to answer the 'why' for all of them.

There was silence for what felt like forever. "Bobby, I'm trying to make sense of this." She sounded upset.

There was nothing to make sense of. He was still her son. He tried to keep his voice steady. "I know. It took me a while. It's a lot."

"But … gay? Bobby, how do you know? Oh my God."

The change of tone told him she was picturing him with another man now. The picture that probably meant one thing, the stereotypical thing. Not being held, or being kissed, or being told 'there is nothing wrong with you.' He wondered if she ever pictured his brother with his wife. "Mom, take a breath. Are you breathing?"

"Mmm." It sounded stifled.

"Mom, you don't have to say anything. I don't expect you to be okay with it. I only wanted to tell you the truth, and tell you I love you." His voice went a little bit wrong, because he couldn't help feeling this might be the last chance he had to say that. He took a slow breath himself. Into the unpromising silence he said, "I really love you, and Dad, and everybody. I'm the same person. But I'm dating men now, and I'm happier, and I thought you should know so that you know who I am. You can decide if you want me in your lives. I want to be in yours. You know how to reach me." He gave it a few more seconds, made eye contact with Jade, and said, "I love you Mom." He didn't want to say goodbye, so he simply disconnected. Set the phone down very carefully. Blew out a shaky breath. Leaned forward, elbows on knees, face in his hands.

Jade stood up, took two steps, and crouched down beside Robert's chair. One arm around his back, saying nothing. He didn't think Robert was crying, but he was clearly trying not to, and the wrong word might set him off. After a silent minute Robert got to his feet. Gave Jade a hand up, pulled him into a hug, and put his head down on Jade's shoulder. Definitely crying now. Jade petted his back, his own eyes wet because he remembered this as if it happened yesterday. Nobody ever got over it. Even if the loved one turned around someday and said, you know what, it's okay, I still love you. Nobody could ever forget that the first reaction was rejection. When Robert's breath was steady and the tremor had eased, Jade said, "You handled that really well."

Robert didn't want to let go of him, but he needed a hand to wipe his face. He turned his head to see if a kiss was possible. It seemed that it was. He kept it brief, but warm and full of gratitude. "Thanks." He stepped back, reached down for his glass, and drained it. Then he drank what was left in Jade's glass. Jade almost laughed. Robert caught his eye. "Sorry."

"No apologies necessary. I know where the bottle is."

Robert stood there for a few seconds, empty glass in hand, staring out the window across his little balcony to the building next door. It wasn't much of a view. All he had to do was turn a few degrees and he could look at Jade instead, so he did that. "Are you hungry?"

"Not yet. Let's have another glass while you settle down. Find a game or something to watch." That seemed to go over well. Jade took both glasses over to the bar, aware that Robert passed behind him into the den and woke up the big flatscreen. By the time Jade joined him on the loveseat, he'd found a baseball game, conveniently at the seventh inning. They watched to the end in comfortable silence. "Any of your clients playing there?"

Robert shook his head. "Not on those teams."

"What's new at work. Tell me while we get some dinner rolling."

Robert thought *could you actually be more perfect* and said, "Sure." He stood up, gave Jade a hand again – it was so unnecessary, only an excuse to touch him, which he surely knew – and they went to the kitchen. Talking about the nothing-much that had changed since they last spoke.

Jade mostly stayed out of the way, watching Robert assemble the components of a meal. It wasn't far from the way he handled things in the kitchen himself, when he had time. A protein, a lot of vegetables, and a little bit of satisfying starch. In this case the combination was pork tenderloin, sautéed cabbage with fennel and onions, and mushroom risotto. "Where did you learn to cook?"

"I took a class at this culinary school in WeHo. It was called Man Food." Jade laughed. "Yeah, I know. There was a separate class on knife skills, which I took because a girl I cooked for once said she was afraid I was going to lose a digit."

Jade couldn't comment on that, because the prep was all done before he got there. He felt free to comment on the results after laying his fork and knife across the empty plate, leaning back, and patting his belly. "That was really good."

Robert poured them both a little more wine. He'd opened a second bottle, because he didn't have to go anywhere and he knew Jade didn't drive himself. He wanted to suggest, or at least ask, if the guy could stay over. That was the same as asking if they could go to bed again, and he didn't know the etiquette. If Jade was a girl he'd know, because the only reason she would be here was if he planned to take her to bed. The thought made him blink, and then frown. "I just realized I never asked a girl over unless I planned to take her to bed. Like, that was the whole point of it. Is that normal?"

Jade bit back a laugh. "I have people over all the time without taking them to bed. Do you ever have guys over?"

"No. If there's a social thing, it's always out in the world somewhere." There were reasons, such as the very annoying parking situation, but the truth was it never occurred to him.

"Would you *like* to have people over?"

"I don't think I've ever thought about it before. I must have thought that was the woman's job. Like, once I had a serious girlfriend or a wife, she would organize things. No wonder nothing lasted." He could tell Jade was holding in a laugh. "Go ahead and laugh. I learned that from my parents, though."

"Hey, I thought the same thing. Same exact pattern for me growing up. But living with a whole gang of other broke artists for so long, we never got over the habit of gathering." He sipped some of the new wine, conscious that he'd had a lot more than usual. Over the course of several hours, but still. "Whatever happened with your new wrestler?"

68

"Oh! I meant to tell you." Robert leaned forward, elbows on the table, smiling. "He got an offer to play a villain in this medium-low-budget action movie. They sent me the whole script, I sent it to him, he said can you rep me for this? And I had to say I've never done a movie deal before, there's a guy here who might do better for you. But if you want to trust me I'll talk to some people and do the best I can. He said sure. So I'm talking to this guy in my office, you know, picking his brain. Trawling through IMDb. Doing a fuck-ton of calling around. The details on deals aren't that easy to find. He's inclined to take the gig for shits and giggles, but if he likes it he might want to do more. So I don't want to put him in there for minimum wage, if you know what I mean."

"Sure." *Could you actually be more perfect.* Jade drank a little more wine. "A villain, huh. Is he a bad guy in the WWE?"

"Oh, they're all bad guys sometimes. He's not super huge. Six foot one, two thirty or so. Makes me look like a broomstick."

Jade almost choked on a mouthful of wine. He gulped, coughed, and laughed for a minute. "You do not look like a broomstick. I could do incredible things with you."

I'll bet you could. "Like what?" Robert was leaning back now, hand on the stem of his glass. Wondering if he was the only one who heard innuendo in that statement. This evening was clarifying one thing, which was that attraction to men was every bit as variable as attraction to women. It was not a case of 'any guy will do.' The guy he went to dinner with was a maybe. Jade was always going to be a yes please. Even though Robert had only half a clue what to do, how to do it, how to ask for it, or when. The man would not be here if he weren't at least a little bit interested. They wouldn't have shared that moment of awareness earlier if Jade weren't open to the possibility.

Jade watched Robert watching him, thought *there is no chance I'm not getting in his bed tonight*, and said, "I assume you've never done drag."

That was out of nowhere. "Uh, no."

"Would you?"

For you, anything. "I would consider it." He let all the caution come out in his tone.

"For a good cause?"

"What good cause?"

"Los Angeles LGBT Center. There's a benefit, the whole silent-auction thing plus a drag pageant. It's going to be a literary theme, so the costumes have to be based on a book."

"You have an idea." Robert was smiling again.

"Ever since I saw you naked." That was a slight exaggeration, but now the word was out of his head and in the air where it belonged. *What the hell*. "Which I'd like to do again."

It took a second for Robert to come up with something that wasn't 'let's go.' "I could be naked as soon as the kitchen is clean."

"Will it go faster if I help?" They were grinning at each other across the table. Jade didn't care if this was only a way for Robert to forget that phone call for a while. Didn't care that he had slipped several more notches toward love over the course of the evening.

Robert didn't care if this was only Jade being nice, taking care of him again, or thanking him for dinner. Didn't care that another night with the man was going to make it even harder to consider anyone else as a possibility. "It might go faster if you don't, actually. I don't know if I could keep my hands off you in close quarters."

"Mmm. I see. Well, I could spend a few minutes snooping through your closet. See what else needs to come out of it."

Robert laughed. "I'm so glad I met you." He stood up, collected the plates, and took them into the kitchen. Jade gave himself a second to savor that last comment, then went to snoop through (first) the powder room and (second) Robert's closet. He wasn't kidding about that.

It didn't take long to clean up the kitchen. Possibly because, atypically, Robert threw everything in the dishwasher instead of doing it by hand. If the machine didn't get things perfectly clean he would deal with it later. Right now all he wanted was to freshen up, get his clothes off, and see what else Jade could teach him. There was something he'd been fantasizing about for weeks. Every time it crossed his mind he wondered if this was always a thing he was curious about. Maybe it was. The first time a girl went down on him, in high school, he predictably loved it. It was more than a year after that before he went all the way with a girl. And he didn't like that as well, which he'd always thought was because of the condom, which they should have used for oral sex too. He didn't start doing that till college, and it was always a battle. His girlfriend never wanted to give head with a condom. That was the one thing he had to ask Jade before they did anything. He didn't want to ask. Didn't want to offend, or ruin the mood. But thanks to pathological fear, he'd made it to thirty-six without any STDs. It wasn't unreasonable to want to maintain that record. *Please let him not mind.*

This apartment was laid out with a master suite, even though it was only a one-bedroom. It was like the

71

builders fully expected the den to be used as a bedroom sometimes, even though it was open to the living-slash-dining room. The full bath was entered from the bedroom. So when Robert went into the room, he saw Jade – sitting on the bed, still clothed, doing something on his phone – and he saw a few things on the nightstand. Tissues (the box from the powder room), condoms, and lube. *Oh my Lord.* He didn't say anything before going into the bathroom.

Jade knew Robert noticed the staging. He put down his phone, went to get a glass of water, brought it back to the bedroom, then took off his clothes. He was already excited. It seemed like a long time since their first night. Apparently neither of them had been with anyone else. He wondered if he should start things, or wait for Robert. It was probably best if he did. He was more experienced, after all. When he heard the fan go off he got on the bed. Sitting on his heels, knees apart, one hand on his dick, as obvious as it was possible to be.

Robert stepped out of the bathroom naked. "Jade." It sounded husky. Seductive. Not his normal voice at all. "You're so beautiful."

"So are you, Robert. Get on this bed."

Chapter 7

Robert put one knee on the mattress. Just looking at the man had him so hard he couldn't stand it. He used to have to talk himself into being with a woman. Shoot down all the lame reasons why not: it's late, one of us has to drive home, whatever. He should have known this was what he wanted. "What are we going to do?"

"What do you want to do?" Jade wanted to grab him, pull him over, kiss him. Pin him down and fuck him like a blow-up doll.

Oh God, he actually had to say it. Jade was not going to let him get away with some weaselly bullshit. "I've been dreaming about getting my mouth on you. I love getting head. I've never done it." That was probably obvious. "But I'm scared. I've never had an STD." Oh *fuck* he just blurted that out as if he totally expected Jade to be some kind of infectious. "Shit, I'm sorry, that didn't –"

Jade shook his head, smiling a little. "It's good, you need to be able to say things like that. I've had chlamydia and gonorrhea. Both a long time ago, both treated. I've been clean for ten years. We can use condoms if you want. That's why I brought them."

"I don't. I don't want to. I want to feel your skin. I want to taste you." He was practically babbling now, and he was sitting close to Jade with his legs folded, hands down, leaning in. Begging for a kiss.

"Good. That's good." Jade lunged at him. A moment later they were stretched out, bodies plastered together, kissing hungrily. In the rational moments that surfaced through the next few minutes of obsession with Robert's mouth, his hands, the feel of his skin, Jade tried

73

to think of all the reasons he should take it slow. All the ways he should remind Robert that nothing had to happen. But he wasn't the one driving the bus now. Robert might be new at this but he was not tentative. It was as if he'd never wanted anything in his life more than Jade's flesh. He was leaning on one arm, one of Jade's legs between his and the other pushed up and open. Fondling and stroking with his free hand. Rocking his hips, making urgent sounds into Jade's mouth, against his throat. If Jade didn't do something they were both going to come like this. He wanted more. He planted his foot, braced his arm, gave a mighty heave and rolled them over.

Robert made a surprised noise, half a laugh. He looked up at Jade's gorgeous face. "What."

"What am I doing? I'm going to get my mouth on you. Take notes." He heard another laugh as he started moving south. Robert's hands were on him, but his body was still. It might have been nerves but Jade thought it was more like attention. Surely some woman had taken her time enjoying this body. Jade had no idea how a woman really made love to a man. Would she have spent this much time on Robert's neck? Would the angle of the jaw, the ridge of the collarbone, the hollow of the throat have bewitched her like this? Did she want more chest hair, or none at all? Did she notice how Robert's breath caught when a tongue swept across his nipple, how he twitched when teeth joined the party? Did she hear this exact gasp and that exact stifled moan when she sucked that nipple into her mouth?

Jesus, this body. He could have been a supermodel. You could put anything on this body and it would look like haute couture. All those people who thought an eight-pack was sexy, who liked overdeveloped pecs and obliques, would never appreciate this sleek, smooth, narrow torso. Muscles elongated, lying close to the bone. Jade had his mouth on a hipbone now. The skin there was like silk. He was looking at a magnificent erection. Robert's hand was in his hair. "Almost there."

"Sometime today."

Jade laughed. Licked down the crease of the groin, heard Robert make a breathless sound, and brushed his nose and mouth up along the side of that package. "Mmm." Delicious. The perfect degree of musk, very well-groomed. "Are you always this neat or were you expecting company."

"You. I was hoping for you." Robert was losing his mind.

Jade licked again, from base to tip. Mouthing around the length of that cock, hand full of balls, the other hand resting on Robert's ribs. His chest was propped on Robert's thigh; he could see the man's face. Slightly flushed, lips parted, pupils dilated. "Are you paying attention?"

"Jesus, yes." Robert moaned as Jade took his cock. From the feel of it, but also the way it looked. He wanted to close his eyes so he could focus on the sensation, but he wanted to see this. He'd never watched before. He looked so huge in Jade's mouth. How in hell was all of that fitting. Was he opening his throat somehow, how was he not gagging. Oh Jesus Christ the feel of it. The sounds Jade was making, as if he liked it. Would Robert like it when he had Jade in his mouth? He couldn't wait to find out. He was quivering with the effort of keeping still. Panting, whimpering, barely breathing. It was almost too much, the heat and pressure and suction, and then the swirl of tongue around the head of his cock. "Oh *God*." It felt like his balls exploded up through his shaft. His whole body heaved as he surged up into Jade's mouth.

Jade got his hand around the base of Robert's cock just in time to keep some control of the situation. Kept his lips tight around it so he wouldn't scrape with his teeth. Held his breath for a few seconds while the waves of climax pumped into the back of his throat. Swallowed, letting his hold soften. A caress now, slowly drawing his head away. Listening to Robert's breath even out. Pressing a kiss to the tender skin below his navel. Sometime soon he'd find out if the man was ticklish anywhere. Find out where the rest of his erogenous zones were. Right now he was so hard it hurt, and he wanted some relief. He pushed up onto hands and knees, letting his cock drool onto Robert's leg, and made eye contact.

There is no doubt what that look means, Robert thought nervously. "Your turn. What do you want? I'll do anything."

Jade huffed out a laugh. Did he have any idea what he was saying? Had he spent the last few weeks watching gay porn? Even if he had, he'd probably missed a lot of what 'anything' might entail. "I want your mouth. I'll settle for a hand."

Robert had no intention of making Jade *settle* for anything. "Should I do it like you?" He meant with all the kissing, all the attention to the rest of Jade's body. He'd love to do that, but maybe more foreplay was not what was called for here.

"No." Even five minutes of that would be too much.

"Tell me."

Well, this was the downside of taking on a virgin. He'd have to talk him through it, at least to get him started. On the plus side, he had the opportunity to get the man trained to do exactly what Jade most liked. Might as well take advantage of it. He stretched out on his back. "Give me a kiss." Robert was more than willing to do that. He did it slowly, too, tasting himself. Some men hated that. Jade smiled against his mouth. "Mmm. Thank you. Now since this is your first time, I'd suggest turning around. If you're facing my feet it'll be more comfortable for you. I won't be able to see your face, but this probably isn't going to take long."

Robert said "Okay," kissed him again, and got himself in position. He considered the optimal arrangement of arms and decided on one across Jade's hips, the other under his thigh. Made a pleased sound. Thought *I am totally not perturbed about having another man's dick a few inches from my face*, and did a version of the thing Jade did. Brushing his face against the close-trimmed hair of the groin, registering the different textures and scents as he examined the crinkled skin of the balls and the hot, smooth skin of the cock. He closed his mouth on the base of the shaft, sideways, licking across it. Jade's body jerked and he said something that sounded an awful lot like 'fuck.' It definitely didn't sound like 'you're doing it wrong,' so Robert did the same basic thing all the way up to the head. Oh Lord, the skin was so soft. So kissable. He held Jade's cock in one hand so he could focus on the head. The wetness there at the slit, a little bit salty. He licked a few times, heard some definite cursing from not far away. Swept his tongue all around, felt the whole package move in his hand. God, he *loved* this. He wanted more of it in his mouth. Jade might have given him some guidance if he asked, but he wanted to try to figure it out. He kept his thumb under the shaft and turned his head, sliding his mouth down that length until he couldn't take any more. His cheek rested on Jade's belly. Jade's hand landed on the back of his neck, stroking from his hair down to his shoulder and back.

Okay, I can take a hint. He moved his head. Up and down, keeping his mouth closed. This was hard on a guy's neck. He shoved up with the arm under Jade's thigh, getting some elevation. Holding on with thumb and forefinger, the others halfway cupping Jade's balls. Wetness under his hand, from his own saliva. He had a rhythm now, and he thought it was working. Jade's hips were rocking and he was making noise. Vocal breaths, pitch rising. *I'm going to make you come. God I hope it feels as good as what you gave me.* How had he not bitten Robert. Oh right the lips, tight down over the teeth. Letting Jade's motion do most of the work but keeping busy with his tongue. Breath coming harshly through his nose, there was a lot to manage here. He wanted to be an expert. Wanted to give the best head in the world, and only to Jade, he tasted so good. The balls were drawing up, cock swelling, was this *oh holy shit oh my God.*

He froze, afraid to move as Jade spasmed beneath him with a cry, thrusting up. The ejaculate filled his mouth, an indescribable taste. The combined forces of the climax almost made Robert gag. He coughed, managing not to lose Jade's cock, swallowing and then sucking in a breath through his nose. Jade's hand was in his hair. Body relaxing.

Jade felt lightheaded for a few seconds. He tried a couple of consciously-deep breaths. He wouldn't have sworn that awkward, eager, inexpert blow job was the best of his life; it probably only seemed that way because he'd been so desperately turned on. And, okay, because it was Robert. What a difference it made when you cared. He knew they both did. Had no idea what that meant, or where they might go with it. He tugged on Robert's hair. "You can let go now, sweetheart." The endearment slipped out.

78

Robert let go slowly. There was another drop of that salty slickness to lick up. "You taste good." Pressed his face into the crease of Jade's groin. "You smell good." Felt suddenly exhausted, let himself settle snugly against the other man's body, didn't even care that they were basically at sixty-nine. He needed to rest for a minute, that was all.

Jade felt it, the moment Robert went to sleep with his head pillowed on Jade's thigh and his arm possessively across Jade's hips. His other arm was still underneath that leg. Well, they could adjust in a few minutes. Switch around. Find a position where all limbs could receive proper circulation. God, he was exhausted. He would just close his eyes for a few seconds.

Robert woke a couple hours later, when the air in the room grew cool. He extracted his arm from under Jade's leg with a wince. Sat up, rubbing some life back into his limb, gazing at his bedmate for a few minutes. Jade was deeply asleep. He didn't wake even when Robert went to the bathroom, came back to pull up the covers, and switched off the lamp. Robert considered the implications of sleeping with someone. He'd stopped doing it, all those years ago, because he never slept well. The first night with Jade, he'd slept like a drugged man. That he hadn't this time was probably due to the entangled way they'd fallen asleep. This would go into a new data set. Every time he slept with someone, he'd try to observe sleep quality. If he ever slept with anyone aside from Jade, it would be meaningful data in his new context.

If he didn't, it would only be data. An addition to the evidence he was accumulating that this man, in particular, was meaningful.

Maybe he should have doubted himself more. Maybe he should be very suspicious of his willingness to accept everything about this situation. Maybe he should see a counselor, and talk all this out with someone other than … well, other than who? His friends? Jade? People who actually knew him? But maybe that was the whole point. To talk it over with somebody who had no agenda. Who wouldn't let him kid himself about things. He'd look into it soon. But for now, he was going back to sleep.

Jade woke up with a hand on his body again. Someone's face in his hair again. Both of them aroused again. But this time when he turned his head, he saw Robert gazing back at him. His expression was warm, happy, amused. His hand was on Jade's chest. "Sorry if I woke you. I woke up like this and was wondering if I should move."

"I have to move. But I'll be right back, unless you have to get out of here soon."

"It's only seven-fifteen." That was as close as he could come to saying 'please don't leave yet.' He watched Jade get out of bed, appreciating that slinky body until it disappeared behind the bathroom door. Then he shot out of bed to go freshen up himself. Should he mention the lube? Should he admit to that particular curiosity? Was it a thing best examined at night, or on a weekend? He wouldn't have it in mind right now if Jade hadn't brought the stuff. If he'd ever thought about gay sex before realizing that was the kind of sex he'd be having from here on out, he would have a better idea if lube was used for more than the one thing. They'd only done it two ways so far. Should he mention the porn he'd downloaded and watched? Blushing furiously, volume almost at zero because the first sounds he heard were so embarrassing. Those guys might have used lube. God, he hoped so. But if so, they didn't show that part.

He realized that he and Jade were making similar sounds the night before. Was he embarrassed? Somehow it was less embarrassing to think someone might have overheard him actually having sex, versus watching somebody else have sex. He needed to be really careful about that laptop. His recent search history was a scandal waiting to happen. The thought made him laugh. He was still grinning when he went back in the bedroom.

Jade was there, stretching on the bed. "What's so funny?" Robert sat cross-legged beside him and told him. Jade laughed too. "Yes, the sound effects can be a little mortifying after the fact. But I've never had a neighbor bang on the wall." He straightened up and sat cross-legged like Robert. "I brought the lube because I wanted to be ready for anything. I wasn't sure you'd want to go to bed again."

"I wasn't sure either, until the second you walked in."

Jade put a hand down so he could lean over and get a kiss. "You're still feeling okay about everything?"

"I really am. Woke up in the middle of the night and was thinking, do I need to talk to someone professional. And I don't feel like I do, but I think I will anyway. Even if everything's fine with this part of my life there are still other parts that I've never dealt with." He had Jade's hand in his now. Running his thumb up those slender fingers. "There's so many things I want to try."

"To see if you like them?"

"Mm-hmm. But." He hesitated. After a few seconds: "Could I ask you on a date? An actual date?"

Jade curled his fingers around Robert's. "Yes." He waited to see if there was anything coming to address that 'but.' It seemed not. "Words, sweetheart." That word again. Well, he *was* a sweetheart.

Robert heard it, promised himself he'd think about that later, and sighed. "I never want you to think that I'm only using you as a, a *tutor* or something. That because you were the first man I kissed I assume I can keep coming to you to try every new thing. I want to try every new thing with you because you're you, not because you're the only guy I know who might be up for it."

Jade studied him for a moment. "I'll bet you know quite a few guys who might be up for it."

Robert huffed out a laugh. "More than I thought I did."

"Are they making passes now? Are you suddenly the hot new piece of ass?" He was smiling. "Because you are a hot piece of ass."

Robert straight-up giggled. "It's so weird!"

"But not scary. Not alarming, or offensive, or whatever?"

"No, nothing like that. Guys are like, hey baby, and half the time I just laugh because I'm like what? But, ugh, we don't have all day. I know you need to get home. I have to get ready for work at some point. What would you suggest as the first way to use that lube."

Jade was pretty sure that question was not what Robert intended to say. Neither of them was desperately turned on at the moment. They could quite easily get dressed and go about their business. On the other hand, what he had in mind probably wouldn't take long, it would feel great, and they'd both go into their day smiling. "Lie down, and I'll show you. On your back," he clarified. "I'll show you some other stuff another time. When we don't have to go anywhere."

82

Robert reclined, smiling, not at all nervous because this was Jade. Even if it was embarrassing he'd still enjoy it. He'd enjoy the memory. He'd enjoy fantasizing about it later. Jade got the lube, then settled himself astride Robert's thighs. They were both half hard. Then Jade squeezed some lube into his palm and wrapped his hand around Robert. Stroked a few times. "Oh wow. That feels … different."

"Mmm." Jade added a little more lube, slicked himself. Robert was watching that intently, face slightly flushed, lips parted, erection at full strength. "You could watch me get myself off like this, and do it to yourself. You could use your hand on me. I could use my hand on you. But personally I thought some more kissing would be nice."

Robert made a sound of something like protest. He wanted some more attention paid to his dick. But then Jade stretched out on top of him, going for a kiss that was instantly hot and hungry. The feeling of his hard slippery cock pressing against Robert's, the friction as they both started to move, was like nothing he'd ever imagined. He had one arm wrapped tight around that narrow back, one leg locked over Jade's. Straining against him, panting, making pornier porn sounds than he'd ever thought could come out of his mouth. The kiss was hard, sloppy, toothy. He could never have kissed a woman like this. He had his fingers clenched tight in Jade's hair when he came.

The sound Robert made was very rewarding. Jade set his teeth in the man's shoulder, one hand planted beside his head, shoving against him. Then Robert's hand was at the top of his thigh, pulling him in even tighter, and the thought that someday he might be inside took him over the edge. "God," he said indistinctly, mouth pressed to Robert's skin, as the climax pulsed through him. They were both still, breathing heavily.

"What were you thinking," Robert said softly, when he had enough air to talk.

"When."

"Something changed after I grabbed your ass."

Jade organized his hands, pushed himself up and away, but not far. Settling on his side half on top of his lover, so they could breathe and cool off. "I flashed on how it would be to be inside you."

"Oh." A bit high-pitched. Not quite a squeak. Robert felt Jade's belly jump with a silent laugh. He tried for a more manly tone. "That's something you like?"

"I haven't done it often. When it went that far, it's usually been the other way around."

"But you'd like to."

"I think I would." The 'with you' was implied. "Maybe I could do it to you, and you can take notes. Then you could try it. It's not a requirement, either way."

"Maybe we could work our way up to that. It looked kind of rough, in the video I saw."

Jade took note of the singular reference to a video. So Robert hadn't been on a porn spree. He was such an innocent. Being trusted with that was such a gift. "It can be rough. Doesn't have to be. I don't like it rough."

Robert heard the reassuring subtext of 'I won't hurt you' and 'I'll stop if you don't like it.' Cast about for something innocuous to say, something that wasn't one of the overly-emotional things sloshing around in his head. "Can you stay for breakfast? Or I could drive you back to your place."

84

Jade thought he might be a little too pleased at both suggestions. Then he thought *if you're going to fall, it's going to happen whether you fight it or not, so why fight it*. He craned his neck to get a look at the clock. "World's fastest shower and option two."

"Go ahead and start the shower. I can at least get some coffee rolling." Robert accepted another kiss, levered himself up off the bed, observed that he was an absolute mess, and went to the kitchen not caring at all.

Chapter 8

They didn't return to the subject of the drag pageant before parting, but Robert hadn't forgotten it. He wasn't at all sure he wanted to do it. On the other hand, it sounded like the sort of challenge that could be transformative, and that seemed to be what 2010 was all about for him. Plus he got the idea it was an important event for Jade. So after he had the day's work under control, he sent an email.

> Hey Jade,
> Last night was great. Thanks so much for lending support, and for everything else.
> You mentioned a benefit for the LGBT Center. Maybe we could talk about that some more this weekend? If you're not booked all the way through. Let's say next time you're free.
> JM approved a counter to the offer on that movie. Waiting to hear back. If they go for it I'll take him out to celebrate. If you want to meet him let me know, I think you'd like him. Maybe you could join us for dinner.
> Take care of those hands. I'll be thinking about them tonight.
> Robert

He almost didn't write those last two sentences, or rather almost didn't leave them in the email. What it came down to was wanting to say everything he thought he could say without freaking either of them out. He knew Jade was expecting Robert to trip over some kind of trigger and have a meltdown. He almost expected it himself. *Focus on business*. On to the next email, the next voice mail, the next way to make some money for a client. The next thing to distract him from the growing certainty that he was falling in love.

Jade was busy on a set from ten till well past midnight. He saw the email come in, took a moment to be pleased that Robert got in touch, didn't read it because his hands were literally full. He was styling a whole group of extras for a black-tie banquet scene and he really shouldn't have even had his phone out on the counter. At the end of the day he'd have to take the Windex to it in order to get the film of hairspray and powder off.

And the end of the day was far too late to call, which was how he would have preferred to respond to that sweet and tentative message. But he didn't want Robert to start the next day thinking Jade wasn't going to answer, so he sent a reply email.

Hi Robert,

When you see the time stamp on this you'll know I really wanted to answer you. It was a hell of a day. Lost count of all the updos, and why don't people know how to shave?

First, I'd be delighted to meet the wrestler. Here are the nights I know I'm free for the next two weeks.

Second, if you really want to talk about the pageant there's something I could show you that might give you an idea what's possible. It's on DVD, we could watch at your place or mine. Same availability.

Aside from that, the book I want to feature is called The Beekeeper's Apprentice by Laurie R. King and the character is Mary Russell. The event is in September so there's plenty of time to work this up if you decide you want to. On the other hand if you really don't want to (which is fine) ((though would I hate to miss seeing you as this character)) let me know soonest because I need to come up with something else, find a model, etc.

I'm back on set tomorrow so don't be surprised if you don't hear from me right away. I'll be thinking about your hands too.

Jade

He could have written a lot more. Might have, if it weren't so damned late. There would be another chance.

The next time they saw each other was business-adjacent, but definitely a date. They were meeting Jonathan Morris at Morton's downtown to celebrate the movie deal. Robert thought hard about what to wear. He'd never seen his wrestler in a suit and didn't want to look too formal. Especially since he was taking Jade along. His solution was his best jeans, a silvery-gray linen blazer that he'd bought for a friend's summer wedding, and a white dress shirt with no tie. The approving look he got from Jade was a reward.

Jonathan was at the bar waiting for them. He looked massive but harmless in khakis, a sport coat, and a button-down shirt. Jade was dressed to kill in black dress pants and another slinky shirt. This one was a snake print in red and gold. When he did the usual thing, offering his hand, the big guy didn't hesitate at all. He took Jade's hand lightly in his, said "Robert told me you're a stylist. He didn't mention you looked like this," and kissed the back of it. Jade was absolutely floored, and also delighted. Jonathan must have seen both; he laughed, let go of Jade's hand, and took Robert's for a normal sort of greeting. Then he said, as if to clear things up, "My second divorce was final this week, I'm a total fuck-up, maybe it's time I should try something new. But if you happen to know any nice women who are looking for a two-time loser, send them my way."

"You're not a loser," Robert said, patting the big guy's back. "You're going to be a movie star. You'll be up to your neck in women."

"Really?" Jonathan sounded interested. That sort of banter continued while they waited for the host to come get them. Once their order was in, Jade asked how Jonathan got started with WWE. They ended up talking sports for most of the dinner, then sports movies through coffee. The big guy might have been surprised that the swish Hollywood stylist could give him chapter and verse on every baseball movie ever made, but he didn't show it.

"He's a lot of fun," Jade said in the car on their way home. "No wonder they wanted to put him in a movie."

"He is a lot of fun. I have a feeling he could be big. He's got a little bit of a complex about not having a good education, but he's plenty smart. He's never been in the obvious sorts of trouble." Meaning drugs, alcohol, reckless driving, or domestic violence. Robert had done a thorough investigation after the movie offer came down, because the contract had some clauses about nullifying behavior and he didn't want to get tripped up. "I asked around and found him an acting coach. Someone to help him get used to memorizing dialogue, trying out different tone and timing."

"By the time he's on his second picture you'll be an expert." Jade was smiling. "Your other clients will be all, find me a movie."

"Oh Lord I hope not. Some of those guys, ugh. No." He heard Jade laughing, glanced over at him so he could see that, looked back at the highway. "Jonathan's got good diction and a great voice. The movie people didn't say so, but I'll bet that's why they went for him instead of some other wrestler. He's not the most villainous-looking guy in the sport."

"I could make him look more villainous. Easiest thing in the world."

"I'll bet you could." Robert navigated the exit to La Cienega. "Could I send him to you? It seemed like you got along."

Jade would have taken the guy on even if he didn't like him. It was never a bad thing to have another connection. Plus, if Jonathan was a big success, that was going to be good for Robert. And anything that was good for Robert was going to make Jade happy. "Sure." He thought about it the rest of the way to his place. Wished he didn't have an early start the next day.

Robert pulled up outside the building, knowing he couldn't ask to come up, wishing he could. "Where do you have to be at oh God o'clock?"

"Pasa-fucking-dena." Jade unbuckled his seat belt, leaned over for a kiss. "I had a great time tonight. Can you send me Jonathan's script? So I could get an idea about the character?"

"Sure." He knew he didn't have to say 'keep it to yourself.' Jade understood about that stuff. He understood everything. "I'll call you."

"I know you will." One more kiss, then out of the car before he could say anything he shouldn't. He let himself into the building, aware that Robert hadn't pulled away. Turned to wave. Went up to his apartment, wishing.

Robert did his usual after-a-date thing, meaning he called Jade. This time he was not relieved to have to leave a message, because he actually wanted to talk to the guy. All he said on the voice mail was "Thanks for coming with me last night. I had a great time. Jonathan texted to say he did too. Talk to you soon." Then he sent a text: *Hi Jade this is not me being a stalker, I swear. I could use your help getting a client to fire me. He's coming in at eleven, any chance you could send me a selfie around a quarter after?*

Jade saw that text, had an idea what Robert was up to, and didn't reply. Not till eleven-fifteen, when he sent a deliberately-sexy selfie without comment. The comment he wanted to send might have been 'go ahead and stalk me.'

Across town, Robert heard his phone buzz at the suggested time and thought *you are the greatest*. Then he picked it up, with an apologetic look at the client he wanted to unload, and nearly laughed out loud. "Sorry, just got a picture. My boyfriend." He turned the phone around and showed it to Kurt, whose expression was exactly what Robert expected it to be.

"Your boyfriend." Flat, disapproving, disgusted. Very much the tone Robert heard from his mother, but he wasn't going to think about that right now. He waited for the next words. Kurt said, "I didn't know you were one of them."

"One of them? Oh, you mean gay. Well, it wasn't pertinent to whether I could represent you effectively. Or was it?" He let that sit for a second. His client was sufficiently self-aware to know that firing his agent for being gay was not going to look good to a lot of people. On the other hand, knowingly working with a gay agent was not going to look good to some other people.

As usual, Kurt came down on the side of the other people. "I don't think I can keep working with you."

"You don't think you *want to* keep working with me," Robert clarified. "I understand. Have your lawyer draft a termination letter. There may be someone else at the agency who can take you on." It wasn't a sure thing, and the guy definitely knew it. But he was a guy who thought he was always going to get away with everything, because so far he always had. The meeting was over. Robert watched the guy walk out with no regrets. He picked up the phone again, enjoyed the picture again, and texted back: *Thanks so much that was perfect mission accomplished. IOU as usual. Let me know how you want me to pay up.* He was strongly tempted to write something about how he called Jade his boyfriend, but he didn't quite dare. And he didn't want to hang around the office, because that business was stressful even though it was a little bit fun. He checked in with his assistant, suggested he could bring back some coffee, got a pleased response, and went for a walk. While he was waiting in the coffee shop another text came in: *Did you have a homophobe?*

Yes. Footballer recently 'cleared' of rape because girl mysteriously dropped charges

Oh gross. You don't need him

Definitely not. That picture was perfect for about a thousand reasons. You don't mind if I keep it do you?

Jade was thrilled. *Not at all. It's nice to be appreciated*

You definitely are. I'll email you that script when I get back to the office. Say hi to Shaya for me

Will do TTYL

Walking back with the coffee, Robert wondered why he'd never missed this feeling before. Maybe it was simply because he never knew this feeling existed. He wasn't sure when he'd get to see Jade again; they both had crazy hours for the next week or so. Right now wouldn't have been too soon. Right now was exactly what he wanted. He wished their regular workplaces were closer together, or that they both had normal office jobs. That they were in the right place for Robert to say 'see you tonight' or for Jade to sign off with something a little more personal than 'TTYL.' He needed to watch himself. It was still possible that this was only infatuation. That he might look back on it someday and think 'what a great way to start being gay' but not 'I will never do better than this.' That the best sex of his life, plus being able to talk to someone about everything, didn't add up to more than the sum of those parts.

When Shaya saw the picture she said, "Yowza."

"It's not that bad," Jade said, biting back a laugh. "I have all my clothes on." Admittedly the shirt was unbuttoned, he'd done a little subtle makeup to give himself a very sleepy-morning-after look, and his free hand was on his neck as if he'd just run it through his rumpled hair.

"Why did you send that particular picture?"

He put the phone in his pocket and got back to work. "Instead of a boring one? Because he said he needed help getting a client to fire him. I would have bet you a pitcher of margaritas he had a homophobe; he was going to make a production out of getting that text; he'd show the picture to the guy, and the guy would walk."

Shaya blinked. "That is a very specific bet." Then she narrowed her eyes. "Wait. Did you talk about this guy before?"

"I think so. It wouldn't have been a fair bet. I was spot on."

"Well, good for you. God knows I've wanted a few clients to fire me."

"That one woman. You keep charging her more." Jade was snickering. That was a common device: jacking up the price, hoping eventually the problem client would give up and go somewhere else. If they didn't, at least you were being well-compensated for unpleasantness.

Shaya shook her head. "Most expensive hair in all of West Hollywood, I think. Maybe every other stylist in the city already told her to gee tee eff oh." Jade was trying not to crack up; he had scissors in his hand. They shouldn't even be having this conversation with a client in his chair. "So I would have ended up paying for the pitcher, huh." Her tone was very judgemental.

"Mm-hmm."

"Cheater."

"Only a potential cheater," he pointed out. "But to make up for it, I'll buy the first round next time." He offered something else, too, though not until they were both done with their clients. "This client of Robert's is coming in for a test style. He got a part in a movie and needs a villainous look."

"Ooohh." Shaya was delighted. "Can I stay and watch?"

"That's the whole reason I told you, honey." He gave her the date.

A few days later Jonathan was at the salon, in the evening because Jade's schedule was packed. The big guy came in with a bag full of enough sushi for four people. Shaya was supposed to be off at eight, but hung around after lowering the blinds and turning the sign over to tell the world they were closed. She kept up some ridiculous banter with Jonathan while they ate,

94

cleaned the place up while Jade discussed his ideas with the wrestler, and promised to be quiet as a mouse while they worked. "Don't be quiet," Jonathan said. "I need you to distract me. I just had these goddamned hair implants and now he's telling me he's going to shave my head."

"They'll grow back," Jade said heartlessly. "That's the whole point." Jonathan sighed, gave Shaya a pitiful look, and submitted.

Robert could hardly believe the before and after pictures Jade emailed the next day. Jonathan's slightly-suspect hair was shaved to the scalp. His olive skin tone now looked paler, because his eyebrows were darker and heavier. The skin around his eyes was subtly darkened, and his lower lashes enhanced. The eyes that were blue-hazel in real life were now golden-brown, surely due to contact lenses. His nine o'clock shadow might have been darkened, too; the shadow beard joined up to shadow sideburns. Best of all, running from the point of one eyebrow to the nape of his neck was a tribal-style tattoo that matched a real one on his shoulder. He looked like a man who stayed up late thinking about ways to fuck people up, and possibly getting off on it. Jade must have painted that tattoo. Robert absolutely loved it. Anyone who saw it was going to think 'this guy is dangerously nuts.' It was exactly what the part called for.

It was, however, a toss-up whether the movie people would want this exact look. Even if they didn't, the after picture could go in Jonathan's marketing kit. Robert sent a quick thank-you, then asked his assistant to send flowers to the salon. "To Jade Derecha." He spelled it for her.

Emily had the florist website open five seconds later. "What kind of flowers does she like?"

95

"Uh, Jade is a guy." Robert was smiling. "And I don't know for sure, but I think he'd like white roses with something purple." Based on nothing but the décor in Jade's bedroom.

"How much do you want to spend?" Emily was extremely interested in this development. The agency-wide rumor to the effect that Robert-who-used-to-be-Bob was seeing men now would seem to be confirmed. She hadn't realized he was seeing anyone in a serious way. The 'how much' would answer a lot of questions.

"I don't care. Make it a dozen roses, with whatever looks good. I trust you. Put a card in that says," he thought for a second, "I'll thank you properly when I see you."

A dozen roses?! Emily squealed a little on the inside. She couldn't help it, she was a romantic. She was also very gratified by the 'I trust you.' The flowers she eventually sent were worthy of a wedding.

They were delivered at the end of the day. Jade was packing up his tools, getting ready to go home, thinking about that almost-brusque email from Robert. He'd sort of expected, or maybe hoped, for something warmer. Maybe including a suggestion for another date. *He's busy too*, he told himself. *Don't be a diva.* Then the door opened and the person at the front desk squealed. Everyone in the salon looked that way.

"Jade!! These are for you!"

Jade was frozen for a few seconds. No-one had ever sent him flowers. Apparently there was something to be said for being with someone who used to date women. *Am I with Robert? Is that what this means?* Somebody gave him a gentle shove and he walked to the front. Put his nose in the roses and lavender, throat tight. Swallowed hard, straightened up, found the card. Blew out a breath through his mouth. Touched a twig of pussy willow. This was beautiful. He was so glad he was going to be in the salon for the next week. He'd be able to see this every day. People were asking who sent the flowers. "They're from Robert," he said. Of course everybody knew who that was. He thought some money might have changed hands. "I'll put them on Tonio's station since he's out this week. We can all enjoy them." The vase weighed a ton. After moving it, he got his phone out and sent a text: *Hi Robert, your beautiful flowers were just delivered. Everyone here is in a tizzy. So am I. Are you free tonight?*

The reply came fast: *I am now*

Come to my place. I'm on my way

See you soon. Robert debated for half a second before adding *OXO*, then sent it before he could second-guess himself.

Chapter 9

Jade saw hug-kiss-hug and thought, *At least.* He took a phone picture of the flowers before he left. On the way home, he stopped to pick up some no-prep-required dinner items from the fancy deli. After that was put away he dithered for a few seconds. He was fairly sure it was still too soon to talk about feelings, so he turned on the TV. They wouldn't really talk while a game was on. The occasional comment or reaction, not a conversation. He needed a shield, something to make this casual.

Robert didn't cooperate. As soon as he was through the door he had his arms around Jade, face in his hair, sighing as though he'd truly come home. "Can I tell you something?"

Oh God not yet yes tell me everything. "Mmm?"

"Last week when you sent me that picture? I called you my boyfriend."

It was a relief, because it wasn't a declaration. It was also a disappointment, because it wasn't a declaration. Jade took a breath and said, "That's okay. Were you worried about telling me that?"

"It's only you said you wanted me to see other people, and I've been doing that, and we've only seen each other four times, well five counting tonight, but only a boyfriend would send me that kind of picture and it kind of slipped out because I kind of think of you that way anyhow." *Oh shit did I really just say all that.*

Jade was still in Robert's arms. He turned his head a few degrees, brushed his mouth over the other man's jaw, and said, "When those flowers came today I

98

thought, so this is what it's like to be with someone who used to date women." A stifled laugh. "And then I thought wait, am I with Robert? I've been fretting about it ever since."

"Why fretting?"

"Because it's been hardly any time since you made this huge discovery. I do want you to see other people. If you want to be with me despite everything else that's out there, great. But it needs to be an informed choice."

Robert thought that through. The third sentence seemed like the most important. "That said, is it okay if I think of you as my boyfriend? When I look at that picture, at least?"

Jade huffed out a laugh. Ducked his head a little to press a kiss to his lover's collarbone, tantalizingly exposed because he'd taken time to change out of his suit before coming over. "Yes, it's okay. So what happened with that guy?" He eased back a little.

Robert allowed it. "He fired me. I was asked for a statement and said something about different viewpoints. His publicist issued a statement trying to cover the fact that he fired me because I'm gay. The next day an out tennis player got in touch to see if we could work together."

"I didn't know there *were* any out tennis players."

"He's not a star." Robert shrugged. That wasn't important. He kissed Jade's forehead. "So are we eating? Watching a game?" *Going to bed?*

Jade thought he could detect an agenda, not so hidden, that was the same as his own. "Both those things. Did you find an overnight parking spot? Because I'd like to thank you for those flowers." He could only assume that the answer was 'yes' because Robert was kissing him. He let himself be moved until his back was up against the wall. Robert's body pressed against his from chest to knees. Jade got his hands under Robert's shirt, roaming all over that sleek skin. Mouth open, eyes closed, fully aroused. Robert unbuttoned his shirt. Moved his mouth to Jade's neck, chest, nipple. "Oh God."

"Mmm. Can I?" Hands at Jade's waist, waiting for the 'yes' before undoing his pants.

Such good manners. "Yes." Pushing Jade's pants down, then his briefs. Steadying him while he got his feet free. On his knees, hands on Jade's hips, face pressed to his belly, then brushing against his erection. Jade made some kind of sound. Then Robert's mouth closed over him. "Jesus!" An answering sound, something like a laugh as one hand went around to grip his ass. This guy was a quick study. Pulling Jade forward, deeper into his mouth. "Fuck, Robert, you're so hot." A sound that might have been 'you are.' A tug on Jade's thigh, as if he wanted that knee up. Jade bent his leg, planted his foot on the wall behind him, and started fucking Robert's mouth.

"Mmm. Mm-hmm." That happy sound told Jade this was exactly what the man wanted. Robert had one hand on the top of Jade's standing leg, the other wrapped around Jade's cock. There was no chance he could get out of control. He let himself go, more conscious of the sounds Robert was making than those he made himself. Enjoying the wet heat of Robert's mouth and then, at the perfect moment, a tighter grip and some suction. Jade's rhythm changed. Shallower, faster, feeling the climax build like an ocean swell until it broke. He heard a startled sound from Robert, a stifled cough, and tried to pull back. Robert wouldn't let him. He took it all, swallowing, holding on until Jade's pulse faded. Foot sliding down, heart pounding.

If this were any other man, he'd make some crack about practice making perfect. Didn't want to cheapen this. He ran his hand through Robert's hair, cleared his throat, and said, "Your turn." Reached down for a hand, helped his lover up, pulled him in for a kiss. Tasting himself. Feeling the fierce erection pressed against him. "Mmm. In here." Jade stepped to the side. Kept hold of Robert's hand, tugging him along to the bedroom. "Get your clothes off." He didn't have to watch that happen; he could hear it, and it only took a few seconds. Then Jade was on his back with the lube in his hand. Spreading some on his inner thighs. "That first morning when I got myself off I was thinking of this. Lie down."

"On top of you?"

"Mm-hmm. Slick yourself up. Get in here."

Robert didn't need any more prompting. He stretched out on top of Jade, erection shoved between his thighs, and started fucking him almost before they were kissing again. Jade had one hand on his ass, fingers right above his balls. Robert was losing his mind. One knee on the bed, the other clamped to the outside of Jade's leg. Pinning the man's legs closed around his cock. The thought of how this must look: Jade with his head pressed back, neck arching, arm wrapped over Robert's back. And Robert's teeth sunk in the man's deltoid as he cried out. Coming hard, shuddering, going still. Moving his head to press a kiss to that abused shoulder, then to Jade's neck. Becoming aware that his dick was on fire. "God *damn*." He detached himself, fanning his crotch.

Jade was laughing silently. "That was a lot of friction."

"How about you?"

"A cool washcloth would be nice right now." They were both wheezing.

"Okay. Don't move."

"I can't." More ridiculous laughter as Robert half-fell off the bed, staggering out of the room. He was back in a minute, wrapping one cold damp washcloth around his dick as he sat beside Jade. He used the other to wipe Jade's thighs, balls, cock. Jade helpfully opened his knees, then rolled over.

Robert cleaned up the underside of his legs. Gave him a light swat on the ass, then wiped the sheet. "So did I need more lube?"

"A little. You went longer than I expected." Jade rolled over again.

"It felt too good. I didn't want to come too fast." It occurred to him that this had not been a problem with women. In fact, he suspected the opposite was the problem. Irrelevant now, though possibly he owed a few ladies an apology. He leaned over for another kiss. "I'm glad you liked the flowers."

Should he say no-one ever sent him flowers before? Maybe so. Robert deserved to know when he did something noteworthy. "That was the first time anyone ever sent me flowers."

"Oh! Really? Is that not a thing gay guys do?"

"Not the ones who were dating me, anyway. It made me feel special."

"You are special." They regarded each other for a moment. "And I am hungry."

Jade sat up. "You're special too. Let's eat." The rest of the evening would have fit Jade's earlier goal of keeping it casual, except for the way they sat together to watch what was left of the game. Wearing only tee shirts, with Robert's arm over Jade's shoulders and their bare legs intertwined. They went to bed together as if it were the most ordinary thing in the world, except for the way they settled close, Jade's back to Robert's front. They didn't talk about feelings. Neither of them quite dared to.

In the morning, when Robert reluctantly got dressed to go, he leaned over to kiss Jade. Softly, lingeringly, meaningfully. Touched the man's face, gazed into those warm hazel eyes, and almost said something. Settled for, "See you soon." Jade watched him leave the room, heard the apartment door close, and thought, *if this isn't love I don't know what is.* He wondered what Robert hadn't said.

Robert was, again, thinking about all the things he wanted to say and didn't dare say as he went home, as he got ready for work, and on the way to the office. He hadn't even told Jade about Jonathan's email. It was partly because he didn't want to raise any hopes. A question as to whether requesting a particular stylist for the movie shoot was a thing he could do, and Robert's reply saying 'let's find out,' added up to a maybe at best. They might not get a response at all, or the response might be 'already hired somebody, sorry.' The start date for filming was only a few weeks away. For all Robert knew, Jade had something else lined up. They weren't at the point of telling each other about every work thing. *I want him to tell me everything.*

This was new, too. This apparently-bottomless interest. He'd never given a moment's thought to how a stylist's day might be. How the business worked. Now he knew that Jade and the others rented their chairs at the salon. They were independent contractors, rather than employees; that was how they had the freedom to take gigs up to and including film shoots. Of course that was also why they had all the work of running their own business. All the record-keeping and other hassles.

Robert knew about that. His father had plenty to say on the subject of self-employment. You should have gone into a law firm, you'd be making twice as much, guaranteed. It could take you ten years to get established. You could be a partner by then. On and on, as if Robert's choice were somehow a personal insult. As if he'd suspected it had something to do with Dad's buddy who had a law office in Salt Lake City and a daughter Robert's age who would make such a good wife. Or as if it were a whim based on 'Jerry Maguire.' So what if he had been inspired by that movie. It was mostly because he'd never even heard of sports management before. He'd fully intended to go into sports law, and get his fix from the sidelines. But this career put him closer. It put him in the managers' offices and the locker rooms. It gave him a legitimate, non-wannabe, non-pathetic excuse to follow the sports his athletes were involved in. And he could use his brains and his expertise to help them succeed. He was as important as a coach, and he was making more than any of his classmates who'd gone into law firms. More than his brother. More than his father.

The money conversation, last Christmas, had been interesting. It started with a comment about the house Lance bought, and quickly diverted to why Robert was still in a rental. Couldn't he afford to buy, blah blah. The mild answer that he could do better in the stock market than the real-estate market led to a semi-snide remark that (for the first time) Robert didn't let slide. He told them his net for 2008. Told them what he had saved, even with his loans cleared and a new car. His father didn't backpedal, exactly. He'd simply not pursued the conversation once it became clear the story didn't include 'you were right' or 'I'm coming home.' Instead Robert's mother pitched in with a comment about how he must be ready to think about getting married. And he made her happy by saying he was. Well, at the time it was true. What a difference a 'no' made. What in the world would he be thinking and feeling now, if Sharon had said yes? Would he be glad? Would he still be convinced he was straight?

The thought of never having met Jade was an almost-physical pain. The occasional moment of confusion, or disbelief, or shock – like that moment in the gym, when a guy said something flirty and Robert flirted back in front of everybody; it didn't catch up to him until he'd been on the treadmill listening to his mp3 player for five minutes – was a small price to pay for those conversations. Those kisses. This … *call it what it is*. This love.

Robert spent the too-many days until his next date with Jade carrying on with business, trying not to think about the silence from Utah, accepting two more invitations to meet other men for coffee or a drink, and reading 'The Beekeeper's Apprentice.' He liked to read, but hadn't taken much time for it. In high school he was busy with sports. His missionary year, he basically didn't dare read anything except the official book. Then he packed three degrees into six years; he honestly couldn't remember reading a single book for pleasure in that time. Since then so many of his leisure hours had gone to work-related research that he'd almost forgotten *how* to sit and read a story that was longer than a magazine piece. He was halfway through the book before it really caught him. The last third went in a single up-too-late session, and he immediately ordered the sequel.

The thought of going out in public, actually on a *runway*, as Mary Russell was so wildly improbable he didn't know how to feel about it. He stripped naked, stared at himself in his full-length mirror, and wondered. Looked up 1920s fashion and wondered. Maybe this DVD Jade was going to play for him would clear things up. When he asked people to recommend movies set in the Twenties, everyone said 'Chicago' and 'Some Like It Hot.' He enjoyed them both, and after seeing Tony Curtis and Jack Lemmon in drag the whole thing seemed a lot less impossible. They weren't fully credible as women, but for that story they weren't supposed to be. He didn't know what 'drag' meant, he decided. He'd let Jade tell him. At least he wasn't coming into this completely clueless now.

The flowers lasted nearly two weeks. Jade had another few days on a set during the second week, but made a point of going by the salon on his way home so he could visit the roses. Watching them fade didn't make him sad. They weren't meant to last. When the flowers were all spent, he collected the pussy willows and took them home. Once he was done with the latest movie gig, he was back to business as usual. In between heads, he chatted with Shaya, who was deeply interested (not to say invested) in his new romance. "It *is* a romance, isn't it?" The question was a bit mangled because she had a rattail comb in her mouth, but he got the gist of it.

He glanced at Shaya's client, noticed the expression of fake absorption she was giving to the magazine on her lap, and bit his lip. Met Shaya's eyes, tried not to laugh, and said, "I think it is. It's different, that's for sure. I lost my head and asked him if he'd be my model for the pageant."

"You did not!"

"Mm-hmm. Of course he's never done drag at all. Barely knows what it is. Who are you doing?"

Shaya couldn't hide her excitement. "Patrick."

"You are not!"

"I couldn't believe he said yes."

Patrick Sarkisian had been Shaya's client for six years. He was a prominent WeHo businessman, in a committed relationship with a man who ran a dance studio a couple of blocks away from the salon. Jade thought about this. He knew both men supported LGBT causes. There was a legendary Pride event featuring a dance performance from Patrick's partner Dmitri and a well-known local theater person. Neither of them, however, was in the drag scene. "And you're doing Amelia?"

Shaya nodded excitedly. "Full Amelia."

Jade giggled. "The Egypt excavation costume, or something formal?" Shaya's client was openly listening now.

"All bustle all the time, baby." They both giggled. "He's getting their friend Kenji Matsumoto to make the dress. It's based on one described in the books somewhere. Red satin."

"Oh my goodness." Jade fanned himself. "I can't wait to see him in red."

Shaya's client couldn't stand it. "What's a bustle?"

"It's a ridiculous wad of fabric perched on a woman's ass for reasons having to do with the patriarchy," Shaya said. Jade snorted. The client was giggling. Shaya assessed the hair conditions, nodded with satisfaction, shot a sideways look at Jade. "So what else is up. Anything happening with that test style you did?"

"Tell you later." He couldn't wait to tell her, but it had to wait until they were at the Mexican restaurant

107

with margaritas and their second basket of chips in front of them. Then it had to wait for Jade to give Shaya a report on the post-flowers night with Robert. Only after she was satisfied with that did she allow him to proceed. "He asked for me," Jade said, as quietly as possible considering he still wanted to squeal about it. "The movie people got in touch to say hey are you available on these days because Mr. Morris requested you. So of course I immediately rescheduled every other fucking thing and then wrote back to say yes."

"Did Robert know about this?"

"He must have. He didn't say anything."

"Probably didn't want to get your hopes up in case they already had somebody else contracted." Shaya ate a chip, slurped some of her margarita, and refrained from squealing. Squealing was premature. This might be the only movie the wrestler ever did. On the other hand, it might be the start of a major career. He was good-looking, funny, and easy to work with. You could always tell. Somebody who wasn't a dick with a service provider was almost never trouble on set. "Well, when you see him, be sure and tell him Hi from me."

Jade sat back, grinning. "Want to get yourself a piece of soon-to-be-famous wrestler?"

She ate another chip. "Maybe. You said he's single." Licking salt off her fingers. "He was a little bit flirty." A decorous sip of her drink. "And he can't work *all* the time."

"So in other words, slip him your business card and let him know you'd be perfectly happy to see him outside of the salon."

"Mm-hmm. When's the next time you see Robert?"

"Soon." Not soon enough.

"What's he up to aside from you?"

"He's dating."

"How do you feel about it?"

Jade gave her a look. She made a 'well, sorry, but' face. "He needs to do it, so how I feel about it is kind of irrelevant."

"Jade, it fucking *isn't*."

"Yes, it is," he said stubbornly. "If he said to me, Jade you're my one and only, and then I saw him out with someone else, that would be different. If I said, Robert, I don't want you seeing anybody else, but he still did, that would be different. I've had open relationships before. The open part was never what killed them. It's," he stopped, because the server was there with their entrées, and a welcome offer of more booze. A minute later, because Shaya was keeping her mouth shut for once, he returned to the subject. "It's a gamble." She nodded grudgingly. "He's playing fair, and if he decides to, you know, with someone else I'm confident he'll play safe. He's Mr. Clean."

Shaya snorted some of her margarita, cough-laughed for a few seconds. "You realize that probably means he's not doing much with those other guys. Not if he's doing stuff with you."

"Yeah, I know." He hoped so. "But the thing is, he's smart. He's not going to think these acts are going to be amazingly different just because it's a different guy. If you can't tell about somebody from a kiss, you're not paying attention." Also, of course, he had an open offer from Jade to provide any new experiences he might want, which was a thing he was not inclined to share with Shaya.

"True." She looked at the chip basket. "Why is this fucking thing *always* empty? And where did all the salsa go?"

"The same place that margarita went. Eat your burrito."

"Whatever. So if J calls me, do I go out with him, or do I stay in with him?"

Jade accepted the change of subject with relief. "He's a lot of fun. And just between you and me, I think he'd appreciate having a social relationship. Maybe especially if it's mostly for fun. I get the idea there aren't a lot of people in his life who let him know they enjoy his company. He was awfully nice to me even before it seemed like I could be useful to him." He shrugged at the cynicism.

Shaya thought about it. "Yeah. Okay. Jeez, I'd better go to the gym though." She watched with satisfaction as Jade cracked up.

Chapter 10

June 2010

There were so many great things about seeing Jade come through his door that Robert couldn't sort through them fast enough to rank them. All he managed to say was "Hi." Then Jade was closing the door, flipping the deadbolt, setting down his messenger bag, and grabbing Robert by the back of the neck. Pulling him in for a kiss. Open-mouthed, hungry, the kiss Robert had been dreaming of since their last one. *Nobody kisses like you.* When they broke for breath, they stood with their arms around each other, foreheads tipped together. "I missed you."

"I missed you too." Probably shouldn't have said that. The guy was still trying to find himself, Jade shouldn't be … oh fuck that. He was thirty-six, not sixteen, and he was one of the smartest people Jade ever met. Even if any given date was the last one, Jade wanted Robert feeling good about their time together. Jade wasn't going to walk away from this. If Robert ever did … well, it wasn't wrong to want to be remembered with fondness. "Do I have you to thank for my new gig styling Mr. Morris?"

Robert shook his head, smiling. "He asked, I queried, they said sure. So you can do it?"

"I can do it. What have you been up to?"

"Doing some research. Want a drink?"

"Sure." He kicked off his Crocs and picked up the messenger bag again. "Game first, or straight to DVD?"

"I've had enough of sports for the day, if you don't mind. Let's see what you brought." By the time he had a bottle open and glasses filled, Jade had the DVD loaded and ready to go. Robert set the glasses on the side tables. "I have a confession." Jade looked up, surprise quickly fading to neutrality. *Oh God don't look at me like that.* "I went on two more dates."

Jade hoped the disappointment didn't show. "Same guys?" He'd heard about several.

"No, two different guys. Coffee and drinks." Jade's eyes narrowed slightly. Robert wondered if he was thinking 'how many is it now, you slut' or if it was 'those are not necessarily dates.' He sat down, not as close as he would have liked. "I only call them dates because we were flirting, and there were kisses. I didn't initiate but I also didn't say get off me. I mean, coffee, that was right in the middle of the day. I was a little bit, eek. We were in this semi-private area at the mall, but I'm not used to kissing anybody in the middle of the day."

Jade bit back a laugh. He was equal parts relieved and charmed. The relief let him say, "You don't actually have to tell me about stuff like that."

"I want to, though." He wanted to hear about it if Jade was kissing anybody else, too, but he couldn't possibly say so. They hadn't made any promises to each other. They'd only known each other for a couple of months. "But I won't if you don't want to hear about it. My therapist told me I shouldn't get too dependent on anybody, because I could mistake that for something else, and project things onto somebody that they might not be feeling. He said I need to be as self-reliant as possible."

"That was probably good advice," Jade said carefully. He didn't mean 'you shouldn't depend on me.' From the slight wince at the other end of the

112

loveseat, though, his meaning wasn't clear. He suppressed a sigh. The last thing he ever wanted to do was hurt Robert. But he still needed to protect himself. "I meant you should definitely be spending time with people you're interested in. People other than me. We all think we want somebody who's only interested in us, but the fact is that's a lot of pressure to put on each other. I'm really glad you like me. I'm really glad you want to go to bed with me." After a second: "Uh, you do still want to go to bed with me." It was almost a question.

Robert huffed out a laugh. "Yes." The last thing he ever wanted to do was hurt Jade. But something had to be said. "Obviously you're my first in this new life. But I've dated a lot of people. I wasn't always the one who got left."

That was a relief, actually. "Who did you leave?"

"The girl in college who always put up a fight about condoms. I caught her sabotaging them and that was it."

"Jesus, what a nutcase."

"Right? I left a girl after the whole law-school-business-school thing too. We met in a sports law seminar and it seemed like we had a lot in common. The sex was no worse than usual." Jade snorted. Robert half-smiled. "I know. I still can't believe I never questioned that. I mean I did, but if someone said she was fine was I supposed to assume she was lying? Anyway. She landed something on the management team for a baseball club on the East Coast. I told her she should take it. She said why don't you come with me and I said no."

"So, your point is you have boundaries."

Robert wasn't at all sure that he did, at least not when it came to Jade. He was sure this wasn't the time to admit that. He wanted to say 'I'm giving myself a

113

chance to see if I like kissing anyone else as much as I like kissing you, even though I'm pretty sure I never will.' Instead he said, as if in agreement, "I have boundaries. There are things I want. Out of a relationship, and out of life in general. I'd really appreciate being able to talk to you about everything. Tell me when, or if, you're not interested. If it's too much, or if it's just the wrong time. This is in my head all the time and it spills out with you because you know exactly what's going on and you're, well, the way you are." *Wonderful. Perfect.*

"The way I am." It was soft. Jade wanted so much to say all the overly-emotional things that were in his head. *The way I am is in love with you, and it's way too soon to say so. It may always be too soon.* He turned his head as if to assess the contents of the wineglass. Picked it up, took a drink, and said, "Why don't we have a look at this disc."

He was surprised when Robert's reaction to the overture music was "Hey! I just watched that! This is live? Cool!" He wasn't surprised at the next reaction, when Robert realized that the entire cast of 'Chicago' was male. There was an introductory parade of showgirls and flappers played by men. Robert said, "Whoa." Something happened with the lights. All of a sudden, as if by magic, there was a long-legged flapper perched on the end of the baby grand piano at one side of the stage. Lit by a spotlight, turned away from the audience. The pianist started the introduction to 'All That Jazz.' The flapper slowly and elaborately re-crossed those long legs, then twisted to face the audience. No, not face; confront. Robert said, "*Wow.*"

Jade enjoyed his lover's expression for a second, then turned to watch the performance. Velma Kelly did the whole first verse on top of the piano. Seated for the first few lines, then getting to her knees, then up on her feet. Down on her back to finish the verse, legs in the air. Turning some kind of double fan kick into a dismount to the stage. Slinking and vamping through the next verse, with other dancers joining in. A full-on production number in the third verse, ending back on top of the piano. Jade sighed with appreciation as he paused the disc at the end of the song. "So now you know why I thought it might be helpful for you to see this."

"Who is that guy?"

"His name's Andy Martin. He was a Broadway dancer for twenty years. Out here he's a photographer. This show was a benefit for the guy playing Billy Flynn. I'll tell you more about that later."

"Okay. Let's watch it." He was looking at Jade. They were not as close as he wanted them to be. He scooted over and laid his arm on the back of the loveseat invitingly. Jade did exactly what Robert wanted: unpaused the disc and moved in.

Jade really loved this show, even though it was bittersweet watching it. He'd tell Robert all about that. He knew something about the guy's history now, it was only fair that he shared some more of his. The part of it having to do with this show was significant for more than one reason.

Robert kept his mouth shut for the rest of the recording. He'd never imagined anything like this. It wasn't quite the same as the movie; the 'Mr. Cellophane' number was missing, which suited Robert fine because it had taken him out of the story. This one was all about the women. He wondered what some of his feminist friends would think about this presentation. He kept hearing that there were few enough great parts for women; having all of the many female roles in this show played by men probably annoyed some people. But it was a benefit. Maybe there were special rules. The closing number … he could watch that over and over again. Andy Martin and whoever was playing Roxie Hart, singing and dancing, sexy as hell, and *terrifying*. There was absolutely no sense that these killers were remorseful, much less reformed. They'd gotten away with murder, and they were going to set the world on fire. When the disc ended he turned to Jade, opened his mouth, and couldn't think of a single thing to say.

Jade tried not to laugh. "You are not the only person who's had that reaction to this."

"Is that what people mean when they say someone is fierce?"

"Mmm, yeah."

"Please tell me that was acting. Tell me that guy playing Velma is a mama's boy who loves kittens."

Jade gave up and laughed. "He loves his mother. I don't know about kittens. He was very fond of Robbie. Billy Flynn," he clarified. "He, I mean Andy, only did this show because he had some history with Robbie. They were in a few shows together back in the day. And I was involved because Robbie and I were a couple then."

"Oh." Robert considered that. "Hang on. I'm going to take a leak. Are you hungry?"

"I could eat." So they took an unhurried break from that conversation. Made themselves comfortable, put together dinner from Robert's well-stocked kitchen, and took the last of the wine to bed. Sitting propped up against the headboard, naked, relaxed, Jade picked up where they left off. "That show was four years ago. Robbie Campbell was dying of lung cancer. The benefit

116

was for his medical bills. The show only played once but it was sold out, because Robbie knew a lot of people and he had a lot of friends. The benefit made enough that he was able to be comfortable to the end."

"How could he sing like that, with lung cancer?"

"Good question. The insult to injury part was, he never smoked. He grew up in suburban New York and it turned out his childhood home was chock full of radon gas and asbestos. He was diagnosed the year we met, two thousand four."

Robert did the math. "You were twenty-nine. How old was he?"

"Twice my age. We met on a set. I was styling the whole cast. I didn't know he was a Broadway legend." He was smiling. These memories didn't hurt. "He made the most blatant pass at me, and I was like really? You're old."

Robert laughed, shaking his head. "No you didn't."

"Oh yes I did. But he was persistent, and he was funny, and as you could see, he was attractive."

"Yes, I noticed that." Robert was still amused. "Really different from Richard Gere though."

"Mmm. So anyway, at a certain point I gave in, and we had a great time together for a year. A slightly less-great time for the next year, because he was being treated. It was," he tried to think of a way to explain this, "not a great love affair. It was friendship, and affection. He didn't want to be alone. I liked him a lot, so I didn't want him to be alone. He had other friends, so it wasn't all on me. There were people to take him to appointments, make sure the household stuff was taken care of. I made sure he never had to go out in public without good hair, even when he didn't have any of his

117

own. He never looked as sick as he was, even at the end. That was important to him."

Robert thought it was awfully convenient for the guy that his boy toy could keep him looking good. It wasn't his place to make that observation. Jade seemed to think the relationship was legitimate, and his was the opinion that counted. "Whose idea was the benefit?"

"The guy who played Roxie Hart. Honestly I think it was fifty percent him wanting to do 'Chicago,' and knowing Robbie played Billy Flynn before. Once they had Andy roped in, it came together pretty fast. You should have heard them all bitching about the high heels, though. Which is maybe a good segue to talking about this pageant." He drank the last of his wine and set the glass on the nightstand.

"I read that book."

"Oh, you did? Did you like it?"

"Took me a minute to get into it, but yeah. I'm reading the sequel now. Do you read a lot?"

"I do. There's a lot of downtime in my profession. There's stretches of eight to ten hours when you never get to sit down some days, but that's not every day by a long shot."

Robert was diverted. "Which do you like better, salon or on set?"

"I like having the option to do both. On a set, or doing a photo shoot, I'm more likely to get a chance to do a whole look. At the salon it's usually hair. And then there's drag things. That's a whole look, obviously, and it's for a performance, so from my point of view it's the best case scenario."

"Which brings us back to the pageant. I'm glad you showed me that recording. I watched 'Some Like It Hot'

118

and that gave me an idea what was possible. Were you thinking a flapper kind of thing?"

"I was. The dress style is pretty well covered up except for the legs. Obviously Andy and the others went with short skirts, because they were all either showgirls or whores. Well, except Matron 'Mama' Morton." Robert snorted. Jade was grinning. "Also it's easier to dance in a short skirt, or so I'm told. Not a concern for you, if you decided to do this. There are other things you could watch. 'Singin' in the Rain' is a classic for Twenties style. 'Bugsy Malone' isn't as good a movie but the design is great."

"I'll watch them," Robert promised. He looked down at his glass, noticed it was empty, and set it aside. "Is it okay if I want to do it for you? Not because I aspire to be a drag queen, but for you. So you can do this."

You unbelievable sweetheart. "Yes, it's okay. I really appreciate it. I think you'll be great. You're great at everything else," he said recklessly.

Robert leaned over, put his hand on Jade's neck, and kissed him. "You don't know that," he said against the man's mouth. "We haven't done everything."

"What do you want to do."

"Teach me something new." Another kiss. Then he moved away, got out of bed, went to the bathroom. Jade blew out a breath, thought *are we doing this?*, and headed for the powder room. A few minutes later they were back in bed. There was a pillar candle burning on Robert's nightstand next to a glass of water. On Jade's nightstand were the tissues, condoms, and lube. He thought he knew what Robert wanted, and he was nervous. This was the kind of thing that could change a relationship. He'd only ever done it with people he didn't love. He couldn't say that. He sat on the bed, made eye contact with Robert, wondered if he was at all in control of this situation. Robert studied him for a moment, still on his feet. "Jade. We don't have to do anything in particular. You know I'd be happy to just lie here and kiss you."

"I would be too. I need you to tell me exactly what you want."

"I want you to introduce me to the back half." He said it fast, and he knew he was blushing. "Could we do that? I've never been touched that way."

"No woman ever did?" Jade thought about that. He knew a lot of women, was friendly with them, talked about sex with them. They were not all disinterested in ass play. He wondered if Robert had somehow discouraged that with women. Body language could say a lot sometimes. Like right now. "Hmm. Come and kiss me for a few minutes. I think we both need to settle down."

Robert didn't say anything, simply flung himself on the bed and let Jade stretch out half on top of him, going for one of those kisses that were familiar now. A kiss that felt like friendship, and affection, and something more. Once they were nicely warmed up, Robert confessed something else. "I really want to touch you. But you have to tell me if you like it. You know I'm making things up as I go along."

"Sweetheart, that's what we all do. Don't worry, you'll be able to tell if I like it."

"Do I need the lube?"

"Only if you're going to penetrate." Robert squeaked, which made them both laugh. "Breathe, honey. Do whatever you want, and don't forget to breathe." Jade shifted off of his lover, lying on his front with a pillow under his chest. He stretched in a deliberate and provocative way, a ripple from his shoulders to his feet. He could feel Robert's gaze.

Then a hand on the back of his head, stroking through his hair, down his neck, down his spine. The mattress shifting as Robert moved to straddle Jade's knees. Both hands on his back, exploring, caressing. They'd touched each other in a lot of ways, but not like this. Jade was already turned on, and this was no more explicit than a massage. Except those hands were sweeping down the outside of his hips, around and in. "You have a really nice ass." It sounded a bit breathless. Jade was about to suggest a change of position when Robert beat him to it. He shifted his weight, pushed Jade's legs open, and knelt between them. Jade imagined how this must look. He felt Robert lean forward again, one hand on the bed beside Jade's chest. Then his mouth on Jade's back. They both made some kind of sound. Jade could feel Robert's erection on the inside of his thigh. Then it was a long time, too much time, or not enough time of being kissed and fondled. Robert still hadn't made it down past Jade's waist and he was desperately aroused. This was torture.

Robert really meant to keep moving down, but the skin of Jade's back was so smooth. Every sound, every breath, every contraction of a muscle seemed to resonate through Robert's body. Finally he forced himself to leave that supple back and put his mouth on that perfect ass. Jade moaned. Robert almost fainted. *Breathe, idiot.* He was kissing, licking, sinking his teeth in. Jade was quivering under his touch. *I'm going to make you come again.* He had no idea how, exactly. Maybe this way. His mouth at the top of the cleft. Licking into it, tentatively. This should have been disgusting. He was licking another man's ass. But it was clean, and soft, and what he was doing was driving Jade crazy. He wanted

121

more. Lower. *There*. He got his hand down to the back of Jade's knee and pushed, bending the leg, opening it.

Jade whimpered, shoving his hips into the mattress. For someone who'd never rimmed anyone before, who might not even know that was what it was called, Robert was doing an exceptional job. No hesitation at all, once he really committed to it. Well, there never was with this guy, was there? Oh *Jesus* that tongue. He was losing his mind. He pushed up from his elbows, then from his knees. Spread open in front of Robert, who didn't hesitate. He reached around, got Jade's cock in his hand, and kept going with his mouth.

It took a minute to find the perfect rhythm. To let his hand move steadily on Jade's cock without disrupting his concentration. He could tell from the vocal breaths that this was working. This was going to send Jade over a cliff. He was so hard he thought he was going to explode, but he was going to make Jade come first. Was he making those sounds himself? He was. He was urging his lover on without words, yes, now, do it, yes, oh God *yes*. That climax in his hand, Jade's head flung back as he cried out. Not a moment too soon, because Robert's neck was killing him. He licked once more, felt Jade buck in his hand, then sat back, breathing hard. He rolled his neck, wondering what to do next.

"I really want you in me right now," Jade said. It was somewhat muffled because he was flat on the bed again. "Would you?"

"What if I do it wrong?"

"Robert, I'll tell you, trust me. Somehow I'm not worried." Still muffled. His body felt like jelly. He couldn't raise his head, or turn around, or do anything but lie here hoping he was about to get fucked. The mattress shifted again. Robert, reaching past him to the nightstand. The sound of lube squirting, and then two fingers caressing where his mouth had been a minute before. "Mmm. Yes." Had to remember to talk him through this. It wasn't obvious. "Get those in me. Have to relax the sphincter." It was so clinical-sounding, but if he thought he was hurting Jade, Robert wouldn't enjoy this at all. He was figuring it out. Circling, teasing, then one fingertip. Nice of him to have such a good manicure. *Was that for me?* Jade's thoughts were hazy. Not even thoughts, really. He was so relaxed. He shifted, accommodating a second finger.

Robert's attention was split between Jade's face (the little of it he could see) and what he was doing with his hand. Things felt fairly relaxed, but how much was enough? He knew from the porn thing and, well, going to the bathroom that this was a stretchy area. He wasn't slinging around a giant dick. It still looked huge compared to this hole. But Jade said he wanted it, and Robert wanted to try. This was the *ne plus ultra* of gay sex. This was the Rubicon, the point of no return, the event horizon. That thought almost made him laugh.

"What's funny." Jade sounded drugged, even to himself.

"I'll tell you later. Are you good? Because I'm dying here."

"I'll bet." Smiling through the haze. "Go for it."

Robert may have gone overboard with the lube. He was so slippery he thought he might just slide all over the place. But when he set a hand down and started to engage, that aperture gave way for him. Slowly, carefully, attention split again. Jade was making soft sounds that were the opposite of protest. He was pushing back somehow, giving resistance, opening up to take this. "Oh holy fucking Jesus." Unbelievable. It

123

felt unbelievable. It wasn't only that he didn't have a condom on. It was the heat, and the pressure, and the way the room already smelled of sex, and Jade's back flexing. Robert was working in him, propped on his hands. The only way it could have been better was if they were face to face. Was that even possible? Could he be kissing Jade while he did this, or while Jade did this to him? Jade was panting. Robert was grunting. Animal noises while he did this animal thing, the most animal he'd ever been, the most *male*. He moved a hand, getting it around the top of Jade's thigh, pulling his hips up.

Jade said "God!" because Robert hit his G-spot. After that orgasm he wouldn't have thought he had it in him, but it seemed there was more. He dug in with his feet, got his knees braced, and let Robert know this was good, so good. Jesus he was going forever, and he was going to take Jade with him.

That was it. This was it. Robert could die happy, and he thought he might. He was close, so close. Jade was going again, he could tell from the sounds, and it had to be "Now. Jesus. Jade. Holy. Fuck. *Now*. Oh *God.*" He shoved in hard, catching his weight on his hands, hearing a sound from Jade that he desperately hoped was a good sound. The climax felt like it went on forever. He couldn't move for a long moment. He was shaking, exhausted, exhilarated. And he had to get out of here. He pushed back, disengaging as carefully as he could. "Okay?"

"Mm-hmm." Jade couldn't move. He was lying on an epic wet spot and he didn't even care. Things were messy, and they were simply going to have to be messy. He couldn't manage a word.

Robert collapsed onto his side, wrapped a quivering arm around Jade, rolled to his back. Pulling Jade with him with strength he would have sworn he didn't have. Jade let his head fall back against Robert's shoulder. They lay there in sweaty silence for a few minutes. After a while Robert patted Jade, somewhat randomly. "Did you come again?"

"Mm-hmm."

"Can that be done face to face? I wanted to kiss you." *I always want to kiss you.*

Jade thought *I wanted to kiss you too*, organized his thoughts, and said, "I never have but I'll bet it's possible. We could get online and look for evidence." He felt a laugh. Patted the part of Robert that he could reach, which seemed to be a thigh. "Think we can stand up long enough for a quick shower?"

"We can hold each other up. You're really okay?"

"Robert. Sweetheart." *I love you.* "I feel great. You were great." Another pat. A slow and careful collection of parts. Crawling off the bed. Robert was still lying there. Jade went to start the shower, then returned to give his lover a hand.

Chapter 11

Two days later, a package was delivered to Robert at the agency. It was from someplace called Worldtone, which he'd never heard of. Deeply curious, he took it off Emily's desk and into his office, closed the door, and cut through the packing tape. Inside the plain brown cardboard box was a shoebox, also taped closed. He dealt with the tape, put his scissors back in his desk drawer, and lifted the lid.

"Oh! Okay." These had to be from Jade. T-strap saddle shoes with a three-inch heel. He gulped a little at that. Black and white, which might be stock colors. If those didn't go with whatever the costume plan was, he assumed Jade knew how to change the shoe color. He was so glad he knew this was actually possible, because he couldn't imagine walking in these things. He put the shoebox down on his guest chair, wishing it weren't so obvious. Hi! Pair of shoes here! He'd never had shoes delivered to his office, let alone high-heeled shoes. He sent a text to Jade: *Interesting package delivered today. Does coaching in how to walk come with these? See you soon OXO*

The reply came back fast: *I'll show you how to Walk This Way*. Robert laughed out loud. He opened the office door, still smiling.

Because she'd heard that laugh, Emily said, "What was in the box?"

Robert debated for a second, thought *it's for a good cause*, and said, "Want to see? Come on in." As soon as Emily was through the door he took the shoes out of the box again and dangled them in front of her. Her expression was priceless. "Jade asked me to be his model for a drag pageant. It's part of a fundraiser. Want to help me learn how to wear these?"

"Oh my God yes!" It ended on a squeak.

"End of the day?" She nodded. Robert had never seen a woman look so thrilled about doing something with him. He was trying not to crack up. "Okay. Back to business for now."

He ended up with an audience, of course. The word spread through the office. By six o'clock nobody was getting any work done. Robert took off his suit jacket, hung it on the back of his office door, stuffed his tie in the pocket. Unbuttoned his collar, rolled up his sleeves. Took off his real shoes and socks, put on the nylon socks someone had thoughtfully included with the shoes, and tentatively slid his feet into bizarro-world. "Emily?"

"Right here!" She was hovering at his door.

"What's the first thing I need to know?"

"Okay. Um." She thought for a second about how she did it. "I've been wearing high heels since I was fourteen. It's like I haven't thought about it for, never mind. Stand up." He did that, cautiously. Leaning forward, feeling like he was about to fall on his face. "Oh no. Can I?" Standing close now, hands hovering.

"Please. Ouch, holy crap."

She took his shoulders, moved them back. "Tuck your tushie. Like, get your butt over your heels. There you go. Wow, you're so tall. All lined up?" She examined the situation, thought about things again. "Think about, um, like your shoulder blades? You want them in your back pocket."

Robert considered that. He had honestly never thought about the mechanics of standing, much less walking. It was simply something he did. Getting his weight back over his heels took the excruciating pressure off his forefoot. "Is this ever comfortable?"

"Oh sure. A well-made shoe that fits right shouldn't hurt. Do they actually hurt?"

"Uh, I can't tell." They both giggled. "Okay, so, I have to walk. One foot in front of the other. Oh, lord." He took a deep breath and tried a step or two. The last thing he needed was to break an ankle. "Do I have the straps right?" Emily crouched down to check, gave him the thumbs-up. He observed the thoughtless ease with which she changed position and tried not to be bitter. A couple more steps, through the doorway. "Oh come on." Everybody was out in the hall, even people from upstairs. "Don't you people have anything to do?"

"Come on Robert. Let's see you. Down the runway." The gabble resolved into a chant of 'Go Robert.' He was trying not to laugh because he thought that would mess up his balance. Emily was trailing along behind, like a spotter, as if the poor girl could catch him if he took a header into the wall. *I'm going to play this up for Jade later, and he's going to laugh his ass off.*

Jade got to the apartment barely fifteen minutes after Robert, and he did laugh his ass off when he heard the story. He then requested a demonstration, praised Robert's heel management, and said, "You look incredibly sexy."

That made up for a lot. "Really?"

"Are you kidding? Your legs are a mile long and your ass is unbelievable."

Robert frowned, looked over his shoulder, couldn't tell. He went to check himself out in the full-length mirror. "Huh." Jade snickered. Robert gave him a look. "I usually only look at myself after I have the whole suit

128

on. So I don't know how this ass compares with my usual ass." Jade laughed again. Robert tugged his shirt out of his trousers, unbuttoned it, stripped it off. Took another look at things. The line of his back was … kind of sexy. The curve of his ass, definitely. "Huh!" Now he wanted to see what his legs looked like. He unfastened his pants, sitting down on the bed to get them off. Jade gave him a hand threading the shoes through. Robert stood up again. Boxer briefs, shoes, and legs. "Wow."

"Sweetheart?"

"Hmm?"

"How short a skirt can I put you in?" They both giggled. "The thing is, for a historically accurate costume it shouldn't be shorter than this." He set the edge of his hand just below Robert's knee. "But if some of that length was fringe, or maybe a car-wash thing." He went silent, thinking.

Robert had no idea what a car-wash thing might be. All he knew was, he suddenly wasn't horrified at the idea of wearing a short skirt. These were pretty good legs. And he had months to get used to the shoes. "Just let me know when you're at a point where you need me to show up somewhere. What's the one thing I should work on aside from walking."

Jade focused in. "Your hands. I don't know if you noticed when we watched 'Chicago,' but Andy did this kind of Fred Astaire thing. Like this." He took Robert's hand, folded the thumb under, curved the fingers. The whole hand looked smaller and less manly. "Whenever you put the shoes on, think of your hands too. You are truly amazing."

"I am?" Robert was ridiculously pleased. He turned his hand over. It looked as though he were holding an invisible cucumber, lengthwise. Or somebody's cock. He glanced at Jade from under his eyelashes.

129

Oh God. "Amazing. I want to do things to that ass." Jade moved in, crowding him a little, tipping his head back because at the moment Robert was five inches taller than he was. He wanted a kiss right now. Robert delivered. They were both breathless when Jade stepped away. "Yes?"

"Yes." *Anything.* Robert wasn't sure he wanted that, but he'd loved everything else he'd done with Jade, so he would probably love that too. So he told himself, anyway, as he took the shoes and briefs off. They both went to the bathroom to freshen up. Robert wasn't uneasy about the clean factor, now that he'd done this with Jade. He'd read online about douching, wondered if that was necessary, but the answer seemed to be 'no.' A choice, not a requirement. *I'm still nervous.* He went to the wet bar and poured a couple of shots of vodka. It was early in the day for that, and they hadn't eaten, but the last thing he wanted to do was give Jade the impression he didn't want to do this. He was not merely consenting, he was participating.

He was sitting up in bed, sipping the vodka, when Jade came back in the room. "What's that?"

"My tranquilizer," Robert said honestly. "I'm a little nervous. This was a gag gift at the agency last Christmas."

Jade picked up the other shot glass, sniffed it, tasted. His eyebrows went up. "Candy in a glass?"

"Cupcake vodka." They made eye contact for a second, then both of them started giggling. "I wonder what somebody was thinking when they gave me that."

"You are a cupcake. And I'm going to eat you up." Jade couldn't believe he said that. Robert was blushing. Jade set his glass down. He'd have another sip later. Right now he had to make sure those nerves went away.

130

He took the shot glass out of Robert's hand, sipped without swallowing, set the glass aside. Leaned in for a kiss with closed mouth. When Robert's lips parted, Jade let the liquor trickle in. Heard a surprised sound that quickly became a yummy sound. *Yes.* Kissing him until he was relaxed, then until he was urgent. Moving down his body. Reminding Robert of the feel of another man's mouth on the inside of his thigh, on his balls. Then going lower. Listening to his breath getting short, those stifled sounds, the pitch rising. Getting to work with the lube while his mouth teased Robert's cock. He was going to try it this way, face to face, so they could kiss. If it didn't work, they'd try something else. Robert was gasping, whimpering, begging. *Should I make him come first?* Robert did that, and Jade was so relaxed after. It would be easier. And he wanted to. Wanted to taste that. It took no time. He held still briefly, letting Robert's breath settle. Then another sip of vodka. Licking his own lips, licking Robert's. Feeding him another mouthful of the sweet liquor. Finally pushing Robert's knees up. Beginning to engage. Robert moaning, hand on Jade's ass, pulling him in. His foot in the air, then on Jade's back. Oh God this was good. He never wanted to do it the other way again. This mouth. This kiss. *I love you.*

Robert felt the pulse deep inside, like nothing he could have imagined. Jade's moan lasted as long as the climax. His own cock twitched in response. He'd felt that midway through, when Jade hit some kind of trigger point inside. It was not impossible that he would have come just from that, if he hadn't already been spent. Jade was flat against him, breathing hard, his face tucked into the curve of Robert's neck. Things were slightly uncomfortable now. Robert shifted, setting his foot down. *Didn't know I was that limber.* Jade pushed up, kissed him again, and moved off him. Disengaging, head hanging low as if he were exhausted. Robert remembered that feeling. He wrapped his fingers around Jade's arm and stroked down to his hand.

Jade organized himself somewhat, settling on his side with their joined hands on Robert's ribs. He wanted to ask if that was okay. How to say it so it didn't sound as if he expected that it wasn't. "I was kind of demented there for a minute," he said after a while. "Did I do anything you didn't enjoy? If so, I'm sorry."

"No, honey." That slipped out. Well, Jade called him sweetheart, so maybe it was okay. "I enjoyed it. I think I would have come if you didn't get me off first."

"Oh! Really?" Jade lifted his head to make eye contact. "It felt like you were enjoying it but, well. Demented." Robert huffed out a laugh. "I loved being able to kiss you."

"I loved that too." *I love you.* "There's one thing though."

"Mmm?"

"I'm starving." He felt Jade laughing. Turned a few degrees so they could kiss again. "Shower first?"

Robert wouldn't have thought he could talk about his sexual education with anyone other than Jade, but he found himself doing exactly that a few days later. He went out for coffee and ran into the guy he'd gone on that first date with. The next thing he knew they were sitting at a table outside, noise from the boulevard masking their words, and he was telling the guy everything. "Shit, I'm sorry," he said, pulling up. "What is wrong with me? That's so rude. I'm really sorry, Liam."

"It's okay." Liam sat back, fiddling with his cup. "I figured you were seeing someone. Didn't realize you were quite so new to this, though."

"I was putting up a front," Robert admitted. "I didn't want to scare you off."

Liam leaned in again. "What would you have done if we really clicked?"

"I would have told you the truth. I did really like you. I mean, I do." He shook his head, exasperated with himself, as Liam laughed. "I have no game. Like, none. The thing is."

Liam waited a second. "What?"

"I grew up believing in God. Believing that God had a plan for me. And I don't believe in much of what I was taught anymore, but I can't help wondering if the plan part is real. Because why, on that day, when Sharon gave me that ring back and I thought why am I relieved, was it Jade who sat down with me? It could have been any other guy in Los Angeles. It could have been you."

"Well, I don't get to Callender's very often, but yeah." Liam realized what Robert meant. "You mean you think Jade is the one you're supposed to be with."

"I do not think I feel this way about him simply because he was there, or because he was kind." Robert gestured helplessly.

"Do you have a word for the way you feel about him?"

"Oh, of course. I'm in love with him. And I'm going to tell him pretty soon, either intentionally or because it just falls out of my mouth."

Liam laughed again. "You're so cute." He glanced at his watch. "Shit, I've got to get back to the office. Keep me posted, okay?"

Robert was startled. "You wouldn't mind? Because I'd love to have someone besides my therapist to talk to about all this."

133

"Robert." Liam was on his feet to chuck his empty cup at a waste bin. "You give me hope." He patted Robert's shoulder and walked away.

Robert was still a little dazed when he got back to the agency. Emily frowned at him. "What happened?"

"Ran into a guy I went out with and basically told him I was never really interested in him, and he wants to hear all about me and Jade. Said I give him hope."

"You give me hope, too," she said. "Who is this guy?"

"He's a dermatologist. Works over on Bedford. He's really nice, but I don't know if he dates girls. I'm going to do some work now." He went into his office, rolling his eyes at himself, trying not to notice that Emily was cracking up.

Meanwhile in West Hollywood, Shaya was getting the latest news from Jade. "So I don't want to be all dramatic and say it was life-changing, but," he shrugged helplessly. "I've almost said I love you about a hundred times."

"What are you waiting for?" Clear and present exasperation made its way past the comb in her mouth. "What the hell do you think is the downside of being in love?"

"Shaya! You know perfectly well. Me being in love does not equal *us* being in love, and I'm scared."

"Give me a goddamned break. If that man isn't in love with you I don't even know what love is."

"You've never even met him."

"Jade, the flowers?" She glared at him. "The texts he sends, the things you tell me he says to you, the way he cooks for you. Taking you out to dinner with a soon-to-be movie star. Agreeing to be your model?"

Jade sighed. "Have I given him enough time? It won't seem like I'm trying to tie him down?"

They'd both been mostly ignoring the clients in their chairs for the last minute. Now Shaya stepped over to Jade, put her arms around him, and spoke very quietly. "I know there are people who made you feel like you don't deserve love, or that you aren't lovable. I'm here to tell you that you do, and you are." She kissed his cheek, eased back, shook him gently. "Let him love you."

He nodded speechlessly, blinking hard. Sniffed, swallowed, and turned back to the head of hair that waited.

There were times when Jade wanted to be alone with his thoughts. That night was not one of those times. Shaya was busy, Robert was busy, and a quick round of texts told him most of his other friends were either busy or on the wrong side of town. A last-minute get-together was not a simple thing in L.A. The person he finally ended up meeting for dinner was the man who played Roxie Hart. Jade was already at Callender's when Mark Valance strolled in. Looking around non-obviously to see if anybody recognized him, the attention whore. Jade tried not to laugh. A few seconds later Mark slid into the booth across from him. "Stop laughing."

"I can't help it. You have that 'oh are you looking at me, well you should be' thing going on."

Mark tossed his head, shaking back his somewhat-long auburn hair. "You know it's all about who sees you."

"Yes. And where, and when, and with whom. I dressed up for you." Only a little, in the same wisteria-print shirt he'd worn out for drinks with Robert. "To make up for bringing you to this relentlessly uncool venue."

"There's pie," Mark pointed out. "That makes up for a lot. So how've you been?" They chatted in a catching-up sort of way while drinks were ordered and appetizers were delivered. Mark was working on a network dramedy now, playing the charming-but-unreliable boyfriend of one of the main characters. "We kept huddling in Jenny's dressing room updating our bets on what they're doing with our arc."

"What are the top three possibilities?" Jade finished his seared ahi salad.

"We get married, I get tragically killed so she can start over in an Emmy-bait kind of way, or I cheat on her and she dumps me." Mark shrugged and set aside the leftovers of his quesadilla.

Jade frowned as much as the Botox would let him. The way Mark listed those options made Jade think marriage (i.e. staying on the show) was the least likely. "Does she like working with you?"

"She says she does. The whole cast is, well. It's such a cliché to say we're like a family. I've been recurring for two seasons now and the new contract is for fourteen episodes, but." Another movement, not quite a shrug. "If they made me a little less unreliable I might think the odds are better. I mean, there's unreliable that you can live with, where it's kind of a running joke. Oh he's never on time. Forgets birthdays. Let the neighbor's cat in and now it's taken over the house. But then there's unreliable that nobody would respect her for living with, and there have been a few episodes where that was me. Whatever, it is what it is. It's been a good credit and nobody hates me. But why am I having dinner with you?" He said that as their entrees were delivered. Had a word with the server about boxing up his quesadilla, then turned back to Jade with an expectant expression. "I really haven't spent any time with you since Robbie died."

"Mmm. I had to back away for a minute. You know we weren't fated mates or anything, but he was still important to me. It was tough trying to talk to people who knew him."

"And I suppose somebody snapped you up as soon as you started looking around again."

Jade glanced up, startled by the warmly regretful tone. He'd never gotten the idea that Mark was attracted to him. And he was firmly in the closet, had to be in order to get and keep that particular part, on that particular show, on that particular network. "No," he said slowly. "There was a guy I dated for a minute, and then a guy I dated for a year. And now there's somebody else. I didn't know you even liked me."

"Of course I did! Everybody did! God *damn* it!" He was playing it up a little, if quietly. Then his voice got even softer. "If I could have a boyfriend you'd have been in trouble." More regret, with a tinge of bitterness.

"I'm sorry."

Mark performed an operatically tragic sigh, trying to turn this back to humor. "Me too. Well, why are you out with me instead of with him? Looking for some business?"

"Always. But I needed someone to talk to, and it's been too long." Jade fiddled with his water glass. He felt a little guilty about calling Mark now. Even though he knew the other guy had good reasons for playing it straight. And maybe an evening out like this, with a guy he liked who he had a good business reason to see – a reason nobody would question – was the kind of thing that helped him get through it. He wondered how long Mark was going to live like this. Glanced up at the professionally-interested face and knew he couldn't ask. "He's a sports agent. There's always something. His schedule or mine."

"You should live together," Mark suggested with his mouth full. He didn't notice Jade's twitch. "Of course, the last time I lived with someone it ended in divorce, so I don't know why I think that's a workable solution." That was a good diversion. Jade asked him about it, and they talked about Mark's long-ago marriage. "The best thing about it was my son. I think a lot about moving back East so I can see him more."

There was subtext. If Mark went back to live theater, on Broadway, coming out would be easier. "Maybe you should." Jade pushed his plate away. He had enough leftovers for another whole meal. And he'd get himself a slice of pie to take home with it. "So this guy is very much not my usual."

"Tell me about him while we have coffee." Mark leaned back, also intending to do the take-home-pie thing. It was always tempting to eat it right there, but then he'd eat the whole thing, and it was altogether better to have a few bites at a time. Every ounce showed up on TV. The server must have been used to it. In very short order, they each had a to-go bag pushed to the side to ignore while they had coffee and continued to talk.

Jade told the whole story. "The only other person I've told is Shaya. It hasn't been very long, so it's not like I'm hiding it, but things are moving fast and I guess I wanted a third opinion."

Mark set down his coffee cup. "Even though we've established that I know squat about having a successful relationship?"

"Just an opinion," Jade said patiently. "I haven't been with someone who was fresh out of the closet since I was a teenager. And that experience doesn't translate. I mean, he's thirty-six. I was expecting things to go the complete opposite way."

"Trauma, denial, rage, drugs, religion?"

Jade was stifling laughter. "Sort of."

"I don't know what to tell you. I mean, it sounds like he has enough brains for three or four people. He's talking to people, he's seeing people, he's got a therapist. And he's down with the whole being gay in bed thing?" Jade's wide-eyed nod got a laugh. "Trust him to know what he wants, I guess. I mean, he was damned lucky it was you who rolled up on him. You're amazing-looking, smart, compassionate. He's not going to do better."

Jade knew he must look surprised. Mark didn't say any more about that. He made a show of looking at his phone, complaining about the time and about the next morning's early appointment with his trainer. Jade was suddenly awash with affection for him. This person he'd never been close to, a man he'd barely seen in four years, who would show up on short notice and talk relationships when it was all too plain how much he wanted one himself. If not for the whole closet thing he'd consider introducing Mark to one or another of the people Robert had told him about. "Thanks for that. I wish," he stopped himself before he could make an indiscreet suggestion.

Mark glanced up and seemed to read his mind. "I do too. But for now I'm going home to emotionally-eat this whole slice of pie." He might have wished it sounded more like a joke.

Jade tried to steer it there. "Don't do it. Don't give in to the dark side. I'll call you soon."

"Yeah, you do that." Mark grabbed his to-go bag, slid out of the booth, and walked away. Jade watched him go, then got the server's attention. He still wasn't sure what he and Robert were doing, but he felt a lot better about it now.

Chapter 12

Robert took Parker out to dinner to thank him for his advice with the whole wrestler-movie-offer thing. "How's your thing going?" He waited until they had drinks to ask.

Parker shook his head, sighed, and said, "Not great. It's sounding as though I'm going to be paying alimony for as many years as we were married, unless she gets married again first."

"Holy *shit*. Why? She has a job!" This he knew from previous conversations.

"It's, well. An artifact of the bad old days when a woman would help her husband get through his career training and then he'd dump her for a fresher model and she'd be fucked. And the truth is, she did help. She didn't pay for my tuition and we always split our living expenses, but her job covered our health insurance. When we traveled, she paid for it." He shrugged. "I'm not happy about it, obviously. I'm paying a penalty for the marriage not working out, but I didn't even know it wasn't working out. Which may be why it wasn't working out. I don't know. It could be worse, it won't be forever, and thank God I've got a decent book of clients." They talked business for a while. Parker didn't have a big star, but he had a roster of actors who worked regularly, including a few with steady gigs on top-performing TV series.

All of those picked up fill-in jobs during hiatus, much as Robert's clients picked up coaching or exhibition work during their off-season. Plus there was the never-ending scramble for endorsements and advertising. On top of all that, TV and movie productions sometimes called for athletes to do cameo appearances. Crossover was king. "So I have to thank you again," he said toward the end of the evening. "Jonathan might have been better off if I just handed you that part of the business."

"Maybe, but maybe not." Parker was smiling. "And you never know. Someday maybe he'll end up on a project with one of my people. I know there are some agents who like a package deal. I always wonder if all the clients get the same amount of attention."

Robert would bet they didn't. Sometimes that was the hardest part of his job: making sure he didn't get so focused on one client's contract negotiation that he lost track of some other deal. "Well, I have to tell you, I sure hope he has fun with it. I caught one of his matches recently and I was like, fuck." He shook his head. The matches may have been staged but the impacts were legit. "I'd much rather get a selfie from on-set where he's getting made up for a fake fight than another one from the corner with him bleeding for real."

"Mmm." Parker glanced at his watch. "Speaking of sets, I have to meet someone at one of those at eight tomorrow. So thanks for this." He reached across the table to shake hands.

"Glad you could make it. Go get some rest. I'll see you around." Robert watched his friend go, thought about the upcoming TV stuff he had to keep in mind for his camera-friendly clients, and looked around for the server.

Robert and Jade were both so busy the rest of the month that they only saw each other once. That was at the Koreatown shop of costume designer Kenji Matsumoto. Robert showed up with an agenda. "The

142

thing is," he said, when they were all perched on stools around Kenji's drafting table, cups of green tea in hand, "you said there's another Twenties character."

Jade nodded. "Daisy Buchanan."

"What are the odds they're not going full flapper?"

"Very poor." Jade didn't think it was a bad thing to have two flappers, necessarily; he knew who the model for Daisy was. That guy was five foot six and sixty years old. The word was, he was going to play it as Old Daisy, living in a dream of past glory. Very Sunset Boulevard.

"Okay." Robert glanced at Kenji; his face was hard to read. At the moment, the impression was of polite interest, which was probably how he would look no matter what. "I was thinking about the part of the first book when Mary goes back to Oxford, she and Holmes are pretending to be at odds, and she changes her look. The expensive skirts and jackets, instead of running around in whatever or in men's clothes. It would be super tailored, right? More covered up, but that might actually play *more* sexy if other women have bare shoulders and their knees showing." He was a little excited.

Jade indulged a moment's regret for the revealing dress of his dreams. If this was fun for Robert, it would be fun for him too, so he could roll with it. "Hmm. This is, hmm. It's not like a fashion show, exactly. But if you walked out in a jacket and then took it off, like a model on the catwalk, we could have something underneath? Something kind of slinky and unexpected?"

"Charmeuse," Kenji said. "A shell, with a low-cut back. Pearls wrapped around the throat."

"Yes!" Robert was delighted. "Like a choker in front but then dangling down the back, and you can only see it when the jacket comes off."

143

God, I love you, thought Jade. "A cuff on one wrist, like a World War One wristwatch. The kind where they took a pocket watch and attached it to a strap. Really butch." Kenji nodded, making a note. "A cloche, with a sparkly pin and feathers, only the pin is an old-fashioned hatpin, the kind you could kill somebody with. What fabric for the skirt and jacket?"

Kenji slid off his stool. "Wait here." Robert was too excited to sit still. He went roaming around the shop. Most of what was on display was dancewear and formal wear. There was a gorgeous wedding dress in the window by the street door. The tuxedo next to it wasn't nearly as eye-catching.

Jade watched his lover studying the dress. "Have you ever given a moment's thought to what women wear before?"

"No!" They both cracked up. "I mean, I guess I noticed? But only to the point of, okay, she looks nice. Or hmm, don't like that color."

"What colors don't you like."

Robert had to think about that. "I don't like yellowish colors. Yellow-green, yellow-orange, the yellowy kind of pink."

"Coral."

"Whatever. Don't like it."

"And yet you live in an apartment with yellowish-beige walls."

"Mmm. Yeah, I may need to get those painted." He got the idea Kenji was coming back in, didn't want to stop looking at Jade, turned his head with a show of polite interest. *Two can play that game.* Then he saw what Kenji was carrying and teleported across the room. "What is that?"

144

"It's a modern take on tweed. Cashmere, silk, a touch of spandex to help hold its shape. I think this color would be good on you." Jade was on his feet too, taking the free end of the fabric while Kenji held the bolt. It was peacock blue, incredibly soft. Jade draped the fabric over Robert's shoulder and made a yummy sound. Kenji nodded. "Yes." A moment later the bolt was laid aside and they were all gathered around the drafting table again. Kenji sketched a silhouette, describing the elements for Robert's benefit. "Asymmetrical closure to the jacket. It falls straight down over the hips. Bell sleeves. The skirt is a faux wrap, with the line following the lapel of the jacket. A ribbon here, defining the neckline. We make the cloche of the same tweed, with a band of the same ribbon." A new sketch, the skirt by itself. "A leather belt, with a knife masquerading as a buckle. I know someone who can fabricate that and the wristwatch."

"That is so *cool*." Robert didn't even realize he was clutching Jade's hand.

Jade was very aware of that. "And we color the shoes to match." He glanced up at Kenji. "They're T-strap saddle shoes from Worldtone. Leather." Not absolutely period-accurate, but a dance shoe was built to be both sturdy and comfortable. It had seemed the most practical, as well as the kindest, choice for his novice model. Especially since Worldtone could make them in any size.

Kenji nodded. "Easily done."

"Contrast for the ribbon? Or no. Something explicitly peacock?" Jade was thinking of a beaded trim he'd seen. Beads would be wrong for a daytime look like this. Embroidery, though … he realized Kenji was gone again. Checked in with Robert. "You like it?"

"I love it. I feel a little strange about loving it, but," he shrugged. "It looks like a suit. If the sleeve was straight and the skirt was pants, I'd wear that suit."

Jade wanted to say something about 'someday,' but he stifled it. "I think you'll look great in it. We won't have to do much with your hair. Maybe next time you come over we could try a thing or two with makeup."

"And you can teach me how to do the catwalk." They were smiling at each other when Kenji returned. He draped a length of ribbon across the drafting table. Bronze satin, with peacock-feather embroidery in green, blue, and purple. "Oh *yes*." There was really only one other directive to give the designer, and Robert had to wait until Jade looked at his watch, grimaced, and made an apologetic move. "You go ahead. And hey."

"Mmm?"

"The movie people are going with your character design for Jonathan. Put that image in your portfolio." Jade's smile was a reward. "Call you later."

"Okay. I'll be in touch about the bill, Kenji." No doubt that bill was going to be awful, but a lot of industry people would be at this fundraiser. It was an investment. Jade had to boogie, no time to deal with it now. He waved on his way out.

Robert waited a minute, making small talk with Kenji, to be sure Jade wasn't going to come back in. "His money is no good here, okay?"

Kenji's eyebrows went up. "Most models don't pay for their own costume."

"I don't care. I'm assuming the price tag for all this is going to be closer to wedding dress than tuxedo. He's my best friend, at least, and I owe him." *So much more than a best friend*, Robert thought.

They spent a few minutes discussing the various stages of production, and what would fall due at each stage. Then there was a lengthy round of measurements. Robert paid for the design and pattern, made a date for the pattern fitting, shook hands, and took his leave. When Kenji got an email from Jade asking for the numbers, he wrote back to say it was taken care of.

Jade read that email and couldn't, at first, decide what to think. Obviously Robert had decided to foot the bill. Should he say anything? Should he object? Should he worry? Or should he accept this as a gesture of gratitude and affection, as he was sure it was meant. It could mean even more. At the very least, it meant Robert was fully behind Jade on this. It was a new and wonderful feeling.

He knew the man pretty well now. Knew that Robert had an active social life. He wasn't hiding from being gay. Hadn't, in fact, from the very beginning. He was seeing other people. He was open to the possibility that there was more than one man in the world he might want to take to bed, though there were no indications that he'd done more than kiss anyone but Jade.

Jade also knew that Robert was ready for commitment. He'd been willing to commit to a woman, even though the relationship was clearly imperfect. Had offered her that stunning ring, even though his subconscious guided him to a ring that would fit Jade. Part of him wanted to simply throw himself over that cliff. Another part kept yelling 'it's only been a couple of months.'

It was the part that whispered 'but you love him' that finally dictated the email he sent.

> Hi Robert,
> I hear from Kenji that your sneaky ass told him not to bill me. Well, thank you. I'm telling myself

you probably would have handed over a boxful of cash at the fundraiser. If so, I think you've done enough on your side (though feel free to strong-arm your associates into ponying up). On my side, thank you. I really appreciate it. I'm considering it a gift, and I think I know why you wanted to give me one.

In case you ever wonder, I'm really glad I met you that night. When there's something you want from me, name it.

Your friend,

Jade

Robert read the email, tried to decode it, and couldn't. Was Jade saying he knew Robert loved him? Was he saying that was okay, he could deal with it? Or was he saying he *wanted* that? Was he saying, ask me to love you? Or maybe … *let* me love you?

He paced around the apartment for what turned out to be twenty minutes. He wasn't upset, only confused. They were so good about saying what they wanted in bed. Actually, they made themselves clear everywhere except in this land-mine-strewn emotional space. "My friend," he said out loud. Jade was his friend. His lover. And he wasn't the only man in the world who could be those things. But he was the one Robert wanted. "What if the thing I want from you is you? Can I say that?" Hearing the words didn't help.

He sighed. Another thing to take to the therapist. With so little actual experience of being gay to talk about, they most often discussed previous relationships. Context was everything. So where else did he have communication problems? Things he, or the other person, hadn't said until it was a moot point. Or maybe had been afraid to say. Leaving aside the whole 'I am not who I think I am' thing, he could remember a few such situations. He'd always tried to be up front about his goals and his limitations. In high school, everyone knew he'd be doing a missionary year or two. In college, he made it clear that he'd go where the job was. A lot of his classmates planned to stay in or near their home towns. A few of them were divorced already. At least Robert never did that. Didn't say sure, let's call this the thing to do, and jump through the hoops, and then run away.

Of course, he'd been about to do that with Sharon. Because … why. Because he was ready, that was all. Ready to make a life with someone, and only a couple of things about her weren't right. The same things that *were* right with Jade.

He felt right, that was all. Maybe that was the reason everything was working. Being in the right place at the right time was definitely key, but who else would have felt, smelled, *tasted* so perfectly right? And then the sports thing. It was exactly the right level of interest in sports. Jade wasn't going to be dragging Robert to a golf course or a tennis court all the time. He had his own reasons to stay in shape, he did that on his own time. When they were together, that was their focus. Robert liked that, he always had. He had fitness and career handled, he didn't need a partner to keep him on track for that. But being able to hang out together at home, watch the same things with the same level of interest, and then go to bed and have incredibly satisfying sex … only a fool would want more than that.

If Jade felt the same way, and it really seemed like he did, then maybe all Robert had to do was give it a little more time. Someday he could ask. He could say, what I want from you is exactly what we have now, but exclusively. And forever.

Chapter 13

July 2010

Jonathan's part wasn't huge, and the movie was on a fast production track. The scheduled release date was in the second week of November. It was the kind of thing that would play in wide release for three weeks, then go to suburban theaters for two months, and end up on cable six months after release. The bread and butter of moviemaking, the sort of thing that kept production companies and actors busy. It was the first time Jade had been engaged for a whole shoot, and he loved every minute of it.

Most of the shoot was happening on soundstages in the Valley, with some live action on locations downtown and in East L.A. Every time Jonathan was called, Jade was there: thirteen days and eight nights spread over six weeks. The producers kept things clicking along with as few takes as possible, as little overtime as possible, and hardly any extras. The script was mostly nonsense, one of those semi-vigilante stories where a law-enforcement person goes rogue in order to take down the bad guy, who does bad things to the hero's friends and family in order to raise the stakes. Jonathan and one of his co-stars were running a book on how many times the LAPD consultants on set would cringe over a procedural (or basic reality) error.

Jade was laughing over the day's tally as he got Jonathan cleaned up at the end of a night shoot. "So I guess you're having fun," he said, wiping the big guy down with a damp washcloth.

"So much fun. God, thanks for that."

"All part of the service." Jade handed over a water bottle. That was part of the service, too. "How much time do you have before your next match?"

"None." Jonathan stood up, stretched, winced as his back cracked. "Two days after I wrap with this. Texas, I think. Maybe New Jersey?"

"How long are you planning to keep that up?" Jade perched on his director's chair, holding a bottle of his own. There was usually a decompression period like this; Jonathan never seemed to be in a hurry to get out and go home, and Jade didn't want to seem eager to leave. He didn't even know where Jonathan lived, but it was clear there was nobody there waiting for him. Someday soon he'd ask Shaya if she knew any more. There had been at least one date, before the shoot got underway.

Jonathan bent down to touch his toes, groaning. "Fuck me. Ugh." Straightened up. "I don't know. I've got all those ex-wives."

"Two."

"Two too many. Never again." He sighed, not making eye contact. Shrugged. "I don't know what else I can do. But I'm thirty-six. I've been doing this for fifteen years. I don't know how many more years I have in me."

Jade knew, thanks to Robert, that Jonathan's current contract ran through 2012. He also knew some of the terms of that contract, which he probably shouldn't. In any case, he certainly couldn't say 'if you don't re-sign you'll still be a millionaire.' There were good reasons for Jonathan to be wary of saying goodbye to that income stream, even though the expenses – and risks – associated with the job were high. *Independent contractor, my ass*, he thought. It was funny how much he'd learned about other sports in the past few months. But they were here on a movie set, and this might well be Jonathan's future. "I'll bet Robert could find you more of this kind of thing."

"We'll see." Jonathan was finally making moves to go. "They'd have to be short commitments, like this." He was usually bound to two weeks per month doing WWE stuff. The movie production did its best to work around his schedule, but he was going to owe WWE a week by the time they wrapped. "Or shorter." He finished getting dressed. Glanced at Jade, half-smiling. "Or who knows. Maybe the next offer is worth breaking my contract."

"Better than breaking your neck. Go get some rest. See you next time." They shook hands. Jade watched him go, packed up his shit, and headed home. He wondered if Jonathan had said anything like that to Robert. Maybe it was worth passing along. A good excuse to text the next day, before he went over to the salon: *Hi Robert, had an interesting chat with J last night after wrap for the day. He's getting a real kick out of this. Said, maybe the next offer is worth breaking my contract. Thought you should know. See you soon OXO*

Robert saw the text on his coffee break and sent an immediate reply: *Thanks for passing that along! I'll see what I can find out about things in the pipeline. Glad he's having fun with it. Are you? OXO*

It took a couple hours before Jade was free to pick up the phone again. Then he fixed himself an iced coffee, sat in his chair, and sent back *Total fun because he's so nice. Which reminds me I have to harass Shaya about something. When do I get to see you again?* He sent that and said, "Damn."

"What?" Shaya had her hands full as usual, but was paying attention, also as usual.

"Incautious text."

"What, did you accidentally say I love you?"

Jade stifled a laugh. "No."

"Are you ever going to say it?"

A not-so-stifled sigh. "Yes. That reminds me, did J call you?" They were all using the initial now, because there was media interest in Jonathan's movie debut and none of them wanted to get pinned down for comments (or even for no-comments). He was looking at Shaya, whose expression could only be described as smug, when his phone buzzed again. "He did, huh." She snickered. Jade shook his head in mock judgement, glanced at the phone, and tried not to swoon. Robert's message was *Not soon enough. Busy as hell. I miss you*

Jade couldn't resist. *I miss you too. Call you tomorrow?*

Yes please anytime after 7 XOX

It's a date XOX

August 2010

It felt like forever since they'd had an evening like this. They were hanging out at Robert's place again, and it was probably a little late in the evening to start a conversation. After watching the tail end of a baseball game, after dinner. Before (if he was lucky) they went to bed. He never assumed that would happen. Hadn't even hinted at the wish that they could be exclusive, even though that was in the top five things he wanted. Things Jade might be willing to say yes to, based on that email after the costume consult. Robert didn't have the nerve to ask. Resolutely did not ask if Jade was seeing anyone else. Surely Jade would say so. They'd always been honest with each other, and that was important information for men who were fucking naked.

He asked about something else. "Tell me about your friend. The first one." Robert knew it was none of his business, except everything about Jade felt like his business. They were lovers, if nothing else. He really thought there was something else. Hoped so, anyway.

Jade was watching Robert think, fairly sure he knew what was going through the other man's mind, wondering when he would simply give in and say everything. It felt too soon, but that was mostly because he kept tripping over the speed of Robert's process. Couldn't help relating it to his own, which was so much rockier. It had been years before Jade felt like he really knew who he was, before 'adult gay man' was a comfortable description. He retrieved the original question. "We were lucky we were friends. There really wasn't anyone else for either of us in that town. There were a few days and nights during the summer after graduation when we talked about should we try to keep it going. We loved each other." It was important to say that. To acknowledge it. Partly so Robert would know there was more to it, and partly to remind himself of that. "But we decided it wouldn't be fair to either of us. We were eighteen, and we were going to be like goldfish dumped out of a bowl and into a really big pond. We were going to grow and change." An uncomfortable movement here, because that was the whole reason he hadn't already handed his heart to Robert. "He went to college and got a bunch of degrees. I came to Hollywood and got a couple of licenses. He's the music director now for a private school up in the Bay Area."

Robert hadn't missed that body language, but he was diverted. "Wow, isn't he young for a job like that?"

"He is. He was the assistant till his boss died of cancer. The school opened a search but they didn't look very hard. Everyone wanted Allen." He knew using the name would make the 'first guy' seem much more real to Robert. Didn't know if that was good or bad.

"Do you," Robert hesitated, then forged ahead, "ever see him?"

Jade consciously relaxed, turning toward Robert on the loveseat and resting his arm along the back of it. "Once in a while. He's married." Robert blinked. Jade smiled. "His interest in women is about on the level of mine, but he always wanted kids. And he met a gay woman who also wanted kids. They got to be friendly, kind of circled around it for a year or so, and decided to get married so they could have kids the old-fashioned way. Now they live in a row house with her girlfriend and his boyfriend. The kids call both women Mom and both men Dad. It seems to be working great."

"Well. I'll be damned." A moment's thought, then, "How many kids?" He mirrored Jade's position, because they were talking and they should be comfortable looking at each other. Hitching one knee up onto the seat, leaning forward so there wouldn't be so much space between them.

"Two. One of each."

"That's actually really cool." He knew the surprise came across in his voice. Another little adjustment to his worldview. Another reminder that people were people, and love was love, and gender was kind of irrelevant to a lot of things. Or more like totally irrelevant. Then he thought of something else, and snorted out a laugh. "I'm imagining what that sex might have been like."

"I hear there was alcohol, giggling, and shrieking." He was grinning.

155

"Like, ew, no, really?!" Robert was cracking up. "Oh my God. That's kind of what I thought the first time I went all the way with a girl."

"But you got over it."

"Kind of. I guess. I feel bad now." It was the first time he'd said so.

"Why?" Jade frowned. "Do you think you were deceptive? As far as I can tell, you always acted in good faith. Literally the day you realized you weren't oriented to women, you stopped dating women."

Robert let that sink in. It was true. "Maybe," he said slowly, "that old script is still looking for ways being gay makes me a bad person."

Jade's heart lurched. He gazed at Robert, thinking *why do I care so much*, but the fact was he did. And if it didn't work out, it couldn't be worse than all those other times it didn't work out. Even if it was worse, he didn't think he'd regret it. "As far as I can tell," he said again, "you're a perfect person." Robert looked startled; he made a confused sound. Jade reached out with his free hand, caught Robert's, squeezed. "Robert. Sweetheart. I love you."

Robert couldn't breathe for a few seconds. For the next few seconds he thought he might cry. Then he launched himself at Jade. It was a good ten minutes before they stopped kissing long enough for him to push himself up a bit, enough to speak. "I love you too. You're so exactly what I always wanted. So exactly what I needed. So exactly everything." Another kiss. "This loveseat is too small."

"Yes it is. Let's go to bed."

After saying those things to each other, neither of them really wondered about the sex that followed. It was slow and tender, with more kissing and caressing than

156

anything else. In retrospect, both of them thought 'that was *all* kissing,' and both were perfectly satisfied. They eventually went to sleep in a tangle of limbs that meant Robert woke up in the wee hours, wincing, to reorganize things.

He woke up again around six o'clock and lay there for a few minutes, gazing at Jade and thinking about how wonderful this was. How glad he was that he had friends he could share this with, people who cared whether or not he was happy. People who didn't mind a bit that he was happy because he was with a man. This man, specifically. Calling Jade his boyfriend was a given from here on out. *My friend, my lover, my boyfriend.* Maybe it shouldn't matter what word he used. Except he'd read far too many contracts not to know how important a word could be.

There was one other word available to them. 'Partner' meant something now, legally. Maybe in a few months, if everything was still like this, they could talk about that.

He didn't want to wake Jade. Wasn't going back to sleep. Might as well get up and make some coffee.

Jade woke up after seven, stretched, yawned, and thought *what's different*. A glance at the clock, the smell of coffee, and a memory. Robert usually came back to bed if he was up early. He must have felt the same way Jade felt right now: last night's lovemaking should be cherished for a little while, before they made the next memory. He slid out of bed and went to the bathroom. Appropriated one of Robert's tee shirts and a pair of warm-ups. Found his man curled on the loveseat in the den, e-reader in hand. "You have a hickey."

Robert glanced up, smiling, and set his book aside. "Wonder how that got there."

157

Jade leaned over to kiss him. Noticed the coffee mug on the side table was empty. "Want a refill?"

"Sure." They were both, Robert realized with surprise, slightly skittish. As if those big words last night had pushed them into uncharted territory. Well, maybe they had. He watched Jade go to the kitchen, watched him come back. "I should never have told Sharon I loved her. I didn't even know what I was saying."

Jade handed over Robert's mug, sat down close beside him. "I haven't said that to anybody for a long time. I said it to Robbie." No comment from the man beside him. Jade glanced over. "I didn't mean it the same way."

"He was dying. I'm sure he needed to hear it." Robert swallowed some coffee. Jade always fixed it the way he liked it. "Trying to think of other people I shouldn't have said it to." A stifled laugh. Robert leaned a few degrees, enough to rest his shoulder against Jade's. "It was part of the progression, I think. After a certain number of non-disastrous dates, after you've found out you can tolerate each other in bed, you say I love you. Most of them said it back to me."

"Jesus, I hope so."

"I wonder if they had the same idea about progression. I've never been with someone longer than six months. Either I lost interest or the girl did. I'm hoping that's at least partly because I was with the wrong gender."

"Me too." Jade appreciated the candor. He would have guessed none of Robert's relationships went very long-term, if he was willing to propose after only a few weeks. "The longest I've been with someone is," he thought for a minute, "about thirty months. That was

Allen. The next-longest was Robbie." He sipped some coffee. He wasn't proud of everything in between, but Robert had a right to know. "When I came to L.A., I was determined to embrace it. The whole new world. No family, no church, no little town where everyone knew everything about me, or thought they did, and everyone had something to say about it. I could do anything, and nobody back home would know. Plus of course it was right after I said goodbye to my first boyfriend. It was worst case scenario. I mean, I set myself up to make bad choices, and that's exactly what I did. Did you make bad choices?"

"I was too scared to. There was always the church. Horror stories about STDs. The occasional pregnant girl serving as an object lesson. Right after high school I did a missionary year, which was me and another guy going somewhere remote to talk to people about the church."

"Ugh."

Robert laughed. "I don't know how good a missionary I was. I was drawn to things like Habitat for Humanity. Usually guys do two years, and the guy I went out with did. But I had guaranteed admission to the college I wanted to attend, so I came back and went to school."

"I'm betting there was nothing approaching a relationship during that year." Robert made a sound something like 'tchah,' which made Jade laugh. "I guess the other guy didn't like long-legged blonds." Now a startled sound. "Didn't you ever think of that?"

"No! Not even since April. Wow." Robert drank the rest of his coffee, set the mug down, turned another degree or two toward Jade. "How bad, exactly? Or no, you don't have to tell me. It's not really any of my business."

"Well, sweetheart, it might have been. It was pure luck I didn't catch one of the viruses. The two things I did catch, timing suggests were from the same guy. After that I cleaned up my act. But it was," he sighed. "Too many men. Too much sex for the sake of sex. You know those five guys you went out with over the past three months? Well, that was me in three weeks. And I went to bed with all of them."

That was a little hard to hear. He didn't really want any more details. "But that was before."

"Before Robbie. There were two men after Robbie. And now you."

They were quiet for a minute, then Robert said, "I've been with thirteen people since I was sixteen. Twelve women, and you. Eight of those women I only went to bed with one time."

"You didn't like it? Or they didn't like it?"

"I never knew if they liked it. My high-school and college girlfriends, there was a lot of fooling around that wasn't intercourse. I always liked that better. The woman in law school, the one who moved across the country? She was ambitious and smart and tough. It wasn't bad, but it wasn't anything like sex with you. I wanted to like it with Sharon, because she was so smart and funny and pretty. All those others," he shook his head. "It was like we agreed that it was an experiment not worth repeating. Why did I not *know*?"

"Why should you? If that wasn't something that was presented to you as a possibility?"

"But you said you knew you were interested in boys, even before Allen kissed you. I simply had no idea."

He seemed to be upset, so Jade wriggled in closer, getting one leg over Robert's, one arm around his chest. "Tell me about your family."

That was a swerve. Robert wondered why. "My sister Lisa is three years younger than me. She's married. My brother Lance is two years older. He's married with two kids, one of each. The son is seven now."

"Your brother's name is Lance?"

It sounded an awful lot like Jade was trying not to laugh. Robert wrapped an arm around what he could reach, and squeezed. "It does sound kind of ridiculous."

"He's been married how long?"

"Nine years."

"Since you were twenty-seven. You went from being a missionary, to six years of higher ed, which you finished when you were twenty-five?" Robert nodded. "Two years later, your big brother gets married and you have another model for what men do in your family. You didn't have a lot of time to *think* in there, sweetheart."

Robert kissed his forehead. "I guess not. When do you do your thinking?"

"When my hands are full of hair. Speaking of which." They untangled themselves. "Shower, breakfast, then I have to go."

"Jade."

"Mmm?" He was halfway to his feet. Still close. Robert's expression said so much. Jade leaned in and kissed him. "I love you."

"I love you." From there it was a normal day, except those words followed them through it. Robert couldn't stop thinking about his history. What if his six-month limit was some kind of inability to commit? He *wanted* to commit. He was determined to commit. He wanted Jade forever, not for six lousy months. And he'd

161

never truly wanted forever before, so he was going to hope, and maybe pray, that the want and the determination went along with this feeling, the one he hadn't had before. The one that made him a new man.

Chapter 14

September 2010

The dressing room for the pageant models was a madhouse. Scarlett O'Hara, Daisy Buchanan, Miss Marple, Anna Pigeon, Becky Sharp, Amelia Peabody, Nancy Drew, Alice (in Wonderland), Lisbeth Salander, Katniss Everdeen, and Holly Golightly were in their own areas, defined by what looked for all the world like hospital privacy screens. Mary Russell's area was toward the back of the room. Like everyone else, Robert had a full-length standing mirror, a bar-height cart with supply shelves and a battery-operated vanity mirror, a couple of folding chairs, a wardrobe rack, and a basket with bottled drinks and snacks. Jade was waiting for him when he arrived. All the styling gear was deployed. Robert made big eyes at him as he stepped behind the screen. Jade bit back a laugh. "Aren't you glad you don't need a wig?"

"Oh my *God*." It wasn't only the wigs. Some of the dresses were insane. His suit was practically menswear in comparison. "Honey, I have to tell you."

You're so cute. "What, sweetheart."

"I tried on those tights and it was like, no. Had to shave my legs. It took for fucking ever and I cut myself three times." He tried to put an exasperated spin on it, but Jade was laughing. Half a dozen people he couldn't see were laughing too. "Shut up, bitches. Oh, and that guy is here. That photographer." He raised his eyebrows. He didn't want to say the name, in case the guy was standing on the other side of the screen.

Jade couldn't think of who Robert meant for a second. Then his lover made a 'tsk' sound, followed by jazz hands, and Jade laughed again. He had to mean Andy Martin. "I was hoping he'd be here. They'll be getting posed photos of everybody once the costume is complete. I heard," he dropped his volume a little, forcing Robert to lean in, "at least two of these costumes are *rented*." He used such a scandalized tone that Robert completely cracked up. That should help with the nerves. Jade broke the seal on a bottle of water, handed it to his model, and said, "Let's see those legs." Shoes, socks, and pants off. Robert was deeply grateful his costume didn't require any special underwear. He sat on a towel-covered folding chair while Jade checked his legs, approving of the shaving job, cleaning off a little dried blood, soothing the cuts with a dab of olive oil. Then into warm-ups, because the air-conditioning was on full blast. Shirt off. Another inspection. "Oh, you shaved here too!"

"Well, honestly." At least he'd managed not to cut himself under the arms. That skin was delicate. He let Jade drop the bronze charmeuse shell over his head. There was a moderate amount of wriggling and shimmying to get it smooth over his torso; it wasn't tight, exactly, but it was cut close to the body and the fabric wasn't stretchy at all. Now the zip-up sweatshirt to keep him warm and protect the silk while Jade did his makeup.

Primer, other strange substances, a very odd-feeling process to hide his eyebrows. "Why do you do that?"

"Because putting your eyebrows higher on your forehead will look more feminine, and it's easier to create that line if the original hair is completely covered up."

"Hmph." Robert could only wait and wonder. So many steps for his eyes. Pencils, shadows, liquid liner. Powder, mascara, a different liquid. Then Jade standing back to stare at him with a completely objective expression, followed by a satisfied nod.

"You're going to be so pretty," Jade murmured, smoothing on the foundation. "And so fierce." A touch of bronzer, not blush. Lip pencil to define the mouth. Filling in with a rosy-tan color. Powder brushed on. Jade assessed things, added some contour and highlight here and there. A powder base down over the throat, blending. Wishing he hadn't done the mouth already, because he wanted to kiss it. "I'm kissing the daylights out of you when this is over."

"Good." Robert could say that without moving his face.

Jade finished shaping Robert's hair – he'd let it grow out over the past few months, so Jade had something to work with – sprayed it, stepped back. "Want to take a look now, or wait?"

"I can wait." They still had some time. The models were going out in reverse chronological order, which was definitely doing a favor for Scarlett O'Hara and Becky Sharp. Katniss Everdeen would go out first. She had props, including a bow, and someone was running a book on whether she would shoot anything from the catwalk. Robert wished he could see the pageant and be in it at the same time. At least there would be a video.

They could hear the emcee in the ballroom, telling people about the silent auction. Reminding them that the big event would start in fifteen minutes. Each model's walk would take less than a minute. All of them would return to the dressing room until everyone had walked. Then they'd all go out again, because they were the celebrities here tonight. Robert was more nervous about that than about walking. He shucked off the warm-up pants. Jade handed him the tights, watched him tug them up, and tried not to laugh at Robert's muttered curses. Now the skirt. It fit perfectly, of course. "Don't forget to show people your knife." It was concealed by the hem of the shell. "Some people really love to see the details."

Robert was mentally running through the mechanics of his walk. He let Jade fasten the pearl necklace around his neck. Felt the long loop brushing against his bare back. That was going to surprise everybody. It surprised him, when he went for the pattern fitting. The shell had a high neckline in front, just below his collarbones. In back it was cut in a deep vee. They'd talked about it, but he didn't anticipate how sexy it would be.

He'd practiced taking the jacket off, dozens of times. Letting it slide off his shoulders, down his arms, catching the collar in one hand to let it swing around before passing it to his other hand and slinging it over his shoulder. *Walk out. Strut, be fierce, don't forget your footwork. Stop, half a turn. Jacket off, walk a tight little circle, sling the jacket. Strut again, done.* He'd practiced those turns about a thousand times. Made Emily laugh every day, practicing in the hallway at the agency, complaining about how he could only do that first, essential half turn if he turned to the left. If he tried turning right it was a disaster. So he had to stop with his right foot forward, even if he wasn't at the absolute end of the catwalk. Jade was holding the jacket for him. Robert shimmied into it. Now he looked in the mirror. Almost there. The cloche. Funny how that one piece did so much to create the illusion that this was a woman. The wire-rimmed spectacles. Finally, the shoes. They were bronze and peacock-blue now. He didn't even notice the heels. "Oh wait! Where's my watch?" Jade found it for him and strapped it on. One more look in the mirror. He couldn't help being pleased.

166

"Ready for your close-up, Mary?"

Robert and Jade both turned. Andy Martin was standing there smiling. They followed him tamely to the area set aside for photos. A backdrop with the name of the event, a pillar with a flower arrangement on it, a little velvet vanity bench to pose on if one so desired. Robert did so desire. After a few standing poses (including one that showed his back) he took off the spectacles, sat down and beveled his legs. Turned half away from the camera, looking over his shoulder, jacket draped over the bench behind him. Pointing his toes, drawing the skirt up an inch or so, and putting on an expression he hoped was sultry. Maybe it was. In any case, the photographer made a pleased sound. Then it was Holly Golightly's turn. And a few minutes after that, someone was rounding them up and getting them in line to walk.

The double doors between the main ballroom and the breakout room were opened. There was a heavy red curtain over the doorway. Some music was playing on the other side. It faded out. The emcee said, "And now, please welcome one dozen fabulous ladies of literature, presented by members of Local 706!" New music: 'I'm Too Sexy.' Robert almost laughed out loud. He looked around for Jade; where was Jade? Oh maybe he went out to the other room. *Breathe.* The emcee again as the curtain was pulled open. "Katniss Everdeen!" And they were off.

Robert was seventh to walk. There were bright lights on the other side of the curtain. An actual catwalk, a foot higher than the ballroom floor. Someone standing by the edge to make sure he didn't trip stepping up. "Mary Russell!" He struck a pose stolen from that fashion-show thing in 'Singin' in the Rain.' Heard applause. Walked, one foot directly in front of the other, toes turned out, hips swinging. Stopped with his right

167

foot forward. *'Do my little turn on the catwalk.'* Shimmying out of the jacket, catching it, hearing the 'oooohh' when people saw his back. *Yeah baby.* Tight little circle, slinging the jacket over his shoulder, a toss of the head. Walking back to the curtain, heart pounding. He might not have breathed the entire time he was out there. When he stepped down into the breakout room again he was trembling. Someone put a bottle of water in his hand. "Thanks."

In no time at all the walks were finished. Becky Sharp stepped down (accepting a hand from the helpful bystander), the curtains were closed, they were all moved away from the doors so those could close too. Becky said, "Jesus Christ why did I ever say I would do a fucking *corset*?" Scarlett said something rude about antebellum gowns, Amelia said something obscene about bustles, and suddenly there was someone with a tray full of champagne glasses. They all had a much-needed drink before composing themselves to join the money people in the ballroom. Robert tried not to notice that Andy Martin was prowling around back there again, taking candid pictures. Then there were a few different group shots; Robert wondered why, until Alice said something to Lisbeth about the calendar. "The what?"

"They're going to do a calendar! Didn't your stylist tell you?"

No he didn't, Robert didn't say. He wasn't sure how he felt about it. There seemed to be a difference between doing the pageant – a one-time thing – and appearing in a printed document. People might actually look at him. See him, for a whole month. Dressed as a woman. Was he ready for that? Was there a difference? This was surely going to end up on YouTube. But he didn't look at all like himself. And the people who would mind wouldn't be looking for him in a place like this. He still wasn't positive he was okay about it until the side door opened and all of the stylists came in to collect their models. Then he saw Jade and thought *but I love him*. This event was big for his lover, ergo Robert was going to support it, and that meant not being a baby about someone taking his picture or, God forbid, looking at him. He watched Jade approach and couldn't help smiling. "Hi honey. How'd I do?"

"So good. So fucking good." Jade tipped his chin up, inviting a kiss. As usual, Robert delivered. Not enough to destroy his makeup, but enough to remind himself why he did this. Jade asked him if he wanted to do a touch-up before going out.

"Do I need to? I mean, there's going to be food, right?" Robert was suddenly starving. And he wanted another drink. Jade was the designated driver. Maybe he knew there would be some medicinal alcohol after this thing.

"There's food. And you look great. Let's get some of that food into you." They joined the slow sashay of models and stylists, heading out into the ballroom. Jade made sure there was a steady supply of champagne, alternating with water. Food came out about a half-hour later. By that time all the models were old friends. Their respective stylists were inspecting everybody else's work. Robert lost track of Jade, but now he was in the groove. Feeling a little bit high. Probably a little bit tipsy. All of a sudden he didn't mind being stared at. Maybe because he wasn't really Robert in this moment. He was having a great time telling people about all the details of his costume, dropping Kenji's name everywhere, lavishing praise on Jade. There was a table off to one side with copies of books featuring the models' characters, DVDs of movie adaptations, movie props and more. Robert had to pose for pictures over

169

there for quite a few people. He posed with Daisy. He posed with Holly. He posed with Amelia. Then Miss Marple, Nancy Drew, and Anna Pigeon joined the two of them for a female-detectives group shot.

Somewhere around that time he realized he wanted to sit down. Amelia was also showing signs of wanting a chair. "Let's go over here," Robert said, offering his arm.

"Thanks, honey. I have an escort somewhere but I'll be fucked if I can see him in this mob. I don't even see my stylist!"

"Who's yours?"

"Shaya. She works with Jade, have you met?"

"Mmm, kind of waved at each other at the salon once when I was picking Jade up." Robert helped Amelia take a seat, which was quite a production with that bustle. Then he stood up as tall as he could, spotted Jade with Shaya about thirty feet away, waved to get his attention. That didn't work. He was not in the mood to be patient. "Derecha!" It was a little bit loud, but the room was so damn noisy. It worked, anyway. Jade looked over with a startled expression, said something to Shaya, and began to make his way over. Robert blew out a breath and plopped down on the chair. "They're coming. God I'm exhausted."

"Me too. Patrick Sarkisian."

"Robert Anderson." They shook hands. "That dress is completely amazing."

"Thanks." Patrick looked at it ruefully. "Kenji made it as comfortable as he possibly could, but I've been hating myself for agreeing to do the formal dress instead of the excavation costume. Have you read any of my books?"

"No, I'm going to start on those as soon as I finish reading all of mine." They grinned at each other. Then

170

Jade and Shaya were there, and a minute after that Patrick's partner Dmitri joined them. Not too much later, they were all headed to the breakout room so Robert and Patrick could resume their true identities and everyone could go home.

Before disappearing behind his screens, Patrick suggested they should all get together for dinner sometime soon. "Come to our house in WeHo. We can watch the video of this insanity and do a postmortem."

"Decide what to wear next year," Shaya suggested.

Patrick's outraged expression made Robert laugh. Jade said, "They won't announce the theme until March. Will you be recovered by then, sweetheart?"

"I'm good," Robert said. It was almost a surprise. "I had fun."

Shaya was smiling. "Your walk was high quality."

"Excellent body mechanics," Dmitri said. Those were the first words Robert had heard from him.

"Uh, I used to play soccer. And baseball. Couple other things. Jade and my office assistant had to teach me how to stand up and walk."

"They did very well," Patrick said. "Dmitri's a dancer, so I have a live-in coach."

"Maybe by March I'll have a live-in coach," Robert said recklessly. "Come on, honey. Help me change." He shook hands with everybody else, then caught hold of Jade and towed him over to their area. Wrapped him in his arms because he had to say this, but was afraid to see his face while he did. "I meant that. I'd love to live with you. I can't stand being away from you. Would you live with me?"

Jade had his eyes closed, breathing in the mingled scents of warm cashmere and face powder and the love

171

of his life. "Yes." Then Robert was kissing him. They kept doing that till the lip color was a distant memory. "Mmm. Let's get you out of those shoes."

"Would you believe I forgot all about them?"

That night, Robert had a very specific agenda. Jade didn't have any problem concentrating on that. The next morning, he said, "I'll bet you're dying for a haircut."

"Oh my God."

They both laughed for a minute. Jade kissed his chest, sat up, and said, "Come by the salon after work tonight. I'll hook you up."

Robert sat up too. "Could we try it like yours?"

"Seriously?" Very short on the neck and sides, longer on top. Not the cut that went with the average business suit.

"I like the way it makes your neck look so long. And I like doing this." Robert dug his hand into the hair at the crown of Jade's head, tugging gently, tipping his chin up to expose his throat. Putting his mouth on that throat. "Mmm."

"Mmm," Jade echoed. "I like when you do that too. You're sure? Because a man our age with a haircut like this, you might as well run around in a rainbow Speedo."

Robert laughed against his mouth. "If I can't take it, you can take a little more off the top. Jade. Tell me we don't have to get out of bed yet."

"We don't." It was a little breathless.

Robert ran into Liam at the coffee shop two weeks after the pageant. The first thing Liam said was, "Nice

172

haircut." The second thing was, "Good job on the catwalk."

"Oh my God were you *there?!*" They stepped out of line so they could talk.

Liam was laughing under his breath. "I saw it on YouTube. One of my staffers has a friend who's a stylist and she was talking about this big event, and I remembered you saying something about a fundraiser with a drag pageant. So I asked a couple of leading questions. Did you get to see the whole thing?"

"Yeah, the organizers sent us all a link once it was posted. Jade and I had dinner with Amelia Peabody and his partner a couple nights ago. We deconstructed everybody."

"I know that guy, too," Liam said. "He gets facials from one of my aestheticians."

Robert lowered his voice a little. "Wasn't he gorgeous? He's fifty-five!"

"Good role model. Anyway, was it fun?"

"It really was. I said I'd do it for Jade, but by the time we were putting together the costume I was really into it. If they do something similar next year," he shrugged.

Liam nodded. "So you're pretty sure you and Jade will still be together, huh."

"He's moving in with me. I'm so excited. And scared to death, because I've never lived with anybody, and the longest I've ever dated anybody was about six months, and what if I screw it up." He took a breath, embarrassed and a little upset. He always did this with Liam, always over-shared. But the other man's arm was around his shoulders, squeezing, reassuring.

"Hey. You love him, right? And I'm sure he loves you too, or he wouldn't be moving in with you. You've already come so far. It'll be fine." Liam gave him a pat and let go.

Robert blinked, sniffed, swallowed. "I hope so. By Thanksgiving it'll be officially the longest I've ever been with anybody. I was thinking maybe we'd have some people over. Would you come? Dinner and a game?"

"I'd be delighted. Let's get back in this line and I'll tell you about my last date."

He made the story funny, so by the time they parted ways Robert felt steady again. The whole thing was strange, though. It wasn't the first time he'd run up against this insecurity. This fear of doing the wrong thing, fear that he didn't know what to do. That was the undercurrent to every date he'd ever had with a woman, but he hadn't been aware of it with Jade. Or maybe hadn't recognized it, because everything was so new that he had other things to worry about. On the way back to the agency he made a mental note to mention it to his therapist. It was definitely something he wanted to figure out on his own. Not a thing to bring into the relationship. Not a problem Jade should have to try to solve.

Except the next time he saw his lover, he blurted it all out. "Fuck," he said, leaning his head on his hand. "I was going to try and work this out with my therapist, not bother you with it."

"Sweetheart, why in the world would you think I'd be bothered? I love that you're so open with me." Jade reached across the table, took Robert's hand, pulled it down and away from his eyes. Robert sat back, not making eye contact. Jade gave it a little more time, wasn't getting more words, sighed. "I want you to feel like you can tell me anything. I am not going to judge you. You've heard what a mess I made of myself. You can't possibly do worse than that."

"You never had a chance to do it right." Robert sat forward again, fingers curling around Jade's. "You didn't get a chance to grow up and figure yourself out before you got your head twisted off. By the time it happened to me I was settled. I had my career, my independence, security. You were a *kid*." Jade was staring at him as if he were speaking Swahili. "Look, even my therapist can't figure out why I made the switch so easily, but what if it's as simple as that? The only trouble I had was dating. The only reason for that was disorientation. Thinking I was straight when I wasn't. As soon as I refocused it was like finding the missing piece of a puzzle. And now I think this fear thing is an artifact of that. Have I done anything wrong yet?"

Jade was confused. "What?"

"Have I screwed up. Have I hurt you. Have I in any way shape or form failed to communicate that I love you, and I care about you, and I want you in my life."

"No." Jade shook his head. "Never."

"Good. That's good. I don't want anybody else. I don't need to roam around looking for someone better than you. There isn't anyone better than you. You're the one I want. So whatever I do, or whatever I say, that's where I'm coming from. I love you."

"I love you too." Jade took a deep breath, let it out slowly. "I am not used to this. I have not been loved this way before." Tears were coming. He tried to blink them away, couldn't keep up, wiped his face. "If I ever seem a little standoffish, or untrusting, or as if I don't believe you, that's why. That's where I'm coming from. It's not about you. Nobody's ever committed," he said in a rush. It was a revelation. His deep and abiding affection for

175

Allen was a real thing, but they'd walked away from each other. It was Allen's suggestion, and Jade went along with it because he couldn't believe it would last out in the real world. Better to make the break while they still cared about each other.

He'd never asked if Allen had the same experience, the weeks – months – of bad nights, of loneliness and regret. Making desperately bad choices so he wouldn't be alone. Maybe he should have asked. All this time he'd thought it must have been so much easier for the other man, but maybe it wasn't. Maybe that marriage was every bit as much about having someone to hold onto as it was about having kids.

Robert could tell this conversation had unlocked something for Jade. It was a good thing they were at home. He stood up and went around the table. Pulled Jade out of his chair. It was still too soon to make promises about forever. But at least they could hold each other.

Quite a while later, after some silent time on the loveseat, they went and cleaned up the dinner things. Both of them were still thinking, not talking. They washed up, got in bed, settled into each other's arms. "Can I ask you something?"

That soft, tentative voice. Jade tilted his head to see Robert's face. "Ask me anything."

"Did your parents *never* say they loved you?"

"My mother did. When we were little."

"We." It was almost a question.

"Oh my God, I never told you. Wow. For thirty years I've tried not to think of him, that's why. I had a brother."

Oh no. Robert filled in the blanks. Wrapped his arm around Jade a little more snugly. "What happened."

176

"His name was Joshua."

"Joshua and Jacob?"

"Mm-hmm. He was six, I was five. Dad was out in a rowboat fishing. We were playing around on the shore. He drowned. None of us ever got over it."

Losing his big brother, at that age when a big brother was your hero. Then growing up knowing there was something off. Something he had to hide, suppress, deny, right up until the day he couldn't. "Please tell me your parents never said it should have been you. That hitting you was the worst of it."

Jade shivered. He'd had that thought himself, many times. Was glad he could say, "No. They never said that. And Dad only hit me once. I almost wanted him to. I wanted to be punished." He'd never said that.

"For living? Or for being gay?"

"Both? I don't know. You're right, I never had a chance to get my head together. Not till Robbie, really, when I let myself accept that caretaker role. It made me feel worthwhile."

"When did you change your name?" It sounded like a digression.

"When I was twenty-five. My parents didn't speak to me for a year."

"Jesus!"

"Why did you tell your family? You could have put that off for a long time."

Robert sighed, accepting the change of subject. It wasn't really a change. "Maybe I thought, if I do this now, they'll have that much more time to get used to the idea. If I waited, and told lies about women I was seeing, and kept up this front about future grandchildren or whatever, eh. I guess to me telling the truth was more honorable."

"Well, of course it was. It was also pretty rough on you."

"But it was always going to be rough on me, and at least I didn't have any lies to apologize for."

Jade pressed a kiss to Robert's chest. "You're a good man."

"So are you. And don't you forget it."

Chapter 15

They were negotiating the terms of cohabitation well into October. Jade said it would definitely be before March. Robert suggested it should be before Thanksgiving, and for a minute Jade wanted to say it was too soon. Then he said, "Give me a second."

Robert wasn't sure why he needed a second; they'd been talking about this since the night of the pageant. But he didn't argue. Simply pulled Jade close, arms around him, cheek against his hair, not-watching whatever was on TV. After a while he heard something like a sigh. "What is it, baby."

Jade turned his head, pressing a kiss to Robert's neck. "Remember how I said nobody ever committed?"

"Mm-hmm."

"Well, neither did I. I remember thinking you were ready to commit. So ready that you proposed to a woman." A silent laugh from Robert. "I guess that's why I wasn't really surprised when you suggested we could live together. And I want to," he added, because that shouldn't be in question. "So I had to take a second to examine why I was trying to put on the brakes."

Robert gave it a few seconds, waiting for more. "Well, it's only been six months since we met."

"Yes, but it's also been five months since I started thinking, I love that man." There was some kissing for a few minutes. Jade eventually put his hand on Robert's chest and pushed back enough to catch his breath. They were both laughing a little. He set his hand on Robert's face, sobering. "The thing I was tripping over was control. If I move in with someone, I'm putting myself in his power. And that's why I've never done it, because there was always a trust issue. Would that man be good for me. Would he support me in the important ways. Or would he use me. Would I give up my independence, my privacy, my *options*, and then one day find myself out on my own with less than I had before. Including less self-respect. I didn't have a lot of that to spare for a while."

Robert was staring at him, wondering how he had the courage to say these things. Wondering who some of these assholes were, that left Jade feeling less-than. "I love you," he said eventually. "I want to live with you because being with you makes me happy. I want to sleep with you and have dinner with you and wake up with you every day. I want to give you anything I can that you can't get for yourself. And I want to be the only man for you."

"You are. And you realize that as of next month, I'm going to be the longest-lasting person in your life."

"Mmm. I did realize that." Robert was smiling again.

"Halloween." Jade watched it sink in. Checked for panic, didn't detect any – on either side – and couldn't have cared less about giving a full month's notice. "Can we go to the parade in WeHo? I'll have to work that day but nobody gets anything done at night."

Robert would have said 'yes' to just about anything in that moment. "I will even let you choose what I wear." He almost regretted saying that a few days later, when he got an email with a picture. He said "Oh hell no" out loud.

Emily heard from across the hall. "What?"

"Jade wants to dress us up in these vintage-looking baseball uniforms for the WeHo Carnaval."

"Well, what's wrong with that?" She appeared at his door, looking curious. He beckoned her to his side. She looked over his shoulder at the image. "Oh." They both cracked up. The top half looked legit but below that was a pair of very short shorts. Emily started to say something, but choked.

Robert could tell she had a comment. "What?"

"Um. At least you have the legs for it." She fled the office while Robert laughed. He thought for a few minutes about how to answer that email in a way that signaled both willingness and horrified disbelief. Finally settled on *This puts a whole new spin on take me out to the ball game*.

Jade picked up the email when he got done with his current client, snickered, and wrote back *We can discuss balls and bats later*.

"Are you guys doing the dirty emails thing again?" Shaya was cleaning up her station.

"No," he lied.

"You're such a liar. Give me." She took the phone out of his hand and read the email thread. Made a 'tsk' sound. "From his business address, too. You should be ashamed of yourselves." Handed the phone back. "Moving day is coming right up."

"Saturday the twenty-third. Gives me a week to get the old place clean."

She plopped down on her chair and gazed at him. "You lived there a long time."

"I'll miss being able to walk to Callender's."

"Nothing else, though, I'll bet."

"Nothing else." He blew out a breath. "I'm half-scared, half-excited. It's like, we get along great. We've been spending three or four nights a week together as it

181

is. This totally makes sense, and I'm glad he asked me, and I'm glad I'm doing it. But wow."

"It's wow," she agreed. "I kind of expected you to put him off a little longer."

"Really?" She made a 'yeah, sorry' face. Jade thought about waving off his hesitation, then thought *this is my friend*. "I almost did. I was like but this, and that, and before March definitely but let's not rush it. And then I thought, why not rush it. Why not dive in. If I'm going to commit then I should fucking commit." He made an 'eek' face, glancing around hurriedly. It didn't look as though anyone in the salon heard him, or if they did they didn't mind the F-bomb. "Anyway, I told him he was right. We've had some talks about history. I already told him nobody ever committed to me. But when we were talking about when I should move in, I suddenly realized I never committed to anyone either, not like this. And the time is now. I'm not going to do better. I know more about him than I've ever known about a boyfriend. I love him." He half-shrugged. "And if it doesn't work out, then maybe I end up knocking on your door asking if I can crash on your couch."

"You know you're welcome. But I really don't think that's going to happen." She left it there. "So are you doing tanner on your legs for the parade, or what?"

"Gross, no. I'm going out there in all my glow-in-the-dark vampire glory. What are *you* wearing?"

Shaya made a dismissive sound. "I'm going to the party at Shall We Dance. Once was enough with that mob scene. I seem to recall you saying never again."

"Yeah, but Robert has to do it at least once. Okay. We'll have you over after I've got the place fixed up."

"Are you doing your princess thing to his bedroom?"

182

"No," he lied.

Maybe doing it in a hurry helped them both get over the 'OMG WTF' factor of cohabitation. They wanted to do it, but they'd never done it: there was so much potential for doing things wrong. Not giving themselves too much time to obsess about it, forcing themselves to concentrate on logistics and practicalities, kept those possibly-unfounded anxieties from overcoming the desire. And waking up together on Halloween morning knowing that they'd be waking up together every day from now on was much more soothing than worrisome.

Robert woke up first, slid quietly out of bed to go to the bathroom, and then went back to bed to lie there studying Jade. Those fine features, the fan of soft-brown eyelashes, the trace of a smile. As if he were dreaming of something good. The plain gold stud in his earlobe. *I'm going to get you a diamond.* Robert hadn't inspected everything Jade brought with him; there was no time for that, and it would have been intrusive anyway. But if he already had a diamond, he would have worn it by now.

It was going to be a struggle not to overdo. Not to overwhelm. Those words about control, independence, privacy: those meant something. Robert had to be careful not to let his ingrained patriarchal script turn this into some kind of offensively conventional dynamic. There was a fine line between chivalry and chauvinism. Jade was his own person. *He will stand beside me, not behind me*, Robert thought. He remembered having a similar thought on that first night.

And if he stayed here he was going to wake Jade up and do things. The guy had put in long hours this week, he needed his rest. Robert got out of bed again, pulled on some warm-ups, and went to make coffee.

183

Jade blinked his way to consciousness some time later. Opened his eyes, noted that he was alone in bed, brushed his hand over the sheet; it was cool. He pushed himself up, cursed silently at moving-related sore muscles, and glanced at the clock. "Holy shit." He hadn't slept this late for a long time. No wonder he needed to pee. That accomplished (along with some minor grooming), he found some clean clothes to throw on and went to locate his lover.

Robert was sitting at the dining table, laptop open, looking productive. He glanced up as soon as Jade came around the corner from the wet bar. "Hi honey. Sleep well?"

"Really well. How long have you been up?"

Robert shrugged. "I haven't had breakfast yet." Which wasn't really an answer, but he was having one of those attacks of skittishness. They didn't happen often, so they were always surprising. Jade must have felt it too. He swung by the table on his way to the kitchen, leaned down to wrap an arm around Robert's shoulders and kiss his cheek. Robert turned his head for a better kiss. A minute later, he'd pushed his chair back and pulled Jade onto his lap. "I'm so glad you're here." Mumbling that into Jade's hair, hands under his tee shirt, fiercely aroused.

"God, me too." Jade put his mouth on Robert's throat, squirmed away, rearranged himself astride Robert's lap. "Are you supposed to be working?"

"Fuck work." They both half-laughed, breathless, and kissed again. Stubble scraping, teeth colliding, tongues tangling. Jade got his hand inside Robert's warm-ups, felt fingers at his waistband, heard an annoyed sound that made him smile. "Why the fuck do you have jeans on?"

"Because all my stretch pants need to go in the wash."

"Mine will too in a minute." Another breathless laugh. They kept kissing somehow while Jade got on his feet to get his jeans off, then settled down again. Robert's hands were all over him. He had one of his hands on the back of Robert's neck, the other wrapped around his erection. Working him fast and hard, listening as his vocal breaths ratcheted up. Making urgent sounds of his own into Robert's mouth, squirming under those semi-distracted hands. One in front, fondling. One in back, caressing up and down Jade's cleft. *Hope the neighbors don't hear us*, Robert thought hazily, before deciding he didn't care. He had his hand on Jade's cock, thumb spreading moisture over the head. Jade growled something and stroked down with his own hand, thumb and fingers wrapping around to squeeze Robert's balls. Then he tore himself away. Robert made a desperate sound, tried to get hold of something, then grabbed the seat of the chair with both hands because Jade's mouth was on him now. Wet, hot, ravenous. Robert surged up with a cry the neighbors surely heard.

Jade laughed around his mouthful, a deeply satisfied sound. Then he swallowed, heard Robert whimper, and gave him one last lick. "I love your cock." He got to his feet, leaning against the table to catch his breath, hand on himself now. Wondering what Robert would do.

The first thing was stand up, palm the head of his dick and tuck himself away. The second thing was kiss Jade so hard he nearly laid him back on the table. The third thing was to turn him around, hold him tight with his back pressed to Robert's chest, and work him into oblivion. He caught the climax in his hand and Jade's

185

moan in his mouth. They stood there breathing hard for a minute or two. Robert collected himself enough to say, "I love your cock too." Jade started laughing. "Can I fuck you over this table sometime?" Jade was wheezing. "Or you could fuck me. Jesus. I had some ideas about how this day might go but clearly I underestimated us." Robert was giggling now too. He let go of Jade. "Who's cooking?"

"I will. You finish what you were doing before I pounced on you."

"You can pounce on me anytime." Another brief kiss. Robert followed Jade into the kitchen, but only to wash his hands. Then he went back to wrap up the morning's correspondence, so he could concentrate on his beautiful, perfect lover until Jade had to go to work.

Robert took a taxi to the salon early in the evening. Jade was in the bathroom changing into his costume. He gave Robert an approving look when he stepped out, saying something about two extra inches of leg. As they strolled down to Santa Monica Boulevard, Robert was trying very hard to ignore the fact that he was basically wearing hot pants. Those shorts seriously felt like swim trunks. Then he got distracted, because the first thing he saw was a man in costume as a one-night stand. "That's really clever," he said, taking in all the details. The box masquerading as a side table, the condom and lube and Stoli bottle glued to the top of it. There were men in dresses, women in suits, all kinds of crazy cosplay and quite a few people wearing quite a bit less than Jade and Robert were. Their bare legs got some attention, but not so much that he wanted to flee the scene.

It was a long, aimless, entertaining evening. Walking up and down, getting a drink here or a snack there, taking pictures with their phones. Deeply grateful for their sneakers. There was music, people were singing, there were performances that might have been impromptu. After dark, there was a screening of 'The Rocky Horror Picture Show.' Robert had never seen it. Jade said, "This is exactly the way you should experience this movie." So even though they were tired and it was chilly, they stood around with dozens (maybe hundreds) of others. Close enough to see the people on stage in front of the screen, playing along with the movie. Jade sang under his breath. Robert barely understood what was going on, but he rolled with it. When everybody started singing 'be it, don't dream it' he swayed with the crowd, Jade wrapped in his arms.

As they made their slow, hand-in-hand way back to the salon, Robert said, "Thank you for this."

Jade glanced over at him. "It's an experience. Not something I feel like we have to do every year, but I thought, once."

"More for the list of things I did for the first time with Jade." Robert was smiling. "I still have a list of things I want to do for the first time with you."

"Oh you do." Jade was smiling too. "What's on the top of the list right now?"

"Get a foot massage." They both cracked up for a few seconds. "I don't even know if you like massages."

"I love massages. Do you?"

"Never had one."

"Jesus, Robert. You really are hard on yourself. I'll give you my version of a foot massage when we get home." He heard himself say 'home,' glanced over to catch Robert's eye, and had to stop walking for a minute so they could hold onto each other.

Chapter 16

November 2010

Jade and Robert's decision to host Thanksgiving dinner for a few select friends meant making some changes to reconfigure the living-dining room for entertaining. A new even-bigger flatscreen was mounted facing Jade's couch. One club chair went in the den with the loveseat; the other was set at the end of the couch. They acquired a set of stackable side tables to provide plate-and-glass surfaces along with Jade's coffee table. Robert's four-seater dining table could be put to use as a dessert station. They would set up a traditional buffet in the kitchen to graze from while they watched the game.

Moving some furniture and investing in the new screen weren't the only changes. Robert wasn't allowed to take down the vertical blinds, but the property management let him put up curtains to hide the godawful things. Jade picked out a few paint colors and they re-did the whole place. The brown laminate bar top looked a lot less tired with a metallic bronze paint on the walls around it. The bump in rent for a second tenant (which included a second parking space) was insignificant compared to Jade's rent; they agreed to put away the difference for the future. They did a lot of talking about what that future might hold. More than once, in the quiet dark of the bedroom, in each other's arms, they agreed that what they most wanted was a lot more years of this.

Both of them had to make adjustments; they weren't used to being accountable to someone this way. After a night when Robert went out for a last-minute business dinner without telling Jade in advance, they agreed on a daily six p.m. text exchange to say when they expected to be home. Robert was especially glad for that on the day when Jade didn't get home till after midnight. "I knew where you were, and I knew you were okay," he said the next morning while they were in the kitchen. "Without our system I would have been frantic. Calling you a thousand times. You would have been all, get a grip."

Jade concentrated on the eggs in the skillet. "I would have turned off my phone." He heard a half-horrified laugh from the man assembling toasted English muffins. "After texting you to tell you where I was and when I'd be home. And then I would have felt guilty all night for making you worry."

"The way I felt guilty after that bullshit dinner."

"Well, I got some more roses out of it." Another laugh, without the horror. Jade was smiling down at the eggs. "Shaya was extremely envious. Actually everybody at the salon was bitching. They're like, okay, flowers once, that's romance. Twice, that's a pattern."

"What did you say." Arms around Jade from behind, face in his hair, voice soft.

"I said the first time was thank you, and this time was I'm sorry. So both times were romance, but it's not a pattern."

Not yet, Robert thought. He kissed Jade's neck and stepped away to get their plates, making a mental note to find non-predictable occasions to send Jade flowers. He was determined not to turn into one of those guys who took love for granted. All the changes he'd made this year, up to and including re-painting the apartment, were part of becoming the man Jade would stay with forever. And the best part was, all those changes made

189

Robert feel like his own person more than he ever had. Everything was a choice, a conscious decision, based on three dozen years' experience. Nothing was based on expectations, or the need to conform. Which reminded him, it was time to replace a few things in the closet.

He took Jade along to the Men's Wearhouse and put himself in the professionals' hands. The end result was replacing that windowpane-check suit with one in a silvery gray with a black pinstripe, and replacing his navy pinstripe with a micro-check in vivid blue. Then he let them talk him into one in a color they called French blue, in a herringbone weave, and agreed to get rid of the tan blazer he wore with jeans sometimes. With that leaving the house, he didn't even need his brown shoes anymore. He gave all the outgoing things to Dress for Success as soon as the new things were tailored. Emily took a picture of him in the blue micro-check to update his bio on the agency website. He stared at the new page for a minute. "What? Don't you like it?"

He glanced up; she looked worried. "No, it's great. I was just thinking, that old picture looked so generic. That was me looking the way I thought I should look, which was basically a Ken doll." She snorted. "And now I look the way I *want* to look, which is not that different, but it feels really different."

"Well, you look, oh hell I can't say that."

"What? You can say anything."

She looked around as if someone might be listening, leaned down, and murmured, "You look sexy in this one."

He blushed. Made some kind of disclaimer, and some excuse about how they needed to get back to work. Told Jade about it later; waited while Jade got online to look at the new page; and blushed all over again when Jade said, "She's right."

Their Thanksgiving guests had only one thing in common: they were all allegedly single. Robert was surprised but delighted when Jonathan said he'd love to come to dinner. They hadn't met up since right after the movie wrapped. It was doing respectable business, and Jonathan was getting noticed. Robert still thought the big guy might be better off with a more experienced film agent, but he wasn't going to make the suggestion himself. They'd have plenty of other things to talk about on the holiday. Such as the fact that Jonathan arrived with Shaya.

She said it was a friends-with-benefits thing. Robert and Jade gave them a minor amount of crap about it, mixed with thanks for the half-case of brut rosé. Some of that immediately went in the fridge to chill down. Parker showed up with a bottle of Calvados; Liam brought a pound of pure Kona coffee beans; Emily contributed a pan of what she claimed was the best sweet-potato bake known to man. The consensus on that was agreement. They'd all been through the buffet at least once when the last guest arrived. Liam was on his way out of the kitchen with his second plate, so he was the last to be introduced to Mark Valance. Jade was very interested in the eye contact that accompanied their handshake. He didn't give them any crap, because Mark was in the middle of his third season on that stupid TV show and as far as he knew nothing else had changed. It was a shame, though. Liam was the best of the guys Robert had been out with.

He and Emily were in the den talking (Liam was telling her about a problem with his front-desk person) when Jade decided to stir things up a little. A few

191

minutes later, Mark said, "I literally have to sing for my supper?" He was trying to look offended. It wasn't really coming off.

Jade said, "Robert loved you in 'Chicago.' I was trying to give him some inspiration for the pageant." He glanced at his lover, who was waving that off. Mark complained about having no accompaniment, about not being a soloist, not being warmed up. Jade wasn't having it.

"Fine, whatever." With obviously fake exasperation, Mark handed his empty glass to Jade. The game was already muted. His shoes were by the door with everyone else's, neatly out of the way. There was plenty of space. He did the indefinable thing that turned a living room into a stage. Everyone was watching. He struck a pose and started to sing. "'It's good, isn't it grand, isn't it great, isn't it swell, isn't it fun? Isn't it, nowadays.'"

Jade and Robert were sitting crammed together in the corner of the couch. Robert was fascinated. He remembered the song, from 'Chicago.' Done without music like this, it had a pathos that he hadn't recognized. Or maybe it was the way Mark was singing it this time. Not the perky 'hire me at your speakeasy' way, and not the heading-into-the-big-finale way. This time what stuck was the line 'nothing stays.' And then the last line: 'but oh it's heaven, nowadays.' *No*, he thought. The gin and the jazz and everything else were like a Band-Aid on a gut wound. If the man sang it this way on stage, the whole room would be in tears. He glanced sideways at Jade, wondering if it was only him, but then Mark was taking a really grand bow. All of them started applauding. Robert would have decided it was all only part of a great performance except Mark did a thing about getting a glass of water and bolted into the kitchen. Jade started prying himself up off the couch, as if he meant to follow. Then he sank back, because Liam was going in there. Robert said, "Hmm."

Jade leaned in and said very softly, "I thought there was a thing when Mark came in. Let's give them a minute."

Robert nodded. Turned the TV sound on again, not too loud. Nobody else seemed to be wondering what might be going on in the kitchen, and it wasn't really any of his business. And before too many minutes had passed, both men were at the dessert table, helping themselves to one of the pies, and going to sit in the den with Emily. Before long they were all involved in the question of whether she should go to work at the dermatology office.

Much to Liam's surprise, Robert was in favor. "I would absolutely hate to lose you," he told Emily, "but the agency's a dead-end job if there ever was one and maybe Liam's gig wouldn't be. Or would it?" That was directed at Liam.

"An experienced medical office administrator has a lot of mobility," he said cautiously. "And we might pay more."

Emily snort-laughed. "I'll bet. Anything entertainment-adjacent, they pay you less because they think you think the possibility of brushing up against a celebrity in the elevator is worth more than money." She belatedly remembered she was sitting next to a celebrity. "Oh my God, I'm sorry. Too much champagne." Robert was laughing his ass off over by the bar.

Mark wasn't offended. "I would be the first to say follow the money. That's exactly what I did. And besides, you don't need that job to brush up against a celebrity. You have celebrity friends now." She gave him a comically starry-eyed look. "Speaking of which." He raised his voice a little. "Mr. Morris, I meant to ask if you plan to make any more movies."

Jonathan might have been watching the game, but he didn't seem to mind being interrupted. He even came to join them instead of talking across the living room. "I don't know about plan," he said, leaning on the bar beside Robert. "This guy tells me his friend over there sees a lot of scripts that might have room for an oversized goofball like me."

"You're not oversized," Parker said from the couch, momentarily distracted from some minor flirting (disguised as football commentary) with Shaya. "The doctor is taller than you are."

"Yeah, but he's like thirty pounds lighter."

"You have to be big," Robert reminded him. "So you can realistically slaughter people in the ring."

Now Jade chimed in. "Besides, you looked like a legit killer. All the reviews say so."

Jonathan waved that off. "If anybody noticed me it's because of that makeup design you did."

"Well, thanks, but that's bullshit. He stole every scene, you guys."

Mark made a comment about expecting Jonathan to put in a good word for him the next time he was in a room with a casting director. The conversation got very silly after that. Only a couple of people (Robert and Shaya, who had a bet) even cared what the result of the football game was. The rest of them started batting ideas around for a movie that could star veterans of Broadway and WWE.

Mark said, "Don't call me a veteran, it makes me feel old." After the game, he made his excuses, saying he hadn't meant to stay quite so long. "I had a great time. Thanks for the invitation."

"You were very welcome. It was great to get caught up again. And thanks for that beautiful song." Jade made a face that said 'I know something was up with you' but also 'later for that.' They shook hands after Mark got his shoes on. "Tell Jenny hi for me."

"I'll do that." He said a general goodbye to the room, which might have included a wave specifically for Liam, and then he was gone. Parker was the next to go, then Shaya and Jonathan. Liam followed, after making sure Emily had his business card and apologizing in advance to Robert.

Emily insisted on leaving the leftover sweet potatoes. "It's not like I won't see you to get my pan back," she pointed out. "I am now going home to email my entire family about how I had Thanksgiving dinner with celebrities." She hugged them both and went out the door.

Robert looked at his lover. "That was fun. We should do this every year."

Jade leaned in for a kiss. "Yes we should. I'm glad you had fun. We'd better get this stuff put away now."

"Who's Jenny?"

Jade went to the dessert table first, because that was easiest. One of the pies was completely gone, another was half gone, the last (pumpkin) reduced to one slice. He moved that to the apple-pie pan, snapped the lid on, and took the other pans to the kitchen. "Mark plays the boyfriend of Jenny Wilson. He says they have a bet on how and when the show will give him the boot."

"Why would they do that?"

"Well, if they don't want to make him a permanent cast member they'll have to eventually. They might

195

want to take her character in a different direction. Give her story a different focus. I think he halfway hopes they kill him off."

"He doesn't like the job?" Robert was transferring leftovers to storage containers.

"Well, this is in the vault." Jade made eye contact to make sure the other man knew he was serious. Robert nodded comprehension. "Mark has been playing it straight for a long time, but he's not. And he's tired of it. He can't come out as long as he's on that show. Not and keep the job. Coming out might mean he never gets a TV gig again."

"Jesus."

"Mm-hmm."

"I was so lucky. I keep running up against all the ways I was lucky." Robert was leaning on the counter now, watching as Jade scientifically packed the fridge with leftovers. "That song really got to me this time."

"Mmm. I was wondering if that's how he meant to sing it, or if that just happened. I'll ask, next time I see him. Are we hand-washing?"

"Hell no." Robert opened the dishwasher and they started loading it.

The following Monday Jade had a very interesting telephone conversation with Mark. He held onto it through dinner and cleanup, waiting till they were lounging on the couch with glasses of fiery apple brandy. "Guess who I talked to today?"

"Mmm, I don't know. Your mom?"

"Uh, no. Mark. Guess where he spent the weekend."

Jade looked gleeful. Robert was paying attention now. "You're kidding."

196

"Come on, say it."

"Liam?"

"Uh-huh." A sip of brandy. "Yikes, that is some serious liquor. Apparently they exchanged numbers during that minute in the kitchen. Liam called him Thanksgiving night. Mark went over to his place Friday night and left about fifty hours later."

"Wow." Robert thought about that for a second. "I'm going to have to talk to that guy. So what's the deal? Is Mark coming out?"

"He says he is. Says he can't take it anymore, and he wants a chance to have a real relationship with Liam. He's going to work with Jenny on presenting an exit plan to the show, and once he's off he'll go public. And he says Liam is behind him. They know they're going to have to lie low till the end of the season, but I guess Liam feels like it's worthwhile."

Another sip of brandy, another few seconds to think. "I suppose if he came out now, the whole rest of the season would be about that, and the show would have to scramble. Jeez, and you said *I* was hard on myself."

"Well, we can help. I said we would. We can invite them both over so they can at least see each other, and not have to pretend they're strangers."

"Oh, of course. After the way Liam listened to me talking about you for the past few months, it's the least we can do." He thought of something. "He's not still planning to steal Emily, is he?"

Jade snickered. "I don't think so? But she's going to help too. Mark needs a date for all this industry bullshit, you know it's awards season. And he always has a date, so if he doesn't take someone the press will be up his ass in the worst way. Emily, and mind you I'm

197

not sure she knows Mark is gay, probably not because it doesn't really matter for her side of things, has agreed to be his Platonic companion." He listened to Robert crack up for a minute. "She's going to come to me for styling, I'll take her to Kenji for wardrobe, and we'll keep it all in the family."

"Oh God," Robert said faintly. It was seriously funny. At the same time, it was kind of heartwarming, and also a little bit enraging because all this subterfuge shouldn't be necessary. "Well, if I don't hear from Liam in the next couple of days I'll reach out. Let him know you talked to Mark, and that we'll help."

He didn't have to call. He got a text the next morning, suggesting a rendezvous at the coffee shop. They met up a couple hours later. Liam said, "Hey Robert. Thanks again for Thanksgiving, that was really great."

"Jade tells me the whole weekend was good," Robert said innocently, watching a laugh chase itself across Liam's face. They got their coffees and went outside to a corner of the patio that was otherwise deserted, thanks to the cool winter breeze. "So. We did not expect that, but we're really happy about it. And we want to do anything we can to help."

"You are good people." Liam sipped his coffee. "There's this feeling of inevitability. Like, of course. Like I've been waiting for him all my life. Which I know is kind of crazy, but you said pretty much the same thing. That you met Jade at a certain moment because he's the one you're supposed to be with. Is that crazy?"

"I don't think it is. I talked about it with my therapist. I was like, bear with me here. He was all, again with this?" Liam inhaled some of his coffee. Robert waited for him to stop cough-laughing. "My idea is that at different points in life, there are different people who might be the right person for us. In that moment. It just so happened that I didn't meet the right person for the person I was when I was, say, twenty-six. Or thirty, whatever. Then I met Sharon, who was very obviously not the right person despite how cute she is, and she knew she was not the right person because of her own reasons, so she bailed. Which left me really questioning everything right at the moment when Jade walked in and showed me what I really wanted. If he'd rolled up on me when I was twenty-six I wouldn't have recognized him, and he wouldn't have given me a second glance. So it's coincidence, but it's also a genuine *rightness*. And in your case it's coincidence that this guy was at our party on Thursday, and that he was in a moment of accepting that he was at a turning point, and that you were there to be recognized." He sipped some more coffee while Liam thought about that.

"But the reason he recognized me, or we recognized each other, is a confluence of right time and right person."

"Ooohh, good word. Yes. So now you can flow on together, and if you want to flog the river metaphor you can say there are bound to be sandbars and rapids and maybe a cascade here and there, but if you can hang onto each other through all that you'll get to a nice calm place where all you have to do is float."

Liam blinked, momentarily lost in admiration. "I have to remember that so I can tell him. He's expecting some pretty gnarly rapids."

"Flotation devices required," Robert agreed. "That's where we come in, I guess. We do not have a problem being the hosts into whose master suite guests disappear for up to an hour." Liam laughed again, this time without inhaling coffee. "I mean, if we didn't have

199

the powder room it might be a different story. So Jade is going to be the style guru, and he's going to hook Emily up with Kenji, who will probably turn her into front-page fashion news. I think we should send her to you, too. Get the whole facial, laser, Botox thing going if she wants. Do you use Botox? Because I noticed I'm getting a frown line and I'm like, fuck you."

Liam leaned on the wall. "I do use Botox. Or actually, a less-pricey equivalent which I will happily inject into your face. Or my partner can, or our physician assistant can. We sell a lot of that. And yes, definitely. Send Emily to me. It won't cost her a thing."

"You going to let me keep her for a little while?"

Liam smiled. "That's up to her."

Robert made an annoyed sound and grumbled something about getting back to work. They shook hands. He pulled Liam into one of those bro hugs. Now was not the time to say 'he couldn't do better than you,' because a lot of things could go wrong. But he really hoped that, six months from now, this friend was as happy as he was himself.

Chapter 17

Christmas 2010

They'd been living together less than two months, but Robert decided there was no point in waiting for 'someday' to ask his next question. Their life together was ninety-nine percent perfect now, and he might have to wait for that last one percent. He could wait, as long as he knew he would get it someday.

They were sitting on the loveseat, with 'Die Hard' ready to start in the DVD player and dinner a recent memory. Jade was feeling warm and lazy. He couldn't remember a Christmas Day like this since … well, maybe ever. Morning sex, followed by breakfast; a long walk while they talked about next year; a shower together, which led to some more fooling around. Then watching Robert do something impressive in the kitchen with his present from Jade (a paella pan). Jade's present from Robert was a new set of top-quality barber tools. He'd break them in on Robert's hair sometime soon.

"Want anything to drink?" Jade turned his head; thought about it; nodded. That question always meant 'from the bar' if they were sitting in the den. Robert stood up, hoping he was acting normal. Hoping Jade wouldn't notice his quick detour to the bedroom. He returned with a couple of shot glasses of Calvados, handed one to Jade, tapped his against it, and sat down. "There's something I wanted to ask you. I meant to this morning but we got busy."

Jade laughed into his brandy. "Yes we did."

Robert set his glass on the side table and turned toward his lover. "This is actually kind of serious. It's something we can't do yet. But it's something I want to do, with you, when we can."

Jade thought *what on earth* and then *oh my God really?* He set down his glass and angled himself toward Robert, who had something in his hand. "Ask me anything," he said, as steadily as he could.

Robert swallowed. "Eight months ago I offered this to someone it didn't belong to. Now I'd like to offer it to you, because I belong to you and I want you to belong to me. I love you so much. Will you marry me?" He opened the box.

Jade stared at the ring. He'd never asked about it. Had always assumed Robert sold it. "You kept it?"

"Because it's yours. If you want it." That sounded uncertain. *Please say yes.*

Jade observed that his hands were shaking as he reached out, steadying the box with one hand as he removed the ring with the other. He slid it onto his finger. It still fit. "I love you too. I do belong to you. Yes, I want it. Yes, I'll marry you. As soon as we can." Tears spilled down his face.

Robert was crying too. He dropped the ring box somewhere and pulled Jade into his arms. It was a few minutes before they both settled down. Then there were a few more minutes of kissing, wiping each other's faces, some shaky laughter. Eventually Jade sat back, reached for his brandy, and gulped it down. Robert did the same. They both hissed at the burn, both laughed softly. "That very first night. That's when I thought, I should give that ring to Jade."

"Well, you knew it fit." Robert made a face that said 'obviously.' Jade reached over and finger-combed his hair, noticing the flash of the diamonds with deep pleasure. "It's been quite a year for you."

"It really has. I asked someone how long they thought it will be before there's a decision on Prop 8. They said, maybe two more years. That's kind of a long engagement."

"But think of the honeymoon we could plan. Oh God, Robert."

"What?" He wasn't worried; that 'oh God' didn't sound like something bad.

"It's so *unlikely*. That I go in for a whiff of pie and I meet you and you're *perfect*."

"I was a mess!"

Jade laughed, he couldn't help it. "You were a little bit of a mess. But you cleaned up really well."

Robert shook his head, smiling. He didn't care about watching this movie right now. But by the time it was over, they'd be ready to go to bed and celebrate. He picked up the remote.

New Year's Day, 2011

One week into being engaged, Jade was almost used to it. He worked at the salon on New Year's Eve – there was always special party hair to be done on that day – and everybody saw the ring. Shaya was speechlessly excited. All of his other friends had already heard all about it. Apparently there was a lot of chatter at the agency, too. The great thing, he and Robert agreed, was that everyone said they were perfect for each other. Neither of them brought up the impersonal Christmas card from Ohio, addressed to Jade alone, or the continued silence from Utah.

They were stretched out on the couch, watching the Rose Parade on the big screen, when somebody's phone buzzed on the coffee table. Jade reached over; not his. He picked up Robert's and almost dropped it again. "It's Lisa." Robert's sister. Jade sat up, handing the phone to

203

his fiancé, who looked like he wasn't sure he wanted to answer the call. "Come on, honey. She wouldn't be calling if she didn't want to talk."

Robert took a deep breath and connected. "Hello? Hi Lisa. This is a surprise." He put the call on speaker, because whatever was about to happen he wanted Jade to hear it. Jade was always on his side.

"Bobby, I want to apologize."

"Okay?" He hoped that only sounded uncertain, and not annoyed. Was somewhat surprised to recognize the annoyance: that was not what he expected to feel when or if one of his family members got in touch.

"For all of us. I know it doesn't mean much for the others. What I guess I'm trying to say is I'm sorry I haven't been in touch, and I'm sorry *they* haven't been in touch. I've been fighting with people about this. With Lance, and Mom and Dad. With Art."

Robert said, "Did he not want you to talk to me?"

"He didn't. We had words. I'm sick of being told what's right and wrong."

Robert gave Jade a big-eyed look. His sister had not, up to now, shown any signs of rebellion. Ever. "Are you okay?"

She gave a wobbly-sounding laugh. "I don't know. I was talking to someone I knew in college. I haven't seen her for six years. She lives in Los Angeles too."

"Do I know this person?" It felt like this call was more about Lisa than about Robert, which was fine with him. He leaned back, getting comfortable on the couch. Jade pressed in close; Robert switched hands with the phone so he could put an arm around his fiancé. *I love thinking that*.

Lisa was saying, "I doubt it. We were only at school together for a year. She's a dancer."

204

"We know a few dancers. What's her name?"

"Michelle Walker. There is actually a point to this. The last time Michelle was here, she told her family about a job she got doing a burlesque show. Pole dance. They said horrible things to her, and on her way out of town she stopped by and said I'm probably never coming back here. Asked me to keep in touch. So I've tried, because they were awful to her – you know how word gets around – and nobody should be alone. And that's what I've been telling our parents, and our bonehead brother, and my bonehead husband, who may not be my husband much longer." She said all that in a rush.

After a brief hesitation Robert said, "Lisa. Weren't you trying to get pregnant? The last time we spoke?"

"I was. But I didn't, and now I don't want to. Bobby, I'm leaving him, because I'm not allowed to say no to him as long as I live in his house. That's what he says. I have to get out of here."

He did not like the sound of that. "Come right now. Take what you can carry. You can stay with us."

"Us?"

Robert closed his eyes. "I'm living with someone, Lisa. His name is Jade. We're in love. We're going to get married as soon as the Supreme Court kicks Prop 8 to the curb."

"Oh." She sounded surprised, but not horrified. She might know what Prop 8 was; rumor had it the church was behind that mess. "Well. Congratulations?"

Jade stifled a laugh. Robert squeezed his shoulder. "Thanks. Do you need a safe place to stay? Because I'm serious. You can come."

"Thank you, Bobby. It's not quite that bad. I'm going to move back home with Mom and Dad. We'll

205

figure things out from there." A brief pause. "But I'd love to see you."

Robert made eye contact with Jade. *I am not taking you there to be stared at and condescended to.* "We could get to Las Vegas on pretty short notice except for certain dates. Jade works on movie sets a lot and that stuff can't be rescheduled."

"He works in the movies?"

"He's a stylist. So do you want to try for Vegas sometime? I'd love for the two of you to meet."

"Yes. That's a yes. I'll call you after I'm settled in with the parents. We'll make a date. Bobby, thank you for talking to me."

"Honey, I never stopped loving any of you. Thank you for calling. Keep me posted."

"I'll do that. Happy New Year."

"Happy New Year to you." He was about to end the call.

"Oh wait!"

"What?"

"Tell Jade I'm happy for you both."

Robert smiled. "I will. Take care."

"You too. Bye now." They disconnected. Robert reached over to drop the phone on the coffee table. Sat back, rested his head on the back of the couch, closed his eyes, and exhaled. It felt like he was breathing out years of things that weren't right, but still. "She only called because she wanted someone to back her up about Art."

"Does it matter?"

Robert thought about that. After a minute he decided, "No."

"I can't believe your brother's name is Lance." Robert laughed silently. Jade gave it a second. Then he said, "Does Lisa look like you?"

"Mm-hmm."

"Maybe we should introduce her to Jonathan. I think he's wearing Shaya out." Robert started laughing for real. He pulled Jade with him as he toppled over, stretching out again. The parade was almost over. Well, there was still the game.

The next time they had Liam and Mark (and Emily) over for dinner, nobody disappeared into the master suite. Emily figured out what was really going on in about ten seconds anyway. None of them were afraid she would spill the beans.

Part of the conversation that night was about Robert and Jade getting engaged. Part was about trips they all had to take pretty soon. Mark and Emily would be flying to the East Coast for the New York Film Critics Circle Awards on the tenth. She had a lot to say about that.

Jade didn't say much about his trip. He was going up to San Francisco to assist at a photo shoot, and he planned to check in with Allen while he was there. Before he left Robert said, "Say hi for me. Actually, tell him thanks."

"For?"

"For being your friend." Robert watched Jade absorb the idea, and the subtext. "If you're comfortable with that."

Jade nodded. "I am. I will. I love you."

"I love you too." A hug, a kiss, and Jade was out the door. Robert felt sorry for himself for a minute, told himself not to be ridiculous – he had some travel of his own coming right up – and went to get ready for work.

Jade's flight was uneventful, the hotel room was adequate, and the shoot well-organized. It still ran long, so it was too late to go out for dinner by the time he was released. He decided to get something in the bar at the hotel. Caught a ride back over the bridge, texting on the way: *Hi Allen, on the GG now. Is brunch tomorrow still good?* The plan was for him to go to the house.

A reply came in before they turned east onto the 101: *Hey cutie brunch is great. What are you doing tonight?*

Watching TV at hotel bar feeling sorry for myself

Aw poor baby haven't been away from your man for a while huh

Not since I moved in

Want me to come?

Jade blinked at the phone. That was unexpected. He hadn't seen Allen solo for years, it was always with the family. *Need to get undomesticated for a minute?*

Something like that. What's your ETA

Should be there in 20

Let me get my shit together, probably 30-40

OK! Now he had to wonder, was this something he should tell Robert about? Robert, who had so scrupulously confessed to every date, even the ones that barely qualified. Yes, he should definitely say something. Another text: *Hi sweetheart done working and heading back to hotel. Family brunch is still the plan, but Allen's going to come and have a drink with me. I think he wants to talk about something without the whole house listening*

A reply still hadn't come when he exited the vehicle, thanking his teammate for the lift. He went into the hotel feeling nervous. Up to the room to refresh himself (and primp a little), wondering what Robert was up to. It was after eight. Maybe he'd met up with one of

208

his friends, or with a client. He was waiting at the elevator when his phone rang. Glanced at the screen, smiled, and connected. "Hi sweetheart."

"Hi honey, I was out with Parker toasting to a still awful but somewhat improved alimony picture." From the sound of things, Robert was in the car. "So you think Allen needs a break from the four adult two kid situation?"

Jade laughed softly, ignoring the open elevator door. He wasn't going to drop this call to save a minute. "I'm guessing. Either that or there's some big change he wants me to know about so I don't ask awkward questions."

"Oh shit, like what? No, let's not speculate. You can fill me in when you get home. Coming home tomorrow, right?"

"Yes." Jade was grinning. "I miss you too."

"I'm going to fantasize about you tonight. What are you wearing?"

"The wisteria shirt. And jeans."

"Thanks for confirming you have pants on. Send me a selfie of you with Allen, I don't even know what this guy looks like."

"Not as cute as you." Jade heard Robert's pleased laugh. "But don't ever tell him I said so."

Robert made a reassuring sound. "Better get down to the bar. Make an entrance."

"You know I will. Love you."

"Love you too." They disconnected. Jade was still smiling when he walked into the bar. Allen wasn't there yet. A few other guys and two women were. All of them noticed him enter, which was gratifying. One of the guys was giving him a very come-hither look. Jade

209

casually lifted his left hand to brush back a lock of hair that wasn't really out of place, flashing the diamond ring. Affected not to notice the guy turning back to the bar, disappointed.

"It never gets old, does it, Prancer."

Jade turned around, smiling. "Allen." They hugged, stood back to study each other, smiled. "You look good."

"Not as good as you. I mean, damn." Allen shook his head. "You don't age."

"I don't have kids."

Allen laughed. "What are we drinking?"

"Whatever you want, plus I need some food. They had craft service on this shoot but it was all garbage." The host found them a table. Before they sat down Jade took the requested selfie, wondering what Robert would have to say about his friend. Allen was an inch taller than Jade, brown-haired, blue-eyed; a nice ordinary-looking guy. A bit soft around the middle now, and in need of a haircut. "I should have brought my scissors."

"Oh, the hair? Yeah, it's a little scruffy. We've been busy."

"So what do you want to say that you don't want to say in front of everybody."

"God, let's get some alcohol going first. It's nothing bad," he assured Jade. "We just got to the end of this long protracted negotiation and there was a lot of compromise and I want to bitch about it."

"No problem." A break for service. Jade ordered a glass of syrah and a burger. Allen ordered a light beer and looked wistful. "You can have some of my fries."

"I shouldn't. I'm getting tubby. How do you stay so slim?"

"You know I've always been skinny. But Robert's as vain as I am. We reinforce each other's behavior."

"You mean you help each other resist shit. Whereas I live in a house with five enablers." He sighed. "Show me a picture. I know you have a picture in there."

Jade woke up the phone again. He had a lot of pictures. "Here he is at Halloween."

"Oh. My. Lord."

Jade laughed. Scrolled to another. "This was the drag pageant." A click of the tongue, rolling eyes. "And this is from Christmas Day." Right before bed, when they were both somewhere in between sleepy and horny because they'd been cuddling for two hours while they watched the movie.

"After he proposed? Oh Jade. I'm so happy for you."

"He told me to say hi for him, and also thank you."

"For what?"

"For being my friend. From the start. And seriously, thank you. The whole night we met I kept thinking, I had someone to help me through this, let me be as good for this guy as Allen was for me."

"Oh honey." Allen blinked, swallowed, fanned himself. "It was so hard to go off to college without you."

"I always wondered. We were both being tough guys."

"It was *awful*. That little town was, well, it was stupid but we knew how to handle it. College town, not so much. And you were going to Sodom and Gomorrah." Jade laughed. "Seriously! I was still in the Midwest, you were going to Hollywood. I was so afraid for you. I wanted to be there for you. Or, really, I wanted you with me. But," he sighed. "It wouldn't have worked.

211

I would have been clingy, you would have been bored. God I missed you though."

Jade gazed at him affectionately. "I missed you too. Those first couple of years were rough."

"At least you put yourself out there. I was like, ew, no. Don't want you, don't like you, get away from me, nope nope nope. When I finally got out here to SF I was like, candy store! Yes please!"

Jade was cracking up. "And then you met Tanya. So how's that whole situation?" His burger arrived.

Allen eyed it hungrily. "It is a *situation*."

"Have a bite. There you go." Jade enjoyed Allen's blissed-out expression for a few seconds. "Hey, I said *a* bite. Gimme that." They were both snickering. "Tell me about the situation."

After a swallow of beer, Allen said, "You know how the mayor let them issue same-sex marriage licenses a couple years ago."

"Mm-hmm?"

"Of course we'd been married for years, we had two kids, Tanya had only been with Noelle for about six months and I had just met George. So we all kind of looked at each other sideways and didn't talk about it, and then that option got deep-sixed anyway. But George stayed, and Noelle stayed, and then we all bought the house. Now our boy is going to be starting school in the fall, and we're like, should we get divorced? Because if Prop 8 falls, maybe Tanya and Noelle want to get married. Maybe George and I want to get married. But will it be even weirder for the kids if we're all still living together but now Mom and Dad aren't married to each other anymore."

There was a pause that seemed to invite comment. "I don't have any idea what goes through a kid's head,

Allen. From everything you've told me, they're cruising with how you do things now. But that doesn't necessarily mean they would crash if things changed. Maybe they just shift gears, and it's fine." He ate one of the fries, dipped another in ketchup and handed it to Allen, took a sip of wine. "But you said there was a negotiation, and some compromises."

"We decided not to change anything until after our daughter starts school. If the four of us are still solid, then we'll revisit the marriage question. By that time, there might be a decision. If SCOTUS upholds Prop 8 obviously there's no advantage to me and Tanya getting divorced."

That last sentence didn't sound like Allen actually believed it. Jade finished his burger. Drank some more wine. "So, compromise? That you wanted to bitch about?"

Allen sighed. "The girls are both really strong personalities, right. And I'm kind of this roll over and show my belly guy. George isn't much better. The truth is, I'm ready to get divorced now. The family unit is fine, and it'll be fine regardless of that. My position was, it's going to be a more honest household if we are four single adults sleeping with our chosen partners and all taking care of these kids, than if we are a fake marriage with boyfriend and girlfriend tacked on. But it's advantageous for Tanya to be married, because of the bullshit company she works for, and I caved." He slumped back in his chair, eyes on the table.

"Oh, honey. I'm sorry." Jade didn't know what he could contribute here. The kids were five and three, too young to have a meaningful understanding of the adult relationships. In a few years, they'd definitely have an opinion. The marriage was largely symbolic, but it was a symbol with a lot of weight. Should Allen be stuck in a marriage he wanted out of for another three years? "If it were me," he began, then stalled.

"What?"

"I think I'd put it back on the table. Say, you know what, we got married for a reason, which was to have kids together. We're co-parenting well and we can continue to do so. We didn't get married so I could be your beard. You're thirty-five, and you're an executive for fuck's sake. That's me talking to Tanya."

Allen huffed out a laugh. "Yeah, I got that. We don't use the F word."

Jade rolled his eyes. "Whatever. This could happen, Allen." He tapped his ring finger on the table, making the diamonds flash. "Marriage could be a real thing for us. Robert could have waited until the decision comes down to ask me, but I'm glad he didn't. It means a lot to me that he asked now. What does George say? When you're in private."

"He, you know, he was really hanging back. And I don't know if that's because he didn't want to argue or if he didn't want to influence me too much. We haven't talked much about it in private. Oh shit, he might think I don't care." Allen sat up, looking horrified. "He might think it's not important to me. That this is all some hypothetical. What if he wants to marry me and I'm all, ho-hum, sticking with the chick. Shit!" He got his phone out. "Excuse me a second." Composing a text. Sending it. Turning the phone around for Jade to see: *Sweetie Jade is counseling me. I told him I don't want to be married to Tanya anymore. I didn't tell him I'd rather be married to you, but I would. Can I ask you? Face to face not over the phone like a loser*

They both sat for a few minutes, waiting to see if there would be a reply. The beer and wine were long

214

gone. The server came for Jade's plate and asked if they wanted coffee. They both said no. As soon as she left the table Allen's phone buzzed: *You can ask me over the phone*

"Oh shit." Allen blew out a breath, texted again. *I love you. Will you marry me?*

I love you. Yes

Allen dropped the phone on the table, dropped his head into his hands, and started to cry. Jade picked up the phone and read the reply, set it down again. Went around the table and put his arms around Allen, face in his hair. "Sshh. This is good. I'm so glad. Can I text him back?"

"Mmmph."

Jade gave Allen a squeeze and let him go. Picked up the phone and texted *Hi George this is Jade, Allen is crying all over the place because he's so happy. Congratulations*

Thank you I'm crying too. Will you help us break the news to Tanya tomorrow?

Of course. I'm going to get him settled down and send him home. See you in the morning

See you!

After getting Allen into a taxi, Jade went up to his room and called Robert. Told him the whole story. "I guess I've turned into that guy. Now that I've got my happy ever after, I want everybody else to get theirs."

"This is not a bad thing." Robert sounded like he was smiling. "Speaking of happy endings, how do you feel about phone sex?"

"Ooohh, Mr. Anderson." Jade settled himself comfortably on the bed. "Why don't we find out?"

215

Chapter 18

February 2011

Wearing the Mary Russell costume to the inaugural Dapper Day was not in the cards. Robert was still amazed at how good he looked in it, but between the tights and the high heels, the comfort level was just not there. Disneyland was big, and he'd be on his feet most of the day. Jade's solution was to finally create Bertie, the character he'd thought of right at the start. Bertie was very well-tailored in gray trousers and vest, white poplin shirt, and a navy-and-gray Mickey Mouse paisley tie. He wore navy loafers and a straw boater hat with a navy ribbon. Robert was thrilled.

Jade was bounding as Aladdin. His seersucker jacket was brilliant purple and white, his trousers were white, he even wore a red fez. He did not dye his hair black, much to Robert's relief. Instead he wore a magic-lantern bow tie, purple-and-gold slippers, and a gold hoop in one ear. They were strolling through the park, holding hands, thoroughly enjoying the afternoon, when they heard a female voice say "Bob?!"

Robert turned toward the voice; Jade turned with him; they both stared at the two women on the path. They were also holding hands, and not in the way that said 'I don't want to lose you in this crowd.' One was as tall as Jade. Bounding as Prince Charming in red trousers and a tailored ivory tunic heavily trimmed with gold, with her black hair in a French braid. The other was a lovely blonde in a fresh open-air take on Cinderella's ballgown. "Sharon?"

All four of them took a long, careful look at each other. After a moment, the tall woman said, "Vicky Russo."

Jade said, "And you must be Sharon Weiss. I'm Jade Derecha. You already know Robert Anderson."

"Well, actually, I don't think I do." The blonde studied them both for another few seconds. "This explains a lot. Is that my ring?" Vicky choked on a laugh.

Robert completely lost it. He turned to the side, hand over his mouth, wheezing with laughter. Jade patted his back, maintaining his gravity with difficulty. "No. I said yes. So it's mine."

"Fuck those Prop 8 motherfuckers," said Vicky. "I would totally go to this wedding."

Sharon was giggling. "So would I."

Robert inhaled, blew the breath out through his mouth, settled down. "Then I'll send you an invitation. As soon as we know we can set the date."

"I told you you'd find someone who deserves that ring." Sharon sounded a little smug.

Robert put his arm around Jade. "It was always meant for him."

Vicky put her arm around Sharon. "It was too big for you anyway, wasn't it, sweetie?" Sharon smiled at her.

Jade hooked his free arm through Vicky's. "I hear there are adult beverages in this park. Let's go find some." They all strolled on together.

The Disneyland adventure provided a good topic for conversation while they were driving to Las Vegas. It was their first trip out of town together. Both of them

217

came home from their January trips thinking 'maybe next time we could go together,' but they didn't say so until now. Jade was definitely open to tagging along on team visits; Robert wouldn't mind hanging out on a shoot. That topic, once embarked upon, proved to be so engrossing that the second half of the trip flew by.

"That's the best part of this," Robert said as he opened the door to their room. "Having a little vacation with you. The only time I've gone out of town with someone I was dating, it was for a destination wedding. Oh my lord." He rolled his eyes. "Barely escaped that one unengaged."

"That must have been before you were ready to settle down."

"Way before. And the destination was Branson, Missouri."

Jade bit his lip. "It sounds very … family friendly?"

"Exactly. Not like our little getaway here and now. I got us tickets to Zumanity tomorrow night. And a welcome basket should be arriving soon."

Robert watched Jade appreciate the room (a mini-suite with in-room spa tub) while they unpacked. As soon as that welcome basket was delivered and he could lock the door again, he was planning to suggest appreciating the king-size bed. He wanted to be thoroughly satisfied, completely relaxed, and possibly marked when they met up with Lisa for dinner. A previously unsuspected mean streak was looking forward to her reaction when she saw him.

Jade was fairly sure his lover was working off some anger issues when he brought up what to wear in Vegas. He'd heard the annoyance in Robert's tone when Lisa made the first apology. By the end of the call, it seemed like she remembered this was her brother she was talking to, and maybe the brother part was more important than the gay part. They'd talked since, conversations reported to Jade after the fact. Still nothing from Lance or their parents, and it didn't sound as though they were being very supportive of Lisa. At least she did have a safe place to stay. Maybe tonight they'd find out whether she'd made up her mind to file for divorce.

Then the welcome basket arrived, and Jade forgot about the Andersons. "Well, well, well," he said, drifting over to the table, where Robert was unpacking a picnic's worth of gourmet snacks. "Are we drinking this now?"

"You bet we are. The rest of this can wait for tomorrow morning."

Before opening the chilled champagne, Jade lifted the heart-shaped container of short-stemmed roses out of the basket and set it on the nightstand. *He's so adorable.* They'd agreed not to do anything for Valentine's Day since they had this trip coming up. Obviously Robert decided that only meant not doing anything at home. For every first thing he'd done with Jade, there was some kind of first thing he did *for* Jade. It was enough to make a man wonder if falling in love ever stopped.

An hour later, sweaty and exhausted, Jade reached for his glass. He was technically sitting up. It was a good thing this bed had about a dozen pillows; his spine seemed to have melted. "The toes," he said, after a long drink of still-sparkling wine. "That was new."

Robert laughed, face-down on the mattress. He organized his hands, managed to push himself up into a more-or-less-sitting position, got a hand on his glass. Gulped down half the contents. Stifled a small belch. "You remember when I called my mother?"

"Mm-hmm."

"Your toenails were done in stripes like that." He pointed. "Same colors, even. I thought, I have never before wanted to get someone's toes in my mouth. They looked like candy."

"And it took nine months to revisit that?"

"We've been *busy*." It was hard to make that sound exasperated when he was laughing again. Partly at Jade's expression, which was so post-coital he had to reach for his phone and take a picture.

"Oh shit, Robert. No. I can only imagine what I look like."

"You look like my gorgeous fiancé who just came all over the place while I sucked his toes." He didn't bother trying to hide his satisfaction.

"Sucked my toes with champagne in your mouth. How do you even come up with stuff like that?"

"I read porn," Robert said reasonably. Jade snorted into his glass. He would have to examine that e-reader again; last time he looked, it was full of Elizabeth Peters mysteries. They both finished their wine. The bed was so big they weren't even touching. Jade would have done something about that if they were staying in. Since they weren't, he set down his glass, crawled across Robert to get a kiss on his way off the bed, and headed for the shower.

Jade was ready first this time. He was wearing something new, a deep-purple evening jacket over a white shirt and black leather pants, with new purple cowboy boots. He loved the look. It was very Vegas: a little bit Sixties, a little bit glam, and a whole lot sexy. Robert's outfit was the same except for color. His jacket and boots were midnight blue. His only jewelry was his watch. Jade was wearing a new platinum-set diamond

220

stud in his ear and, of course, his engagement ring. His hair had grown out, almost brushing his collar again; Robert's was short on the sides, slicked back on top, with platinum highlights. The finishing touch was the smudge of soft gray eyeliner pencil under his bottom lashes. He was truly spectacular. "This is a very good look for you."

Robert checked himself out in the mirror one more time. "I knew you were the guy to ask." He'd requested the most confrontationally, sexily, gay semi-formal evening look Jade could come up with. Jade didn't ask why. He surely guessed that Robert meant to show his sister exactly who he was now, instead of going in looking like the brother she remembered. Other men in the restaurant (one of the best in the city) would be wearing jackets. Some might even be wearing tuxedos. Every head in the room was going to turn toward these two birds of paradise. Jade was almost nervous about it. He would have said Robert wasn't – he had his negotiator face on – until he caught the deep inhale, the slow exhale, and the slight nod. "Time to go."

Lisa was already seated when they walked in. She looked toward the entrance like everybody else. For a moment, it seemed she didn't recognize him. Then her eyes got big and her mouth dropped open. "Aha," Jade said, satisfied. He glanced at his fiancé. Somewhere along the line they'd talked about Robert's discomfort with being looked at. There was no sign of that now. His posture was perfect, chin up, a faint smile on his handsome face. Crossing the room with wolfish grace. *Like a fucking supermodel.* Jade was a step behind, putting on his own best 'watch me' face, feeling delightfully tall in the boots.

Lisa had managed to close her mouth by the time they reached the table. She hadn't pushed back her

221

chair, the way she might have if she intended to stand up and try a hug. Robert held out a hand. "Lisa. It's great to see you."

She took his hand, then looked at it. "Why are we. Oh." Dropped his hand, shoved back the chair, and seized him. Hugging hard with her face against his chest. "You're so tall!"

"Mmm. Wearing heels." Robert was almost laughing, but his arms were around her and his voice was soft. "Hey. This is Jade Derecha." He eased back a little and let go with one hand, reaching for his lover. "He designed this look for us tonight."

"Holy cow. Wow. Nice to meet you, Jade." They shook hands. When Lisa let go, Jade put his left hand on the back of a chair. "Oh my goodness. That's some ring."

"I told you we were getting married. We want to do it in California, so we have to wait, but our day will come. Let's sit." Everyone in the room was still looking at them. Robert was close to cracking up over Jade, flashing that ring. They could laugh about that later. Right now a server was on her way, and they had some catching up to do.

At first it was mostly about Lisa. She was definitely filing for divorce, and working out a plan to get her own place. "Mom and Dad have been kind of," she hesitated, "I want to say disappointed? Like I failed them somehow. Which I can't help being kind of annoyed about, because they used to tell me I should stand up for myself. Be true to myself."

"Well, now you know how I feel." Robert took a sip of wine to cover his surprise that he actually said that. "Have they been dragging you to church?" Another thing he hadn't meant to say.

"We've been going, wait. Dragging?" She stared at him for a moment.

222

Robert glanced at Jade, who raised his eyebrows. Saying clear as day, might as well get this out on the table too. "Lisa, I stopped going to church in college. I've only been to services when I was home to visit."

"But … why?"

"Because I don't believe in it. I think the book is nonsense, sixty percent irrelevant and forty percent pernicious. The actual Bible does a little better, that's about fifty-thirty, with ten percent history and ten percent useful examples for living a moral life in a civil society." Another sip of wine. Her face was such a WTF face, as if she'd never even considered questioning the dogma that was hammered into their heads for all those years. "My undergrad was anthropology, remember? And I'm a lawyer. I studied the history of law, comparative religion, all kinds of stuff. It was important for me to be prepared to deal with all kinds of different people. I have clients who are Muslim, Buddhist, Jewish, Jehovah's Witnesses, Southern Baptist, atheist. Whatever. It is not my job to come at them from a place of 'this one way is the right way.' It's my job to understand where *they're* coming from and stay out of their way, because their work has nothing to do with religion. Or very little," he amended, because a few of his people did have observance exceptions in their contracts. "You can't understand other people if you're too caught up thinking you're right."

Lisa seemed to grasp that they weren't only talking about religion. "I need to think about that for a while. I've never, wow. So all those years, that was something you did to avoid …?"

"Avoid conflict. Keep the peace. I never wanted to be at odds with my family over something that was so irrelevant to me." All kinds of subtext there. He kept saying things he hadn't fully intended to say.

223

She gulped down the rest of her Arnold Palmer as if she wished it were something alcoholic. Blinked at Robert's wineglass as if only now realizing what he was drinking. Looked a bit lost. "And being … ."

"Gay. The word is gay, honey."

"Being gay. Was that something you covered up too?"

Robert narrowed his eyes. "What did Mom tell you?"

"Something about you were dating a girl and asked her to marry you and she said no and you were relieved and then you realized."

At least she'd related those things accurately. "Mm-hmm. I truly did not realize until last spring. Maybe I was lying to myself, but I wasn't lying to anyone else."

Jade finally said something, because he could tell Robert was getting a little wound up. "And as soon as he came to grips with it, he talked to your mother. Let's take a break for a minute, this food is too good." That might have been exactly the right approach. Lisa and Robert both sat back, relaxed, addressed their meals. After a while Lisa asked about Jade's work. Robert thought she might be trying to put Jade in the 'wife' category. It wasn't accurate at all but was better than a lot of other ways she might have been thinking about his lover. The work discussion carried them for a while. Jade didn't mention the drag pageant, or the Disneyland thing, or any of their gay friends. Well, they'd already laid a lot on her.

At the coffee stage, Lisa studied the dessert menu. "I shouldn't eat one of these all by myself. Would one of you help?"

Jade leaned over to see the options. "If you get the chocolate thing we'll both help."

"Okay." When the server had their coffee on the table and they were waiting for the cake to arrive, Lisa stared at her cup for a few seconds, fiddling with her spoon, as if she had something to say and didn't want to say it.

"Are they here?" Robert was suddenly sure of it.

Jade glanced at him, startled. "Your parents?"

"I'm betting Lance, too. Did they ask you to set up a meeting, Lisa?"

She sighed. "They did. You don't have to. They're all expecting me to come up and tell them that they're right and this is a phase. But it's not, is it? Any more than you becoming an agent in L.A. instead of working in some crappy office in SLC. Yeah, I know about Dad's buddy. They had plans for you." She said it with a rueful shake of her head that made Robert laugh. "Mom said maybe we could have brunch up in their room and talk things over in private."

"Not brunch. Jade and I have plans for breakfast." Plans involving the rest of the champagne, some room service to supplement the gourmet snacks, and the spa tub. "And we have plans in the evening, too. But we're free in the afternoon."

Jade didn't much want to be in that meeting. If Robert needed him, he'd be there anyway. "One condition," he said. The others looked at him. "No amateur conversion therapy. I was with Robert the night he figured this out, and I've been with him all along." Robert took his hand. "This is not a phase, but it's also not a choice. And it's part of who he is, but it's not all of who he is." She nodded.

"Another condition." Lisa turned to Robert. He said, "If Jade comes with me, which I'm hoping he will but I'm not going to make him, he is treated with respect. Like a normal guy, a sports nut same as me, who happens to work as a stylist and who happens to be gay. That last thing should be completely irrelevant to how he's treated. Nobody has to watch us kiss, or anything else. If you choose to imagine that instead of seeing the people in front of you, that's your collective problem. Got it?"

Lisa swallowed, nodding again. The cake arrived in what might have been the nick of time. They all managed to make small talk, easing the tension until the cake plate and the coffee cups were empty. Then Robert took care of the check. They all walked out together. Lisa hugged her brother again, made a nervous feint toward Jade that almost made him laugh, and accepted a hug from him too. She said, "Thanks for dinner. I'll call you in the morning."

"Okay. Good night."

"Good night." She walked away.

Robert took Jade's hand again, squeezed ever so lightly, and blew out a breath. "You are the absolute best, you know that? I love you so much."

"I love you. We'll be okay. Let's go up and raid the minibar." Jade let go of Robert's hand, but only so he could slide his arm around his lover's waist. A nightcap after wine with dinner (and the champagne before) might be a regrettable choice. On the other hand, nobody was keeping score, and they needed to sleep. They could work off all the extra sugar in the morning.

Knowing there was a stressful thing happening later did not prevent Robert and Jade from fully enjoying their semi-aquatic room-service brunch. They were both slightly sore and distinctly pruny when they finally hauled out of the spa tub to dry off. "We need a tub like

226

this on our honeymoon," Jade said, checking himself out in the mirror, smiling at the bite mark on his shoulder. "Only in Hawaii or something."

Neither of them had ever been there. Robert thought this was a great idea. He finished rubbing down with the towel and went for the unscented lotion. By the time he was done doing Jade's legs and back, he was turned on again. "Down boy," he told himself.

"We probably have time." Lisa hadn't called yet. Jade wouldn't at all mind being completely worn out when they finally went to the Anderson suite. It would be obvious what state he was in, but he wasn't averse to making people uncomfortable sometimes. *This isn't about you*, he reminded himself.

"Later." Robert kissed Jade's knees, which were still a little bit red from kneeling on the bench in the tub. Then he used up the lotion on his own legs. "We need to stretch. Get fully hydrated, make up for all the alcohol. Decide what to wear."

They got into briefs and tee shirts, debating that while they started the stretching and hydration process. The decision was jeans and long-sleeved sports tees, the kind that actually fit. Secured through Robert's team connections; his was from the Jacksonville Jaguars, and Jade's was from the Denver Broncos. Lisa called a little before noon. Robert had his phone near at hand, so he leaned over to get it, connected, and put it on speaker. "Morning, Lisa. How's things?"

"Things are okay. If you're still willing to talk, is two o'clock good?"

Robert was watching Jade. "Yes, that's fine. Of course I'm still willing. Conditions accepted?"

"Yes. I'm not sure about Lance but Mom and Dad seem like they really want to work this out."

God, that was infuriating. As if there was an argument to be settled, or a compromise to be made. Jade's face told him to take a breath, so Robert did that. He didn't put on a fake smile, though. He didn't care if his voice sounded a bit cold. "What's the room number?"

"Fourteen oh six."

"See you there at two." He disconnected. "God *damn* it."

Jade scooted over, got an arm around his lover, laid his cheek against his back. "You really don't have to do this."

Robert sighed. "I really do. I have to at least try. I'm about to be thirty-seven, Dad's about to be sixty-three, we're grown-ups. We need to talk. I don't want to be on the outside for the rest of his life. I don't want them pretending you don't exist. Or that you're not as much a part of my life as Lance's wife is part of his. Not that I think of you as my wife."

Jade laughed. "I know you don't, partner."

Robert twisted around for a kiss. "Partner. That reminds me."

"Hmm?"

"Do you want to do the paperwork on that, or do you want to wait until we get married?" He tried to make it sound casual.

"Let's wait. Why go through all that hassle twice." Another kiss. "Do your pec stretches."

Robert thought he might have done a little too well at sounding casual. Well, he could wait. "Jeez, bossy, okay."

They got in bed again for a while after stretching, but only to watch TV till it was time to get dressed.

Robert felt almost guilty about not dealing with the business-related texts and emails he knew were piling up. He could do that tomorrow, on the way home. Jade was going to take the first leg this time, and there certainly wasn't much in the way of scenery. At a quarter to two his phone alarm pinged.

Jade turned off the TV. They didn't really talk while they got dressed, or on the way to the Family Meeting. He couldn't help thinking of it with capital letters. This wasn't a thing he'd ever been part of before. He hoped having him there was going to be helpful, or at least useful. Then they went through the door, and in the midst of the awkward meeting and greeting he lost his temper. They were acting like this was a funeral. Offering coffee, avoiding eye contact, playing musical chairs. Brunch would have been a nightmare. "Can I say something?"

Everybody but Robert looked at him with surprise, as if they didn't expect him to speak. Robert looked grateful. "Please."

"Let's sit. Just sit," Jade said sharply, when Lance seemed like he was afraid being gay was contagious. "Between your parents if you need protection. No." That was to stop Lance from saying anything. Maybe he was too surprised to protest. Maybe he didn't expect the gay wife to have any balls. Jade took his unwanted coffee – at least it would occupy his hands – and sat down between Robert and Lisa. It was obvious Mrs. Anderson was uncomfortable with her son, and didn't know what the hell to think about Jade. There they all were, in an uneven circle at the lounge end of the mini-suite. He started talking. "I realized I was gay when I was fifteen. I told my parents, and my father hit me." Lisa flinched. "The next day we sat down and talked. Amazing, right? We talked. Dad apologized. We came to an agreement about how to have a relationship that included this new information. After I graduated from high school I moved out to the West Coast. My parents were not exactly glad that I was leaving town, but it was easier for all of us. We're not close, but we talk." He took a sip of coffee. Everyone else was silent. "A good friend of ours, when he was seventeen, his parents asked who he was taking to prom. He said, I'm going with Francisco. And they were all oh, you're going stag? And he said no, I'm taking him as my date. I hope that's okay." He glanced at Robert.

Robert picked up the thread. "This friend, his family is Catholic. His dad and grandfather were in the Navy, his two brothers are now too. So he didn't know what to expect. He said his parents kind of stared at him for a minute, then looked at each other. And his father said, well, do you want to bring him with you to the tux shop so you can get something that goes together?"

Mrs. Anderson looked as though she might be about to cry. Jade kept going. "Another good friend. High-profile family in New York City. He was a theater kid. His mother talked to him about stuff before he even knew what was going on. It was never an issue. She wanted to make sure he was safe, working in a business where he had to make a lot of decisions for himself. He and his parents are very close. So," another sip of coffee. "The reason I'm telling you these things is to illustrate that it's possible. You may not know any other families who have been through this."

"It's not a negotiation," Robert said after a moment's silence. "I am gay. It is what it is. I'm going to marry Jade, because I love him. We're going to live together, and watch sports on TV together, and maybe join a softball team. He's going to be working at the salon and on movie sets. I'm going to keep doing what

230

I do. We will invite his parents to the wedding, with the full expectation that they won't come. But maybe they'll surprise us. We'll invite you too, and maybe you'll surprise us. Our friends will be there." The slightest emphasis on 'friends.'

Jade couldn't resist. "Which, incidentally, includes the woman Robert proposed to last year. Turns out she's gay, too."

"Oh come on." That was Lance. It could have been laughter or outrage.

"No, really." Robert smiled. "We ran into her at Disneyland with her girlfriend. She was all, is that my ring?"

"Is it?" Lisa sounded a bit dazed.

"Well, sure. The night she said no, I met Jade. I still had the ring with me. We were talking in the bar at a restaurant, and I put the box on the table. Jade put the ring on, and I was like, what?" Jade snorted. "And then later, when he talked me off the ledge – figuratively speaking – I thought, I should give it to him. So, you know." There still hadn't been a word from Robert's parents, not since they'd sat down. "Here's the thing. Mom, Dad, Lance. I told Mom on the phone that I still want to be part of your lives, and then I didn't hear anything from anybody, not even a Christmas card, until Lisa wanted backup about Art. It's okay," he said to her, feeling her shrink a little. "You needed backup, and I'm glad you came to me. But aside from that, it's been nine months. Long enough to have a baby. And in all that time none of you seem to have thought, gee, he's still our son. He's still my brother." He had to take a breath. "I am not less of a man for being gay. You three are not somehow less, either. I don't see how me being gay injures you in any way. So I don't feel like I have anything to apologize for, and if that was what you wanted here today, you're not getting it."

Yikes, Jade thought. He might have underestimated how angry Robert was. Or maybe it was the overall lack of response. Making them do all the talking, after having not even said 'we're glad to see you.' Come to think of it, he was still pissed off too. They'd done their best. Kept it civil, kept it light, tried to give scenarios these people could latch onto for a model. He took Robert's hand, not at all surprised to feel a tremor. "Maybe we should go now." Complete silence. He stood up, closely followed by Robert. They set down their coffee cups on the dresser and were out the door seconds later. "Fuck. Sweetheart." In Robert's arms, both of them shaking, holding each other tight for a minute. Then walking to the elevator bay with their arms around each other, not talking, because there really wasn't much to say.

"Bobby. Robert." Lance's voice.

They turned around. Lance and Lisa were there together, approaching. Lisa was saying, "I'm sorry, so sorry," and Lance was reaching out.

Robert glanced at Jade, then offered his hand. A second later he and Lance were hugging. "You're right." It was muffled. "It's got nothing to do with me. None of my business. I don't want you thinking about what Stacy and I do in bed, and I shouldn't be thinking about what you and Jade do."

"It has honestly never occurred to me to wonder." Robert sounded half-annoyed, half-happy. "Is that a thing? Do people sit around picturing their siblings fucking?" Lisa squeaked. Jade stifled a laugh.

"I'm really sorry." Lance stood back. "It's like, when Mom told me what you said, I could tell she was freaked out about it, and I needed to be freaked out too

232

because otherwise that meant she was wrong to be freaked out. Does that make sense?"

"Not really," Jade said, even though it kind of did. "You're thirty-nine years old."

"Ugh, don't remind me. Look, could we go somewhere and sit, and talk some more? Really talk?"

"The four of us," Lisa said. "I don't know if we're going to get anywhere with them. I'm still trying to sort out if what I've been worried about is my own actual feelings or if it's all this keeping-up-appearances conventionality. I keep catching myself thinking it's my fault, what happened with Art."

"It's not your fault." Robert made an all-encompassing gesture. "Let's go down to the bar. You guys can get Arnold Palmers or whatever. Jade and I are going to drink."

They ended up staying in the bar till five, talking about all kinds of things, including baseball. A sidebar about little league turned into Lance talking about what he called his mid-life crisis. "I know Dad expects me to take over the business. It's been this unspoken thing for the past five years. And it's not like I don't want to, but I'm a little bit, eh. Because I'm going to want to change some things and I don't want to start a fight." He rolled his eyes at Robert's derisive sound. "I know. If I'm taking over, then it's mine and I can do what I want, right? Well, obviously, there's more to it than that."

"That's why you're still working somewhere else, I'm guessing." Robert was relaxed now. They were just talking, about the kinds of things they'd always talked about. It was the best way to get past the things they still weren't sure how to talk about. Or maybe they didn't need to talk about those things, after all.

"Yeah. I'll probably make the switch pretty soon, though. Let the staff start getting used to me."

"You'll be screwed if he decides not to retire till he's, like, seventy." Jade and Lisa both laughed. Robert turned it around, getting her talking again about her job.

She was the one who eventually looked at her phone, sighed at the time, and said, "We should probably get upstairs. And you have somewhere to go tonight. I'm really glad we had a chance to, you know."

"Me too." Another glance at Jade, who'd been awfully quiet once they started talking family business. "Keep in touch, okay? I do really want that. I do really care about both of you."

"Same goes." Lance was on his feet. They shook hands. Then everyone was up, the siblings hugging. "Jade."

He was standing a little aside. "Mmm?"

"I want to apologize to you, too. I'm sorry." Lance offered a hand. Jade shook it gravely, appreciating that the other man didn't try to get all hearty and we're-all-guys-here. Then Lance surprised him. "If you do the softball thing, help him out with his pitch, okay? Because it kind of sucks."

"That was twenty years ago!" And it was silly enough to have them all laughing as they left the bar. They were in separate parts of the hotel, so they didn't have to share an elevator going back up. Robert huffed out a breath, leaning on the wall of the car. "God, I'm exhausted. How are you doing? I hope that wasn't too much."

"It was right on the edge of too much," Jade admitted. "I don't actually give a shit about the family business. But it was an important conversation, so I'm glad you got to have it. I'm glad at least half of them have come around."

Robert didn't want to say 'the important half.' He loved his parents, too, but the family's future was his siblings. They were back up at the room. Unlocking the door, stripping down again because they planned to dress up for the Cirque show. For now there was an hour to relax, nosh on what was left of the snacks, and simply be together. "I will never stop being glad I'm with you."

Jade patted his leg. "We're good together. Was it me putting this ring on that really made you click in?"

Robert leaned over for a kiss. "I think it was. In the moment, I was like what in the actual fuck, but then it was like okay, that looks right, but I should be outraged, and I'm not. So." He did a 'mind blown' thing with his hands. Jade was laughing silently. "Cuddle up with me here, honey. Let's be quiet for a minute and think about all the filthy things we're going to do after this show."

"Mmm, okay." Jade squirmed in under Robert's arm, wrapped an arm over his chest, felt both arms go around him. He didn't think filthy things. He thought about the day, maybe two years out, when they could finally fulfill the promise of that ring. It seemed like such a long time. Maybe they should do the other thing, after all. Register as partners, and prove to the world (and maybe to each other) that they were in this for life. He'd mention it on the drive home, after Robert took over the wheel. Or maybe while they were taking that break. Because Robert mentioned it, so it might be something he really wanted. He wouldn't push – he never did – but maybe he hoped Jade would say yes, let's do that. In which case there might be some hugging and kissing to be done before they got back on the road.

Chapter 19

The post-show fooling around and solid eight hours of sleep that followed were, they agreed, very restorative. After a leisurely room-service breakfast, they indulged in another splash in the spa tub. Even with that, they were on the road back to Los Angeles by noon. Jade plugged his mp3 player into the stereo, Robert got busy returning messages, the traffic wasn't too bad. Jade pulled into Barstow ahead of schedule. "You're a speed demon," Robert observed as they headed into a fast-food place for a snack.

Jade shot him a laughing glance. "I was keeping up with the flow." How to start this conversation again. Robert seemed very normal today, but he had to still be feeling the effects of yesterday. Jade was, and those weren't even his parents. Maybe he should just come out and say it, even though there wasn't a smooth way to do that. Snack, beverage, and bathroom break accomplished, they headed out to the car. "Before we start," he said, then stalled.

Robert looked over, alerted by something in Jade's tone. "What, honey?"

"What you said yesterday. About doing the paperwork. I changed my mind."

After a second, Robert said, "You what?"

"Let's not wait. Let's register the partnership. If you still want to."

"If I *want* to?!" Robert seized Jade, kissed him, squeezed him. They were both half-laughing, half-crying. "I know I keep pushing us forward. Are you sure? We don't have to. I know you love me."

"I do love you. And that's why, because what if the other thing doesn't happen? I belong to you. I belong *with* you. Or we could get married back East. We don't have to wait for the law to change here."

"But I want to get married here. I want our friends to be there." Standing by the car, arms wrapped around each other. So indiscreet, out here in not-L.A. Robert didn't care. He kissed Jade again. "It's important to have our people there. As many as we can get."

Jade nodded, pressed his lips to Robert's neck, and put a tiny bit of distance between them so he could make eye contact. "So let's register. Then we can start looking for the best place to get married. Because it will happen. We have to believe it will happen."

"I think so too. I want to get married at the beach."

Jade blinked. "Really?" They weren't generally beach people.

"I read this thing." Robert felt himself blush. "I was looking at a wedding blog online."

"You're so fucking cute."

"Okay, all right, whatever. It was this symbolic thing. You walk into the water like you're walking off the edge of the world, and you're two separate people. Then you walk back onto dry land and now you're married, and it's a new world. It's going to be a new world. All these hundreds or thousands of years that men like us haven't been able to do that."

"Men like us," Jade echoed. "It hasn't even been a year."

Robert knew what he meant. "I've never felt more sure of anything in my life. I love you." One more kiss. "Let's get going. We can talk about how to find the perfect beach on the way home."

March 2011

Jade was between heads, taking a load off, and messing around with his phone because Shaya wasn't in that day to chat with. Among the usual messages, there was a hush-hush update from Mark. The show was definitely killing him off, but after a proposal. So there was going to be a string of big drama moments for Jenny, a good clean exit for Mark during sweeps, and then he'd be able to make that announcement. Jade was relieved.

There was a celebration dinner at Vibrato – Mark was singing there – after registering their partnership. Emily was there, as usual, to help keep up appearances. She'd been in on the real reason for all this since the first week of January, when she caught Mark and Liam hugging in the kitchen. All signs pointed to genuine delight. The next day at work, Robert asked her if there was someone waiting in the wings for her, and she said, "No, but I have to confess I'm getting kind of inspired." She also said, after the next rendezvous at their home, "It's wearing him out. Thank you for giving them nights like this." It felt like so little, but both of their friends swore an evening without pretense – being able to touch, embrace, kiss – was enough to get them through it.

After reading Mark's message Jade sent a typically cryptic reply, avoiding overt reference to the coming-out countdown and promising another evening at home the following month. Then he went to the next email and sat up straight. Switched to text mode, and composed a message to Robert: *Sweetheart the LALGBTC sent a thing about this year's fundraiser. Another pageant. Theme is Bond Girls. Please tell me we can do it*

The response came fast: *Pussy Galore get our claim in NOW*. Jade laughed out loud. Switched back to email, sent the message, was amazed to receive a confirmation by return, sat and giggled for a minute. Back to the text app, and a message to Shaya: *It's Bond Girls for September. We have Pussy Galore*

She wrote back: *Bahahaha that's what she said. Shit now I have to watch all those ridiculous movies? I saw that email but I'm kind of tied up right now*

I don't want to hear about it. Except yes please tell me all about it

Later. Who's the next best Bond Girl?!

You need May Day. The Grace Jones character

OH YEAH but who could my model be obvs not Patrick wait I know never mind gotta go

See you tomorrow. Jade disconnected, leaned back in his chair, and stared at himself in the mirror, smiling, seeing something else entirely. Six months to get ready; more than enough time. He could already see Robert in a flight suit, with high-heeled black boots. Doing his little turn on the catwalk.

THE END

If you enjoyed A LITTLE TURN, please consider leaving a positive rating or review. It really helps! Thanks for reading.

Want more? Mark & Liam's story is **GIVING IT UP**. Discover this story universe at

www.thelastories.com

Author's Note:

The Los Angeles LGBT Center is a real organization. Local 706 is the Makeup Artists & Hair Stylists Guild, also a real organization. Dapper Day is yet another real thing.

The fundraiser drag pageant described in 'A Little Turn' is completely fictional.

****

About the Author

Alexandra Caluen lives in a small purple house with her husband, a bottle of Laphroaig, a lot of books, and nine pairs of ballroom shoes. She works in patent law and has enough hair for three people.